Also by David M. Salkin

Military, Espionage & Action Adventure Thrillers

Science Fiction & Horror Collection

Crime & Mystery Thrillers

A POST HILL PRESS BOOK
ISBN: 978-1-68261-439-6
ISBN (eBook): 978-1-61868-859-0

African Dragon:
The Team Book Three
© 2017 by David M. Salkin
All Rights Reserved

Cover Design by Christian Bentulan

Post Hill
PRESS

Post Hill Press
posthillpress.com

Published in the United States of America

AFRICAN DRAGON
THE TEAM BOOK III

DAVID M. SALKIN

ACKNOWLEDGMENTS

The Team series has been fun to write. Obviously, these are fictional tales, but I have tried to create stories that are feasible in today's world. The original concept for the team was based on a real operation run in Vietnam, and I don't lose sight of the fact that brave men and women are out fighting for the United States of America every day.

Several warriors have been extremely helpful in sharing their own stories, advising on technical issues, and offering support in various ways. I'd like to thank LCpl Connor O'Brien Hamill, USMC, Col. William L. Peace and Col. Jeff Cantor. It's not a coincidence you see names like these in the story.

Any technical mistakes are mine, either by accident, or by artistic license. While my warrior friends have explained equipment and technical things in great detail, I sometimes worry that readers may get bogged down in too much technical detail, so I tend to "make things up that are easier to understand." If you're a War Fighter, active or retired, you have my utmost respect and thanks for your service. Some of my Wounded Warrior friends have made huge personal sacrifices for this country. Rory, that includes you. Semper Fi, brother~

As a side note, the African Rift lakes in the story are, in fact, the source for the African cichlids you see in the fish-keeping hobby. I have plenty of these smart, colorful creatures swimming around my own fish tanks. Many of these fish only exist in the tanks of fish-keepers, as the perch introduced to the lakes for food have eaten some of these beauties out of existence.

For my family, my friends, and you...
the readers who keep me writing.

"The secret of Happiness is Freedom, and the secret of Freedom, Courage."

–Thucydides (460 BC - 395 BC)

CHAPTER 1

Senior Chief Petty Officer Chris Cascaes drove the twelve miles to the VA Hospital in silence. He didn't even have the radio on, which was very unusual. 'Car time' usually meant earsplitting Led Zeppelin or some other classic rock. Instead, he drove in the peaceful hush, holding hands with Julia Ortiz, just enjoying her company. Julia was a little nervous. CIA operative or not, meeting the man that her new boyfriend called "Pop" was a little unnerving.

Pop was eighty-seven years old, and starting to fall apart. His mind was still sharp, but his body had betrayed him. The injuries sustained on Iwo Jima had left him with enough problems over the years—a perforated eardrum, shrapnel in his arms and chest that would occasionally surface through his skin without warning, and skin rashes he had picked up in the jungles somewhere in the South Pacific that no doctor could quite cure. None of that had ever slowed him down, though. He was a marine and tough as hell. That was, until the cancer had started to eat him alive.

Chris's own degenerate father, Chris Sr., never discussed his time in Korea. Whatever hell he'd gone through had left him a mean alcoholic that physically abused his wife and son. Chris Jr. avoided being home whenever possible, and had been somewhat adopted by his neighbor "The Major," Adam Stone. Adam would tell Chris Jr. stories about fighting in the Pacific and Korea for hours and hours. His stories usually ended the same way—he would tell a story and then get that funny look in his eye and say, "Ya' know, sometimes I wonder if I was really there or I just watched a John Wayne movie." It was only a half-joke. To Major Stone, Korea and the Pacific were a lifetime ago. Some of the memories were still painful even to this day, but so many details had started to fade. He would occasionally forget a name, and that always broke his heart, as if he had betrayed the man by not remembering every detail.

Now, in the haze of morphine, some of the memories were clearer than ever, and it was the *present* moment instead of the *past* that was confusing. Chris had talked a lot to Julia about Pop Stone—much more, in fact, than his own parents. It was Pop Stone that had helped him make his decision to join the Navy when Chris turned eighteen, basically an orphan. His mother had died in a car accident, and Chris hadn't seen his father since the day he defended himself and his mother against one of his drunken assaults. With nothing holding him at home, the navy was Chris's gateway to seeing the world.

Chris had set his goal of becoming a navy SEAL before he ever signed on the dotted line. It took longer than he wanted to make his way to BUDs training, but he excelled and was immediately noticed for his leadership abilities. He made it through the first time, something not every SEAL manages to do, and loved the challenges, both mental and physical. Now, nineteen years later, Chris was a SEAL team leader and senior chief petty officer (who had been awarded the Navy Cross, Defense Distinguished Service Medal, two purple hearts, and a chest full of other campaign ribbons) and was on loan for "special assignment" to the CIA.

It had been several months since Chris had worn his uniform. He had just returned from the rain forests of South America where he'd been with a group of missionaries that weren't missionaries. Prior to that, he'd been doing special operations with a "baseball team" that wasn't a baseball team. His only "uniform" had been that of a second baseman on the US Navy All-Star Exhibition Team. Today, however, he was taking his girlfriend Julia to meet Pop, and for *this*, he wanted his dress uniform. It was the first time Julia had seen him in his dress uniform, and she was more than suitably impressed. (In fact, she had undressed him before allowing him to redress himself). As they walked into the VA hospital off Irving Street in Washington DC, Julia squeezed his hand and tried to relax. Chris had told her that she was the first woman he had ever bothered to introduce to Pop Stone, and she was not only honored but slightly terrified. What if he didn't like her?

They went through security and walked to the elevators. The place was somewhat sterile-looking, but extremely clean and fairly busy. They stood in the elevator, still holding hands and looking like what they were, a couple of people who obviously loved each other. They walked down the hall until Chris stopped near Pop's room.

"Listen, Julia, when I spoke to Pop last week, he sounded pretty lousy. I haven't seen him in a few months and I don't know what to expect, so prepare yourself for someone that might look a little rough." He kissed her cheek and led her to Pop's room. They walked in and saw Major Stone, now a very frail-looking old man in his bed with an oxygen line under his nose. He had an IV attached to his arm. It dripped morphine when he pressed a button if he felt uncomfortable. He didn't like feeling so loopy, and tried his best not to use the extra dose that he could summon manually. When he saw Chris walk in with his beautiful girlfriend, Pop smiled ear to ear.

Pop waved them in. Chris smiled, and went to the old man to give him a hug. He almost cried when he felt how skinny the tough old marine's arms and shoulders were.

"Hey, Pop," he managed to say without losing it.

The old man pulled the oxygen tube away from his nose and let it lay around his neck. His voice, hoarse from his throat being so dry from the constant oxygen, was weak and didn't sound like the strong marine that Chris remembered growing up. Pop held Chris's hand and looked at him.

"You're one squared away sailor," he said, his voice barely above a whisper. "Is that the Navy Cross I'm looking at on your chest? Son of a bitch," he said with admiration, a smile slowly spreading across his face.

"I bought it at the PX, Pop—to impress the young lady," said Chris.

"And who is this beautiful girl you've brought with you?" asked Pop, holding his hands up towards her.

Julia walked over and took his hands and smiled. Chris introduced her as she held his hands and Julia bent down and kissed his cheek "hello."

"Chris has told me so much about you, Major Stone. It's an honor to meet you finally," she said.

"*Pop*—you call me Pop, like Chris. If he brought you to see me, you must be family. Did he tell you you're the first girl he's ever introduced to me?"

"Yes," she said with her beautiful smile still beaming.

"I was starting to think the boy was, well, you know—don't ask, don't tell…" He smiled weakly.

She patted his hand and whispered, "Don't you worry about him, Pop. He definitely likes girls."

The old man laughed, which brought a small coughing fit. Chris poured him some water off the nightstand and helped him drink a little, then made him put the oxygen back under his nose against minor protest.

When Pop's coughing had subsided and he was relaxed again, Chris asked, "How are you holding up?"

Pop shrugged it off. "I'm ready to meet the Supreme Commandant whenever he calls me up. My wife and most of my friends are already up there waiting, anyway."

After a pause, he said, "I tell you something though, Chris. This morphine is amazing stuff. Some days I don't know if I'm dreaming or awake. I think I've talked to half the guys in my old outfits the last few weeks. It's been kind of nice, actually. Even got to see that one kid Wally something-or-other. Can't remember his last name. But we were in Iwo Jima together. He was a great guy. He was visiting last night—I swear to God, Chris, he was right here in the room. He made me laugh until I coughed my head off. Crazy stuff, this morphine."

Chris could see that Pop was getting tired fast. "Pop, I might be heading out again soon," he said. "Might be gone for a while again."

"Oh yeah? *I* see what's going on in the world. The news is on the TV most of the day. Some world you inherited, huh?" He coughed again a few times, and Chris let him continue. "I always knew you'd be a SEAL. I told you a military career would be good for you. You were squared away even when you were ten, Chris."

Chris smiled and said, "Thanks, Pop."

"So can I ask where you and your SEALs are headed? You know your secret will be buried with me—maybe by next week," he said, trying to smile.

"Well, Pop, you know they never tell us anything. But I do have a little secret for you."

Julia shot him a look; afraid he was going to say something about being on loan to the CIA or about the baseball team.

Pop grunted, as if to say, "go on and tell me."

"Pop, you see this girl over here? She doesn't know it yet, but she's going to marry me."

Pop smiled broadly and squeezed each of their hands, as he began coughing again. Julia's mouth fell open and she stared at Chris. She looked back at Pop. "Well, he wasn't kidding about the 'me not knowing it yet' part!" Chris put his arm around her and squeezed her close, still facing the old major.

"She's a keeper," Pop said hoarsely. "You two will be great together. You a squid, too?" he asked Julia.

It took her a second to understand "squid" meant navy personnel.

"Um, no. Maybe I'll just stay home and have five or six kids," she said with a nudge to Chris.

Pop grimaced and forced a smile. He nonchalantly reached over and pressed the button that released the morphine into his arm, and after a few seconds, his face relaxed.

"Chris," he whispered, as he motioned him closer. Cascaes leaned over, putting his ear closer to Pop's mouth. "You grew up to be a good man. You're a SEAL. The best of the navy. I was always so proud of you, kid. You're the son I never had, you know that, right?"

Chris fought back the tears and hugged the frail old marine. "I love you, Pop," he managed to get out.

"I love you, too, kid."

He held the old man for a few minutes until the morphine kicked in harder and the Major started to fall asleep. He was holding him, with Julia rubbing his back when a doctor walked in and cleared his throat to announce his presence.

"Sorry to intrude, how's the patient?" asked the doctor, an older man in a white coat.

"I was just going to ask you," said Chris.

The doctor looked at Chris's chest full of medals. The Navy Cross wasn't lost on the doc. "Are you family?" he asked.

"Yes," Cascaes said, without explaining further.

"Well, you know he didn't even come to see us until he was very sick. Typical jarhead—too stubborn to see a doctor. At his age, we wouldn't have recommended anything other than pain management, anyway. He's been holding up pretty well, but the last two weeks he's been here full time, and relying on the morphine. He's been in and out with it. Strong stuff. But honestly, I think it's been good for him. I think he's made his peace."

Chris wiped his wet cheeks with the back of his hand. "Yeah, he was telling us about his visits with some of his old friends."

The doctor smiled. "Yeah, he's an entertaining guy. I'm sure you know that without *me* telling you."

Chris smiled. "Yeah, I grew up on his stories. Funniest son of a bitch I ever knew. Anyway, how much time you think he has?"

The doc shook his head. "Hard to say, he's a tough old bugger. But the cancer had spread throughout his body and all of his organs. I'm not sure what's keeping him going now."

"He wanted to see me," said Chris, matter-of-factly. "I needed to see him, too."

The doctor could see him getting upset and shook hands with him and Julia. "Stay as long as you like," he said politely, and turned to leave.

Chris pushed a card into the doctor's hand. "Anything happens, you call me, okay?"

The doctor agreed, and left them alone.

Chris hugged the old man, who was fast asleep. "Thanks, Pop. For everything. I love you, major. I love you."

The tears flowed freely down Chris's face. Julia was crying too, and didn't even know the old man, but felt Chris's sense of loss. She rubbed his back while he sobbed on the Major. Finally, Chris stood up straight, stood at attention, gave the Major a stiff salute.

"Goodbye, sir."

The Major may have heard him somehow in his sleep, a little smile crossing his thin lips as the senior chief snapped his salute so crisply the air seemed to pop.

Chris and Julia walked out, arm in arm, back to their car. She leaned her head against his arm as they walked. Neither spoke, but they comforted each other just by being there.

"Thanks for coming with me," said Chris quietly. "I just wanted to make sure he knew I wasn't gay." He was trying to break the mood as best he could.

"Ah, I see. So you just used me to cover your sexual orientation? So much for having half a dozen kids and learning to bake."

Chris stopped walking and gently pulled her around to face him. "I was serious about the 'you marrying me part.' It's going to get a little complicated, though, don't you think?"

She laughed. "Come on, we've known each other for what? Two months?"

"Well it *has* been a busy two months," he said with a smile. "How many of your *other* boyfriends have brought you out into the jungle for combat operations?"

She laughed. "Unfortunately, all of them," she said. Then quickly added, "Just kidding."

They looked at each other, neither one moving a muscle. Finally, Julia spoke. "You know, if the boss found out we were sleeping together, he'd take me off the team."

"You think so?" Chris asked.

"I *know* so. I don't know how it works in the navy, but in the company, there's no overt fooling around between agents. I'm not saying it doesn't happen—it just doesn't get out in the open. If we actually were engaged or something—and I'm not saying that's going to happen, but if it did, everyone would know. And I'd be pulled in two seconds."

Chris felt his heart sink.

"It doesn't change anything between us, it just means you can't get down on one knee. Yet," she added, and gave him a kiss. They had been standing there kissing for quite a while when both of their phones buzzed at the same time.

They leaned back away from each other and laughed. "Speak of the devil!" said Chris. "But listen—seriously, Julia. It will be a little weird working together in the field now, don't you think? I mean, the last time we ran around in the jungle together getting shot at, I wasn't head over heels in love with you. It might be a little distracting now…"

"Yes, you were *so* in love with me, Admiral. And yes, it *will* be distracting. But it also means we get to be together, so deal with it."

They smiled at each other. It was going to be interesting, to say the least.

"Okay," he said. "I'll try my best not to drool on you in front of anyone, but I can't make any promises." He made sure that no one was looking, then squeezed her butt.

"And you can't squeeze my butt in front of Director Holstrum. It would be a dead giveaway," she said, smiling, and then squeezed his.

"You can squeeze mine anytime you want," he said.

Their phones buzzed again, and they hustled off to their car to get back out to Langley.

CHAPTER 2

The team assembled in their usual muster room at CIA headquarters. Julia looked at Theresa, sitting next to Moose, and smirked. Theresa returned the little grin and looked away. They were best friends and knew each other's love lives. The door opened and Desk Chief Darren Davis walked in, followed by his assistant, Dex Murphy. After some informal greetings, Darren and Dex sat down with the team.

The team had been invented last year—a mixture of navy SEALs, marine recondos, army rangers, and CIA operatives. They had used the cover story of a "US Navy All-Star Baseball Team" to get into Saudi Arabia the previous year for an operation intercepting fifty million dollars of insurgent money, and then traded their baseball uniforms in for church group t-shirts for an insertion into Paraguay to take out terrorists and drug smugglers in the tri-border region. After a couple of weeks off to debrief and decompress, they were recalled to their "ready room."

"Welcome back everyone," said Darren as he took his seat. "Most of you were military so you know how this works: you train for desert warfare and you get sent to the mountains— you train for mountains and end up swimming up a beach at night. Evidently, we are learning from the army. You trained to be a baseball team last year and played what? Two real games on a job? Then you became a church group for the Paraguay job. So you come home, train hard again out on the baseball field, and guess what? It's time to start learning about boats and SCUBA diving from your navy buddies."

The team members all looked at each other and groaned, except for the SEALs, who were smiling.

"Yeah, I knew *you* guys would be happy to hear it," Darren said, looking at the SEALs. "I hope the rest of you don't get seasick. Don't laugh, but do any of you have any background with tropical fish? You know, like fish tanks when you were growing up."

Jon Cohen looked around and finally cleared his throat. "Um, I always had fish tanks growing up," he said softly.

"Anybody else?" asked Davis.

No one responded until Theresa laughed and said, "Moose has a goldfish!"

Davis looked at her and asked, "And you know this *how*?"

Her face turned red and she said, "He told me," not wanting to admit she had been inside his apartment. Julia and Chris made sure they didn't make any eye contact with each other for fear they'd start laughing or something.

"Okay, so Moose has a goldfish, Jon has had some fish, and I have a half dozen SEALs that can dive and know boats. Jon, you ever hear of African cichlids?"

Jon smiled broadly. "Yes, sir! That's what I used to keep— from Lake Malawi and Lake Tanganyika."

Dex and Darren looked at each other and smiled. "Hallelujah," said Dex.

Davis said, "Congratulations, Jon. You just became the resident expert on fish collecting in the region. All of you will be heading to Africa on Canadian passports to collect fish from Lake Tanganyika. You are a new company out of Canada that will be exporting fish back to Canada, air freight, out of Luano Airport in Lubumbashi."

The African sounding names brought a few chuckles.

"Don't laugh—you are all going to have to do some homework on the Democratic Republic of Congo as well as tropical fish. The fish export business for the tropical fish hobby in the US and Canada is big money for the locals down there. Unfortunately, so is their newest export—uranium."

That got everyone's attention.

"As a point of historical reference, it was uranium from the Shinkolobwe Mine that was used in the Fat Man and Little Boy which we so graciously dropped on Nagasaki and Hiroshima. There has been new uranium mining activity in the past couple of years in that region, which has been monitored on and off between wars, but more alarming is the discovery of a new uranium deposit in the eastern part of the country, near Lake Tanganyika. We had a few local resources keeping tabs for us, but they seem to have disappeared. The rumor mill says that China, North Korea, India, and Israel have all had folks down there looking to buy uranium. Nothing is confirmed other than Israel admitting it was 'keeping tabs' just like we are."

The members of the team listened intently, trying to see where they fit into this unusual briefing.

Darren continued, "So...your new fish export company is going to get set up in a small village on the lake. Our Africa desk chief was kind enough to have one of his men purchase an existing fish farm down there. Everything you need is down there already, including a few workers who stayed on after the old owner sold out to us. He actually *was* Canadian, so it makes the sale look routine. The workers will keep things running until you get there, then split. You will live and work right there in the small compound. You will collect enough fish to look like a real business while you snoop around and see who the players are. I'd also like to know what happened to our assets down there. They either changed teams, took off scared, or they're feeding the fish from the bottom of the lake.

"Starting tomorrow, you'll spend some time with the Assistant Africa Desk Chief, Deirdre Gourlie. She will catch you up on the DRC's history, which is a bloody mess, and the local customs and languages. We have a fish guy lined up from the aquarium next week to give you a crash course on African cichlids and fish collecting in the wild, and our doc will start taking care of your shots tomorrow."

They all looked at Theresa, a navy corpsman, who had once made them all drop their pants for shots that she later admitted could have been administered in their arms. She smiled and feigned innocence at the looks from the men. "*What?*" she asked as naively as possible.

Davis missed the joke and continued. "Shots for malaria, typhus, a few exotic fevers, and some other crap you never heard of will be started over the next few weeks to build up in your systems before you go. Trust me, you *don't* want to get sick in the DRC. Their idea of hygiene is spitting on the knife before they hold you down and cut you open. Occasionally, their patients live."

"Nice," said Theresa, thinking back to conditions she had experienced in Iraq out in the field.

"Okay, that's a start for now. There are some other details that we are still working out, but you need to head down to 'the shop' on the fifth floor and get your headshots done for your new Canadian passports and driver's licenses. After your paperwork is done, go out and get drunk or do something entertaining, because starting tomorrow at noon, you are all going to be very busy."

Vinny "Ripper" Colgan, the team's catcher when playing baseball, and Moose's dive buddy when doing SEAL operations, smiled and asked, "Did you say *noon?*" When Darren gave him a yes, he high-fived Al "Moose" Carlogio, the team's pitcher.

"First round is on me," said Ripper. "We get to stay up with the grownups tonight!" The team was used to hitting the rack early and being up working out by oh-five hundred. Showing up late was a special treat that would be utilized to the maximum of their livers.

Julia pressed her leg against Chris's under the table, with her own ideas of how she wanted to spend the extra few hours. Across the table, Moose was doing the same thing to Theresa, who was trying her best to look serious.

CHAPTER 3

The team reassembled in the conference room, showing up in dribs and drabs starting around quarter to twelve. A "noon start" *seemed* like such a late hour at the time it was announced, but "boys will be boys," and as usual, when they were together for a night off, they went *way* overboard. Even starting six or seven hours later than a usual day, they were all hung over and tired, except for Chris, Julia, Moose, and Theresa, who were a little tired, but not hung over—just very content.

They sat sipping strong coffee, quietly trying to wake up. At noon, exactly, Darren Davis walked in with Assistant African Desk Director Deirdre Gourlie. She was about as Irish looking as a woman could be, which made her assignment to the Africa department somewhat comical. Her skin was creamy white—she would definitely stand out in a room of African nationals. Her blondish-red hair was past the collar of her suit, and she had green eyes that smiled when she smiled. The men sat up straight when she entered.

"Good morning, everyone," she said, sounding wide-awake and confident. Evidently, she hadn't been out getting hammered the night before. "Looks like this will be a series of 'firsts' for all of us. I have never worked with a team larger than three agents at once on a job, and you have never been fish farmers in Africa."

The group smiled, already liking her demeanor.

"And which one of you is Jonathon Cohen?" she asked.

Jon smiled and waved.

"Mr. Davis tells me that you are familiar with fish to some extent and you are a navy diver. You will be picking three of your SEAL buddies that you want to do some diving with in Africa, and taking a crash course in African cichlids, the live fish exporting business, fish farming, fish diseases, and water conditions, etc.

"While the other members of the team work on other parts of the assignment, *your* job will be to have a small core of people that actually know the business. There are not a lot of folks in the area working the lake anymore because of the security issues in the DRC. Most of the fish are collected on the Tanzanian side of the lake these days.

"That means that a group this large is going to be very visible on the west side of Lake Tanganyika. That isn't necessarily a bad thing. You will have lots of local fishermen swarming to you, offering to sell you fish. As you get to know some of the locals and they start to trust you, you may have opportunities to pick up local assets, and at the very least catch the local rumors. But—these fishermen have worked the lake for decades with foreigners in the tropical fish trade. If Jon and a few others can't convince them you know what you are doing, they'll see it right away. You'll be happy to know that we have an expert on all of this coming to see you this afternoon. He will do a presentation to the entire group so you all have some exposure to the information, and then Jon and his group will spend a few days learning greater details of the fish farming industry out there. Any questions so far?"

Everyone sat quietly, a few of the SEALs wondering if Jon was going to pick them to learn "Fish 101." Pete McCoy figured he was a "given," having been Jon's dive buddy for most of the last three years.

Deirdre continued with her briefing. "Okay, so Jon and company will get the detailed crash course on the fish industry and the rest of you will start learning local geography. Bringing in gear won't be much of a problem. The last guy there had used fish finders, laptops, and sonar, so you won't look funny bringing in equipment, although what the box *looks* like and what it *does* may be slightly different. Weapons will be slightly trickier. Even though Luano Airport in Lubumbashi is pretty lax about security, you still can't walk into their country with rifles and machine guns. Our shop on three (the 'gadget room' on the third floor) is working on that for you. They are making SCUBA equipment crates that can hold your disassembled weapons. There won't be much equipment on site that any of you would want to dive with anyway, so bringing your own SCUBA gear won't raise suspicion."

Deirdre turned on a laptop that projected a map of the Democratic Republic of Congo on the wall. "You might want to take notes," she smiled. "Most places in Africa have two or three names, depending on who is running the government that day. The DRC was formerly Zaire. City names have mostly been renamed since the formation of the new DRC government."

Jon Cohen, because of his background with African cichlids was confused, and raised his hand. "I thought the Democratic Republic of Congo used to be called the Belgian Congo?"

Deirdre smiled. "I told you this would get confusing. The Belgian Congo, The Congo Free State, and Zaire are the same place. Same place as the DRC—but don't get *that* confused with the Republic of Congo, which was formerly Republique du Congo under the French. Also known as Congo-Brazzaville. French Congo is now the Republic of Congo, and Belgian Congo is now the Democratic Republic of Congo, and they're two *totally* different places. Have I lost all of you yet?"

Everyone nodded, yes. What the Hell was she talking about?

Deirdre laughed. "Look, don't get all worked up over this, I'll have maps for you to look at later and study present names. The only reason I brought it up *now* is because some of the cities have two and three names, and you may need to be familiar with all of the names for each place. Depending on who you are talking to down there, you may get different names for the same places. You will be in Katanga province. It used to be called Shaba province, and some of the older locals still call it that. Lubumbashi is the former Elisabethville or Elisabethstad. It's one of the larger cities around the area, and you'll be working in and out of there for resupply and hopefully making contacts.

"Lubumbashi is known for its copper smelting and the outlying areas are busy with mining. As you may know, world copper prices are way up, partly because the Chinese are buying it as fast as it is coming out of the ground. This led to expansion of copper mining activities in the region, and the accidental discovery of uranium. If you think the Chinese are excited about copper, you ought to see them around uranium. The Koreans and Indians have also been trying to get in on the action as well. US—DRC relations are still very good because of the amount of aid we pump into their government every year, and they are trying to cooperate with us regarding the control of uranium exports, but let's face it—Africa is the Wild West. If somebody shows up with a trunk full of money, the sale is going to get made.

"We need hard intelligence on who is down there, and from where. We also need to know how much uranium is in the ground. That may be impossible for you to find out, but we need you to try. You will have radiological testing equipment with you to make life easier. Keep in mind that there is no OSHA in the DRC. The uranium miners are probably glowing at night, so they'll be easy to spot." That brought a few chuckles.

Deirdre pressed a button on the projector and showed a closer map of the area showing rail lines and roads, with cities, towns and villages marked out. There was a red dot on the shore of Lake Tanganyika that showed the location of their new fish export business.

"Okay, this is a closer look around Lubumbashi. Rail lines from Ilebo, Kindu, and Kolwezi all converge here. The trains only run when whoever is in charge *decides* they are going to run, but it may be handy, nonetheless. It will give you greater appreciation for the local subway, trust me. Kolwezi is west of your position, on the Angolan border. There have been uranium mining activities there for many years as well, in between wars. Keep in mind that distances on the map generally can't be equated to time it takes to travel. There are almost no paved roads outside the major cities, and if you venture too far, bands of bandits, rebels, and general thugs may try and charge you a 'tax' for passing through their area."

She took a deep breath and drank some water. "Everyone still with me?"

Moose said, "You lost me right after the part about the name of the country." After some muffled laughs, Deirdre continued.

"Moose, right?" she asked. He smiled. "You just call it the Congo and we'll try and make sure you don't get lost. Okay... where was I? Right—the crooks in the outlying areas. Okay, so no one goes on safari out there unless you are with a large enough group and are well-armed."

Ripper couldn't help himself. "Sheeeeit...Moose and me are a large enough group to change governments down there."

Deirdre laughed. "Yes, you probably aren't that far off. Which will be a good segue to my next topic and the major reason for your mission in the DRC. And unfortunately, this can't be taken lightly. By African government standards, the DRC's presidential democratic republic is considered stable, however, in Africa the scene changes with the seasons. There have been rumors of a new rebel faction forming and being pumped up with Chinese money and arms. Obviously, a Chinese puppet government would give them unlimited access to uranium, copper, gold, and tantalum."

Everyone exchanged glances, and finally Cascaes had to ask. "Okay—you stumped me. What's Tantalum?"

"Tantalum is used for a variety of things, including alloys used in the electronics industry, super-alloys for jet engine components, nuclear reactors, and missile parts. It is highly sought after and is worth a lot of money to the DRC. It is also responsible for a lot of environmental problems down there and local wars over mining rights. Over a third of the children in the area have left school to work the mines. While it may help their families in the short run, the cycle of ignorance and poverty continues. Don't get me started on my soapbox."

Cascaes was now paying closer attention, having heard the word "China."

"How hard is the intel on Chinese involvement in the area?"

Deirdre crinkled her face in a pained expression. "That is the big question, senior chief (she was letting him know she had read his file). We had assets that were reliable down there, and they went missing. No trace. This includes one of our own agents. I was going to get to this later, but since you asked, we'll jump ahead." She pressed the computer keys a few times, jumping ahead of the geographical information and showed a slide of two pictures of the same man. He was a black man of about fifty, with salt and pepper short hair and a beard. The first picture was a headshot off of his passport in a suit and tie. The second was a picture taken in knee high grass out in the DRC with a bush hat on and sunglasses, a large camera around his neck, obviously enjoying a day out photographing animals.

"This is Nigel Ufume. He was born in the Belgian Congo and came here with his parents as a child. A smart kid, he was educated at Georgetown, and ended up working for us. Besides English, he speaks French, Swahili, and Tshiluba— the prominent languages of his native country. He had been working as our primary operative in the DRC for four years. Nigel had developed almost a dozen reliable assets over that time period, from government employees to an army colonel. He and every one of his contacts simply disappeared almost three weeks ago."

She paused and took a drink. She wasn't used to standing up and lecturing for so long, and felt like a professor. "It wasn't uncommon for a week or so to go by without contact with Nigel, but after the maximum span passed, we tried reaching out to his people out there and came up with nothing. So—you can add search and rescue to your list of things to do while in the DRC."

The mood changed in the room drastically. The team had been in Paraguay working only a couple of months earlier, and had lost one man and rescued Smitty after *he* had been captured. In the couple of hours of Smitty's capture, he had been roughed up pretty good. Hearing about a CIA operative possibly captured and missing for weeks made everyone's hair stand up, especially Smitty's, who had permanent scars all over his body from his experience.

Cascaes asked Deirdre, "Any guesses on who has him? Think it's the Chinese?"

"Well, we're still trying to follow some leads, but we had to bring in another agent and he didn't have any contacts there. He tells us that the People's Army of Congo, or 'PAC' for short, seems to be getting very organized in the shadows out there. Apparently, they are the recipients of the Chinese weapons and money, and have been actively recruiting in the countryside. If the PAC grabbed him, they may have turned him over to the Chinese that are in the DRC, or even worse, smuggled him out on that proverbial 'slow boat to China.' God help him if they did. Our guess is, they broke him and got the names of his assets, hence the disappearance of his entire organization. All speculation at this point, of course. Maybe we get lucky and they're all in hiding somewhere." She didn't sound convincing in her last sentence.

"Okay," she said sitting down and turning off the projector, "That's the overview. Use the next few days to learn as much as you can. Your date with Mr. Fish starts in twenty minutes. Jon, pick your dive buddies. We'll break into smaller groups after the fish lecture and start getting into more details of the assignment. Who's it gonna be there, Mr. Cohen?"

Jon looked at Pete McCoy and said, "Pete's my other half. And unless somebody else is dying to come with me, I'll take Jensen and O'Conner."

Ray Jensen and Ryan O'Conner were also typically paired up during SEAL operations. Moose quietly breathed a sigh of relief. Not only had he no interest in learning about tropical fish, but he hoped he might get more time with Theresa in a different assignment. She was thinking the same thing.

"Okay, congratulations. Cohen, McCoy, Jensen and O'Conner are now the brains behind 'Tanganyika Imports.'"

CHAPTER 4

The team took a quick break to grab new coffees and get rid of old ones. Dr. Hans Rutter arrived a little while later, after clearing security and being escorted all the way to the briefing room. He handed his laptop to Dex Murphy, who plugged him into their computer and projector. Dr. Rutter introduced himself and began a formal lecture about African cichlids in the fish hobby. He began with a brief history of the geography surrounding Lake Tanganyika. Lake Tanganyika and Lake Malawi were the two primary sources for African cichlid exports, although Lake Victoria to the northeast was also a valued source of cichlids.

Unfortunately for the cichlid population of Lake Victoria, the Nile perch had been introduced into the lake as a food source. And while it did help feed the indigenous peoples, the perch also wiped out many of the species and varieties of prized fish in the hobby. In fact, many fish existed only in hobbyist fish tanks around the world now, having become extinct in the wild.

Lake Tanganyika was bordered along its long western shore by the Democratic Republic of Congo, Burundi to the north-northeast, Tanzania on the long eastern shore, and Zambia to the south. The fish export business for the pet hobby was limited mostly to Tanzania where things were slightly safer. The DRC did have a few small operations, however. Foreigners mostly stayed out of Burundi, one of the world's poorest countries, and very unstable. Zambia, ravaged with AIDS and poverty, didn't make many tourist guides, either.

23

Dr. Rutter explained the high alkalinity and hardness of the lake's water, and then started showing slides of the fish, the names of which had most of the team grimacing. "Lepidiolamprologus, Julidochromis, Cyphotilapia"…it was a different language. Only Jon had ever heard of any the species. When he explained the reproductive cycle of the fish, the room got very quiet.

"Cichlids are, for the most part, mouth breeders. The female lays the eggs as the male does his little courtship dance. He has an egg spot on his anal fin, which he wiggles near where she is laying the eggs. As the female picks up the eggs to keep them in her mouth, she goes for the egg spot on the male's anal fin, at which time, he fertilizes the eggs in her mouth."

At first, no one spoke as they did the instant replay of what he just said over again in their heads. Earl Jones, a young marine that had grown up on the streets of Harlem, just about fell off his chair.

"Oh *damn*, man!" he screamed, laughing out loud. "You mean he fires off a round right in her face? Holy shit, man! I wanna be a fish!"

That opened the door for another solid two minutes of chaos in the room. Dr. Rutter, used to speaking to scholars, was not prepared for the response and was mortified. It took Cascaes pulling rank to restore order, although even he was laughing at the comments of his crude men. Theresa shot Moose "the look," and he never said a word. Julia gave Cascaes an "eyebrow," and he felt it in his trousers.

Dr. Rutter quickly moved on to capturing fish in the wild, explaining how they were kept and sorted at the "farm," treated with chemicals to reduce stress during transportation, and then the packing part of the business. Jon and his three men would be going into much greater detail later, but at least everyone had some idea of what life would be like as a fish farmer in Africa. The more pictures they looked at, the less intriguing it sounded and the more it just looked like hard work.

Once a week, they would bag fish—a half full bag of lake water mixed with pure oxygen and stress reducers, temporary home to a dozen or so fish depending on size, which went into Styrofoam crates, and was then trucked over to Luano Airport in Lubumbashi for a very long flight to Canada. Well trained, experienced fish farmers might lose ten or fifteen percent along the way, which was only one of the reasons the fish were so expensive at the pet shops. Dr. Rutter, still slightly exasperated from his lecture on the reproductive cycle, was hoping ten percent *might* live with these clowns.

The team took notes and tried their best to remain focused on the information being given to them, but their hangovers were not helping them. Their success would depend on Jon and his team paying better attention to detail in the days that followed.

The rest of the team joined Deirdre Gourlie and two of her assistants for further briefings on the geo-political happenings of the DRC. No matter how bad things looked in the US on the news, they paled in comparison to what was happening almost anywhere on the African continent. When they broke for lunch, Julia had an opportunity to speak to Chris privately. She looked sad.

"It's like seeing Paraguay all over again," she lamented. "South America and Africa are two continents bursting with natural resources and people willing to work hard, but their governments and leaders are all so corrupt that the people suffer and die by the millions. It's unconscionable to me. And no one gives a shit."

Chris could see her getting wound up. "That's not true. *Lots* of people try to help. The problem is getting the help to the right people. How many shipments of US aid ever get to where it's needed? *That's* the problem. It ain't for lack of trying."

"Then we need to try harder. And not just the US. *Everyone* should be helping."

"Yeah, well, I bet the Chinese are going to start helping quite a bit now," he said somewhat sarcastically.

"And that's just it, Chris. China will help because they want something in return. Just like when we give aid to countries that have oil, or something we want. But poor countries in Africa and South America, Hell—everywhere, if that don't have anything we *need*, they get *shit*."

"That sounds about right. You think the American taxpayers are going to work a few extra hours every week to send more money to someplace they never heard of to make some warlord richer? It's a shitty world, Julia. Just be glad you live here."

Deirdre happened to catch the last part of their conversation as she walked past. She stopped and smiled at Julia. "He's right, Julia. And I heard about all the work you did in Paraguay with the Guaranis down there. It's nice that you care and you try to help. But I've been covering Africa for ten years, and honestly, it is a depressing mess. You don't need to get heartbroken in the DRC. Do your job, get home safe, and forget you were there. Trust me. Africa will break your heart." She turned and walked away to begin the next briefing.

CHAPTER 5

Deirdre was standing at the front of the briefing room facing the team. Jon Cohen, Pete McCoy, Ray Jensen and Ryan O'Conner were in another room with Dr. Rutter, learning how to run a fish farm. Deirdre was looking at Julia when she began speaking.

"The DRC, like most African nations, has seen more than its share of violence and war. The First and Second Congo Wars were brutal by *any* standards. The Second Congo War took place between 1998 and 2003. Best estimates are approximately four million dead. Four *million*. The short version is the Hutus of the DRC, backed by Namibia, Zimbabwe, Angola, and Chad fought the Tutsis of the DRC. The rebel factions called the 'Mouvement pour la Liberation du Congo' were backed by Uganda, Rwanda and Burundi. To say they were brutal to each other doesn't really paint the picture. As bad as things were in the DRC, in neighboring Rwanda, it is estimated that three-quarters of the entire Tutsi population was slaughtered in '94. The irony of the Tutsi-Hutu war is that the two cultures are almost identical. It brings to mind Jonathan Swift's satire about a war over which was the proper way to open a soft boiled egg."

Deirdre flashed through almost twenty slides in thirty seconds, showing piles of corpses and destroyed villages to make her point.

"This is beyond the scope of your mission. You are not the UN, and most of this is behind us now. The reason I'm showing you this nightmare is to remind you of where you are

27

going. I know most of you have served in Afghanistan or Iraq or both. As bad as things are there, they're worse in Africa. In Iraq, a death squad shows up and kidnaps a few men, maybe decapitates them after a night of torture. In Africa, a rebel force arrives at a village and kills everything that moves. That's after raping the women from eight to eighty years old. I can't begin to impress upon you the conditions these people have been living in for their entire lives. It is important to understand, because most of these rebels are not fighting for a cause, they are fighting for a meal. Literally. A *meal*. Keep that in mind down there when you're trying to acquire assets. You can trust no one, but you can also buy real information from almost anyone."

Deirdre walked around the desk in the front of the room and sat on it facing the room. She crossed her athletic legs, every pair of male eyes on them as she did so. Again, she looked at Julia.

"You all served together in Paraguay and I'm familiar with the operation in great detail even though it was in South America. I want you all to understand that you are not in the Congo to build a school or feed the hungry."

Julia felt her face flush, and fought off the urge to respond.

"While I appreciate your good intentions and your humanity, I am trying to mentally prepare you for what you will see when you are there. You will *want* to give away all of your food and medicine the first minute you arrive. You are human, and you are good people. Forget it. Resupplying you is not easily done, and once you go down the road of being the Peace Corps, you will never be able to operate. You are operating a fish farm, not an aid station, and if you aren't careful, you'll have a thousand refugees loitering around your camp."

Cascaes, starting to get annoyed at the lecture on Julia's behalf interjected. "I think we get the point, ma'am."

"I hope you do, because you'd be the first." She let that sink in. "*Every agent* that we have sent into remote parts of Africa has called in for immediate aid to the local population. There are legitimate reasons to aid the locals, I understand that. It builds good will and maybe wins you some friends, but it also escalates faster than you can imagine down there. Many of these people have *nothing*. There will be hundreds, maybe thousands, of people that will be dying or damn near close to it. You will be driving by children dying of malnutrition while you eat your lunch and want to cry, but *eat your lunch* and look straight ahead. I am telling you all this because I have been all over Africa. Everywhere you look you will see disaster and you'll want to help. You all need to be mentally prepared for this, and I don't think I can stress that enough. Maybe this will help. I apologize in advance."

Deirdre walked back around and turned on a slide show from her computer. For the next six minutes, the group sat in silence as they looked at hundreds of slides of dead and dying men, women, and children—victims of war, famine, disease, and total hopelessness. By the time the slide show ended and Deirdre turned the lights back on, every face in the room had fallen. Deirdre looked around the room and folded her arms across her chest.

"I know," she said quietly. "And the DRC is not as bad as it gets. Burundi, Rwanda, and Zimbabwe are worse. The life expectancy in Zimbabwe was sixty in 1990. Today it's thirty-four for women and thirty-seven for men. And it isn't getting any better. If the HIV/AIDs epidemic gets much worse, there won't be *anyone* living there in fifty years. Almost half of the population is currently infected. So—Julia and the rest of you, if you think I have been hard on you or belabored this information, maybe you understand now.

"Africa is a very difficult place to work. You will see some of the most amazing natural beauty in the world, in countries full of natural resources and people who want a chance at a better life, and you will also see the most heart breaking and depressing living conditions on earth. If you think the slides went overboard in any way, think again. There is nothing I can do to fully mentally prepare you for this operation. But at least now you've been warned. Just remember to stay on task and harden your heart. Get in, do your job and get home safe. That's it. That's all you can do. Everyone go take a walk outside and meet here again in twenty minutes."

⊕

Deirdre went back to her private office and closed her door, then put her head on her desk and cried. She had been through those slides many times to try and prepare agents for their time in some of the most depressing places on Earth. What she hadn't told anyone was that she had taken those photos herself some years back. Almost every face in those pictures was burned into her brain. She knew what those people had sounded like when they were crying for help, for food, for anything. And all she could do was take pictures.

Outside, the members sat in the fresh air in total silence. After twenty minutes, Cascaes looked at his watch and told everyone to get back to work. The team walked back inside, still not speaking, except for Cory Stewart, who stood leaning against the brick building. Cascaes spotted him.

"You okay?" he asked quietly.

Cory looked at the blue sky for a moment and then at Cascaes. "Yeah, I'm good. Before I joined the team I spent some time in Africa. That continent gets inside your soul and never leaves, man. Some of the most beautiful landscapes and animals, some of the friendliest people—hell, they'd be starving and *still* offer you half of what they had. And some of the most brutal, inhuman shit I've ever witnessed. I thought I had seen it all, man. But until you walk into a village and see a pile of arms that's taller than you, you just don't know what people are capable of. Anyway—I hadn't thought about that stuff in a long time. On purpose, you know? I had some close calls over there, myself. I hope the missing agent is just on the run, and not being taken apart piece by piece. I'd put a gun in my mouth first."

Cascaes smacked his arm. "We've all seen some shit, no doubt. You gotta let it go or it'll kill you."

"Hey, man, I'm good. Like I said, I don't think about that shit anymore. But when it's shoved in your face, it comes back a little, you know? I was in Africa five times for five different missions, totally unrelated to each other. And every single one of them was a fucking disaster, including Mogadishu. I just hope this one goes better." He faked a tight smile. "I'm good, Skipper."

Cory walked back inside quickly with Cascaes following. It was the most Cory had ever said to him at one time.

CHAPTER 6

When they returned to the briefing room, one of Deirdre's assistants was there. Jesse Daniels had worked for Deirdre for the past eight years, first as a field agent in and out of Africa, and then "inside" for the last four years after getting sick in-country. It was four weeks of intense drug therapy before the parasites that almost killed him were finally eradicated. He welcomed everyone back and had them get seated. As soon as all were sitting, he dimmed the lights and began showing photos of some of the contacts that Nigel Ufume had made before he disappeared. They took notes on names and locations as Jesse explained the network that Nigel had built over the years.

The next slides were of press clippings from the last few months. One of them showed a statement from the DRC's Mining Minister, Djumi Ofama, requesting help from the world community to help police the mining of uranium in the country. While the DRC had "officially" closed down the mines at both Shinkolobwe and Lubumbashi, over 7,000 miners still worked the locations by hand, selling the ore to private companies owned by Chinese and Indian "businesses."

One of Nigel's contacts had talked about large numbers of sick children who had worked in the mines for a few months. Their low body weights made them the "canaries in the coal mine," and they were the first to show signs of radiation sickness. Based on what Nigel had been told, the quantity of uranium must have been vast.

Jesse handed out maps of local roads, rail lines, and villages. Some of the villages had names penned beneath them of key contacts—some to use for help, some to stay the hell away from. After over an hour of detailed information, Jesse put the lights on and shifted gears to a more relaxed mood.

"Okay—I know you've had a long day, and we'll break for dinner in a bit, but 'food' is a good segue to my next topic, which is food." He smiled and everyone groaned, having flashbacks to the Guaranis eating monkeys, caterpillars, and lord knows what else back in Paraguay. "I worked in and out of Africa for several years. I've covered Somalia, Angola, Uganda, Burundi, you name it. My last stint was in Somalia, and I ended up getting sick as hell. Almost died from some type of parasite that we never did figure out how I got. Might have eaten something, might have been bitten by something, who knows? Anyway—you don't eat anything unless you see it killed and butchered in front of you. Vegetables and fruit are usually okay, but cook the hell out of them. Your best bets are your MREs. I know they suck—but you won't die from them."

He smiled broadly. "Now I am going to tell you a true story." That got a groan.

"When I first started working in Africa, I was with one other agent—just us. So we positioned ourselves in a small town posing as businessmen looking for opportunities in metal mining. After we made some contacts, we spent a couple of months in a tiny shithole of a village near the mining operation, where we were trying to sort out who the players were. Anyway, I couldn't eat *anything* except the local raisin bread. Anything else I ate made me sick. I lost about twenty pounds in two months. So every day, I'm eating raisin bread, baked fresh right there. Great stuff, except that I was getting pretty damn bored of it. Occasionally I would eat some porridge or shit with it, but honestly, everything turned my stomach other than the fresh bread, right out of the local oven.

So anyway, after about three weeks of living on the stuff, one day I go and get some bread for breakfast, and there aren't any raisins in it—just plain bread. I figure the raisins are probably the only real nutrition I'm getting, and I want my damn raisin bread. So I ask the baker where the raisin bread is. He asks what raisin bread? And we go back and forth with my shitty language skills until I understand that they just got new bags of flour, and that's why there aren't any 'raisins' in it yet. Maybe I should come back in a few weeks."

It took everyone a second to figure out what Jesse was actually saying as he was speaking, but as they caught on, the heads began shaking.

Lance Woods, an army ranger famous for eating just about anything, asked, "Didn't you notice the wings, man?"

There were a few chuckles and comments about not complaining about MREs anymore. Jesse laughed. "No shit— that's a true story. And when the raisins finally *did* show up back in the bread again, I ate it." He shrugged his shoulders. "And that ain't what made me sick, either. At least those little suckers were cooked."

Julia leaned over to Chris and whispered that they could skip dinner.

Jesse handed out briefing sheets that listed known foreign companies working in the eastern region of the DRC. There were over a hundred companies listed from China, India, North Korea, and South Africa. Sorting the legitimate companies from government shells would take some work, but in any case, the export of uranium had officially been made illegal by the DRC government. Any company exporting uranium, usually through Zambia or directly onto ships in Muanda on the Atlantic coast, was breaking the law.

A rail line ran west from the mining areas through the skinny western arm of the DRC to the Atlantic, the DRC's only access to the ocean. Muanda, a city of about 50,000 people, had seaports and an airport, and refinery operations had sprung up along the rail lines. It wasn't a huge leap to conclude that ore was being mined, transported, smelted and refined, and then either shipped out by boat or plane. Gathering information on that process was another item on their "to do" list.

Jesse went into great details of the operation for another hour and then finally put the lights back on and walked closer to the team sitting in front of him. His demeanor went serious and he looked at his shoes for a moment while he tried to find the right words.

"We work in a dangerous business. Most of the time, we work without a safety net. I know most of you come from specialized military backgrounds where you don't necessarily get to call in air support or expect someone to come get you if things go south. You are all used to being self-reliant, which is a good background to have. Nigel was no different. He knew the risks, same as all of us. But the people here at home see what are called abuses at Abu Ghraib or Gitmo and get outraged because prisoners were humiliated, sleep deprived or scared shitless by big growling dogs. The difference between an American interrogation and a Chinese interrogation is that the Chinese will release the dogs.

"If they *have* Nigel, and I think they *do*, they will not have any qualms about taking him apart piece by piece to find out whatever they can. Once they're finished with him, they'll kill him just as sure as I am standing here. The chances of rescuing Nigel are almost nil, but I expect you to try. Other than your team, he has no chance. No one else is going to look for him. Anyway—that's all for tonight. Go grab some dinner and get a good night's sleep. Tomorrow we start again at seven."

CHAPTER 7

The briefings and training continued for ten long days. At the end of the ten days, Jon and his crew sounded like tropical fish experts, Theresa, the navy corpsman, had studied African diseases and parasites, and the rest of the team knew their way around the southeastern DRC. Places, people, and businesses had been memorized, and they knew more about metals and mining than a college geology student. It was time.

At six pm, Darren Davis and Deirdre Gourlie entered the large conference room where the team was helping themselves to a large buffet at their "graduation party." Darren had ordered a huge amount of food—all of it first class. Sushi rolls, prime rib, shrimp, crab legs, Chinese food, lasagna—you name it, it was on the long table. So were cold beers, a bottle of sake, and a couple of bottles of red and white wine. Cascaes saw them enter and called out, "Attention on deck." Everyone stood at attention, most of them with plates piled high with food.

Darren and Deirdre laughed. "So formal today?" asked Deirdre.

"Anyone that feeds us like this gets a salute, ma'am," said Cascaes, snapping a sharp salute to her and Darren. They laughed and gave their best salutes in return, and everyone chuckled. "I apologized to my men when I saw the food. I hadn't realized this was a suicide mission."

Darren laughed and grabbed a cold bottle of beer. "It's not a suicide mission, but you also aren't staying at the Mandarin Oriental. I hope everyone has their favorite food in here *somewhere.* Trust me when I tell you that you won't be eating very well in the Democratic Republic of Congo."

Chris looked at Deirdre. "Yeah, Jesse told us his bread story. I think we'll be sticking to MREs."

Deirdre smiled. "The snake tastes just like chicken," she said, "But the water buffalo can be a bit stringy and gamey, especially if it's been out in the sun for a day or two."

"Thanks," Chris mumbled.

Darren filled a plate and sat down next to Chris, who was sitting next to Julia—no big surprise. If Darren was curious about their relationship, he kept it to himself. Deirdre picked up a bottle of wine, but Jake Koches quickly took it from her and said, "Allow me." When he had poured her the glass of Merlot, she walked to the head of the table and asked for everyone's attention. Everyone stopped speaking and looked over.

"Here's to a successful mission. Come home safe, and bring Nigel back home, too." She paused and cleared her throat. "And *fuck* China."

Everyone cheered at the pretty little Irish girl using sailor's language. They cheered and toasted and returned to gorging themselves. Darren leaned over to Chris Cascaes.

"I spoke to Mac yesterday," said Darren.

Chris Mackey was the baseball team's "coach" from their last mission. It had been Mackey who originally came up with the idea of the baseball team cover story. He had led the operation, along with Cascaes, in Paraguay, but had contemplated retirement and dropped out of sight.

Chris smiled. "How is ol' Mackey?" he asked. "He must be on some little island somewhere getting drunk and chasing skirts."

Darren leaned closer. "Actually, he told me to tell you to move your ass and bring him a decent bottle of scotch. He's in the DRC waiting for you. He'll be waiting for you at Luano Airport in Lubumbashi when you get there."

Chris laughed out loud and shook his head. "Well isn't that like a good friend, to pick me up at the airport. When did he get there?"

"A week ago," Darren said quietly.

Chris felt himself get angry. "And you're just telling me now?"

"Not my call," he replied. "The boss isn't thrilled with your team concept as it is. He says the group is already way too big and "you guys are going to be the death of him." That's a quote, by the way. Anyway, the director spoke with him personally yesterday and Mac says the Chinese have been very busy. The PAC is much further along than we anticipated. We changed your weapon load after we spoke to Mac. You are ready for a full scale war, and the president has redirected a troop ship of marines from the Middle East to the African coast.

"While the president doesn't want another Somalia on his hands, and certainly doesn't want to antagonize the Chinese, he also won't sit back and allow the Chinese to fund the PAC and overthrow a pro-American government. You will be stepping into a sticky wicket, my friend."

Cascaes clinked Darren's bottle and drank back the second half of his beer in a long chug. He muffled his burp and smiled crookedly at Darren. "So much for a little recon and rescue mission, huh? Well, no matter. My men are better at breaking things and killing people than they are at search and rescue anyway."

Darren kept his voice low, the room getting louder around him as the team drank and ate and laughed a little too loudly, feeling the jitters of getting ready to head out.

"Look, Chris. The PAC may already number over six or seven thousand. Mac is trying to find out who the leaders are, and hopefully, if you can take them out, the rebellion will fall apart. But don't go toe to toe with a friggin' *army*. If the president calls in the Marines, it won't be to rescue *you* guys, it will be a political decision that has nothing to do with you guys. All I'm saying is, stay in the shadows. This is not a military operation."

"I understand," said Chris. "But I would like to go over the new weapons and ammo list with you after dinner."

CHAPTER 8

The flight from Virginia to Canada was via private CIA jet. Once there, they switched passports and boarded a commercial flight to Spain, where they had to change planes to South Africa. Once in South Africa, it was a smaller plane to Luano Airport in Lubumbashi. All in all, from Virginia to Lubumbashi was over thirty hours, and no one was in a particularly good mood when they arrived at the sweaty Luano Airport customs line. It was over eighty-five degrees inside the airport, which might have been cleaned once or twice in the last ten years. While there were a few fans visible in the terminal, not one of them was operational. The weary travelers stood in line fanning themselves with their counterfeit Canadian passports as a bored looking man stamped them in front of a security guard carrying an ancient machine gun. Hodges, the resident marine sharpshooter leaned over to his buddy Earl Jones and whispered in his southern drawl that if the guy fired his weapon, it would blow up in his face. He was probably correct.

After the group cleared customs, they walked down another dirty hallway to freight pickup. They cringed as they watched a half dozen sweaty men manhandle their large crates into the airport. The crates were heavy, having double and triple interior walls to hide weapons, ammunition, and other equipment that would get them arrested. The lead lining to shield from x-rays made them even heavier. The men were screaming at each other in frustration trying to deal with the weight of the crates when an official looking man in a military looking uniform walked over to find out what all the fuss was about. He approached the group, the only ones in the area, and asked what they were importing.

"We aren't importing anything, sir," said Chris. "We are actually in the *export* business—live tropical fish export. This is SCUBA diving equipment and materials we need for our business at the lake."

The official looked at the manifest list on the outside of one of the crates and mumbled to himself for a while as he pretended to understand what he was looking at.

"Extra heavy packages like these are subject to import taxes. Are you in charge of this group?" he asked Chris.

"Yes," he said, sensing the impending shakedown. The official had Chris follow him down another dirty hallway to his small office. When they walked inside, it had an ancient wooden desk and one chair, and nothing else.

The official was tentative. "You have American dollars?" he asked.

Chris shook his head. "No, sir. We're Canadians. I only have Canadian currency."

The official rubbed his chin. "How many Canadian dollars equal an American dollar?" he asked, obviously clueless.

"One Canadian dollar equals two American dollars," Chris lied.

"Well then you will have to pay one hundred dollars as a special tax," he said, trying to be smooth. To him, it was almost five months salary, and he wasn't sure if he was asking for too much.

"Wow, that's a lot," said Chris, waiting for some reaction. They stood and stared at each other for a moment, and then Chris broke out a small wad of bills. He had intentionally stuck his cash in small wads in a dozen different places, for this specific reason. He counted the money, which came out to eighty dollars Canadian. "I didn't go to the bank yet, it's all I have on me."

The official swiped it from his hand and shoved it into his shirt pocket. "My cousin has a truck. Maybe you need a ride somewhere to transfer your cargo?"

Chris fought the urge to smile. *"I bet he does,"* he thought to himself, *"and your other cousin sells gas, and your other cousin…"*

"Well?" he asked, now getting nervous.

"Actually, my business associate is here waiting to pick us up," he said. The official grunted and left the office, with Chris close behind. When they got back to the group, he disappeared. Chris's men pushed the cargo on ancient wooden dollies with wheels that were worse than any wobbly grocery shopping-cart. By the time they got to the main entrance of the airport, they were soaked and cursing under their breath. Mackey's voice echoing off the walls broke the tension.

"Hey!" he yelled, a genuine smile on his face as he saw all of the familiar faces.

Chris smiled and walked over to exchange a big hug. Cascaes whispered, "We cool here?"

"So far. But let's get your shit and get the hell out of here. We have a lot to talk about. I'll go pull the truck up to the door."

Cascaes couldn't help but laugh at the big fish cartoon on the back of Mackey's t-shirt as he walked away.

Mackey pulled up in what looked like an ancient school bus with the roof cut off. Seats in the rear had been removed to make a sort of cargo area. It squeaked and rattled as he pulled up, and the men were laughing hysterically at the heap.

"Go ahead and laugh," said Mackey, "It's the only thing I could find that can carry your fat asses, ladies excluded, of course," he added, catching himself.

The team loaded up their cargo in the back of the bus and piled in. The seats were torn, and most of them were missing the arms. Theresa joked that she couldn't find her seatbelt.

Mackey cranked the engine back up, which belched black smoke, and pulled away from the airport. As they bounced off to begin their mission, Cascaes looked back to see the official standing outside the airport with his arms folded across his chest, watching them closely. He quickly told Mac about the shakedown at the airport.

"Welcome to Africa," said Mackey.

CHAPTER 9

The bus coughed and sputtered as they drove, but kept going. Mackey was driving at just about top speed, almost sixty, on the paved road that led out of Lubumbashi. The steering was similar to driving a boat, with Mackey working the wheel like crazy just to drive straight. Cascaes laughed as he watched him drive.

"Nice ride, boss. You pay more than twenty bucks for it?"

Mackey flipped him the bird and kept looking straight ahead, trying to find the sign for the road to the railroad station.

"Hey, Mac, for real—is this hunk of junk going to make it all the way to Lake T?"

"Not a chance," said Mackey. "I rented this piece of crap from a guy at the rail station. We are taking the train back to Kalemie, which, if we hustle, we'll make by about ten minutes. It took three hours yesterday to get here. If you think this truck is a piece of shit, wait till you see the train."

Cascaes laughed and held on to the door as Mackey swerved all over the road, avoiding people on bicycles, people walking livestock, people with chickens on their heads, people everywhere. It was all he could do to stay on the road and maintain some kind of speed. The rest of the group in the back were mostly quiet, just soaking it all in. The sights and sounds of a new country—new languages being shouted in sing-song mixtures of local dialects mixed with French; goats, cattle, and chickens being moved along the road, each with its own smell and noise, little corrugated steel shacks that were homes and businesses, wood fires with things being cooked and sold—it all painted a sign that said "you are in Africa now, so forget everything you ever thought you knew."

Mackey got them to the train station and pulled the truck-bus-jalopy up in front of the same place where he had rented it for forty dollars Canadian. He turned off the engine, and they all laughed as they listened to it cough itself to death slowly twenty seconds later. The same African man that had rented him the truck also ran the small rail station. There was no train.

"Did we miss the train?" asked Mackey in decent French.

The man laughed. "No, mister. She late again. She always late." He laughed and walked away, leaving them there to unload all of their crates. Moose and Ripper did most of the heavy lifting, carrying crates by themselves that four men at the airport had trouble moving together.

Theresa brushed by Moose and whispered, "That's my man," as she watched him work. He and Ripper were the two biggest members of the group, and they were both unusually strong.

Mackey disappeared inside the rail station and returned with a case of Coca-Cola. It was warm, but it was wet, and in sealed green bottles. He started tossing them out to the group, ladies first.

"I'm not sure what year these were made in, but it's wet and won't give you malaria." The coke didn't taste anything like what they drank at home, probably because it was made in South Africa instead of Atlanta, but it was a welcomed treat just the same.

The train arrived over an hour later, well past the posted arrival time, but the man in the station smiled and told Mackey they made good time. After some discussions with the man about loading their cargo, and the extra money that entailed, they boarded the train. The cargo was put on an open flat car, and the group sat on top of the boxes. The other choice was going inside the one passenger car, which was built to hold fifty passengers, but instead held eighty, along with goats, chickens, a large steer, several crates of pigeons, boxes of supplies, and smelled worse than the Bronx Zoo lion cage on a hot day in August. Besides, they had to guard their cargo anyway, and sitting on it would be a perfect way to keep an eye, or butt, on it.

After a day and a half of rebreathing stale airplane air, the members of the team smiled and enjoyed the warm sunshine and fresh breeze as the train chugged along out of Lubumbashi. The steady rocking and clackety-clacking of the train had them all ready to fall asleep within a half hour. They stretched out on top and between the crates, wherever they could find room. The entire flatcar was theirs. Mackey and Cascaes sat against one of the boxes, their legs over the side of the car.

Mackey spoke quietly. "Man, I thought Paraguay was messed up until I got here. In a little over a week, I've heard enough stories to make me want to quit the human race."

"Yeah, Deirdre from the Africa desk gave us a little slide show to try and prepare us mentally for this trip. Not stuff you can forget too quickly."

"Yeah, well, with all due respect, the slideshow isn't going to prepare you for *shit*. There are more diseases than people out here. Everywhere you go, people are sick or homeless or starving. I'm not talking about Lubumbashi—that place is like a first class hotel compared to the countryside. Most of the villages are made out of mud with thatched roofs like they were made a thousand years ago. Every few months, some group of maniacs raids a village and kills everybody and steals everything they can carry, and there are no police outside the cities, really. This country is fucked, man."

"Yeah? So what the hell are we doing here?" asked Cascaes.

"It's called uranium, maybe you heard of it. They make big fucking bombs out of the stuff. Apparently, the Chinese would like it. All of it."

"Any news?" asked Cascaes.

"Yeah. Lot's of it. Never sure how reliable any of it is, but a dollar will buy you hours of stories. And an MRE might get you a friend for life."

Cascaes thought back to Jesse's speech about the people fighting for a sandwich, not for a political agenda. He asked, "So you hear anything about the Chinese or Nigel disappearing?"

Mackey closed his eyes and pointed his face to the sun, catching a ray. "Lots of talk about the Chinese and the People's Army of Congo. Just say 'PAC' around here and people shit in their pants…or loincloths, whatever the case may be."

"And?" asked Cascaes.

"And evidently, the rumors are true. Chinese agents are spreading lots of money around. They opened a 'humanitarian aid station' not far from Kalemie. When did you *ever* hear of China doing a humanitarian mission?"

"Uh, never," said Cascaes.

"Exactly. I drove by there to see what was going down. Couldn't even get close, man. 'Security guards,' they're calling them. Security guards my ass. There was a whole fuckin army down there, all carrying new Chinese machine guns. Even had pretty little yellow berets so they could resemble an actual army. We'll go pay them a visit one of these nights. You brought night vision equipment, right?"

"Affirmative. When the stories came in about the size of the PAC, the company was kind enough to double our combat load. There is also a float of marines heading to the coast, although I'm told they most likely won't be allowed to land."

"Too bad," said Mackey. "Give us a couple of rifle companies and we could wipe the slate clean in two days."

"Hell, Executive Outcome took Angola with a group not much bigger than what we have now." Executive Outcome was a group of mercenaries hired by the Angolan government to bolster their army. Oil companies had also hired them to secure the oil fields from UNITA forces during the war. It was estimated that a force of some five hundred mercenaries defeated a rebel army over ten times its size.

"Yeah, well, I spoke with Director Holstrum himself last week. He specifically told me not to start World War Three with China."

Cascaes grunted.

"So anyway, China is giving away food and money to anyone who will join the PAC, and the DRC government doesn't want to face the music yet. Instead, they are asking the UN to send peacekeepers for fear of increasing instability. They asked that same great organization for help securing the uranium mines six months ago. You see any white trucks that said 'UN' on the side? 'Cause I sure didn't."

"Yeah, I seem to have missed those little blue flags, too," said Cascaes sarcastically.

"Right. And while the DRC government sits around waiting for the UN to come rescue them, China is going to help build an army to overthrow their ass."

"Well, we won't be bored," said Cascaes. "Any hits on Nigel?"

"Unfortunately, that's been a dead end. Maybe if he had been a white guy, somebody would have noticed something. He just totally disappeared. My guess is the Chinese took him. If he *is* still alive, he's either in China or down at their little aid station surrounded by a few thousand guerrillas. Either way, it doesn't look good."

They sat in silence for a while, contemplating being captured by the Chinese. They independently decided in their own heads that they would die fighting first. Cascaes finally broke the silence.

"You see our new home away from home yet?" he asked.

"Yeah. That's where I've been staying this past week. Hot and cold running crocodiles, ants bigger than small mice, lots of rocks...hmmm...am I missing anything?"

"Sounds charming," said Cascaes.

"Actually, it isn't that bad," said Mackey. "There are a few small cabins and a large building for the fish right on the lake. Two generators actually work, and they run the pumps and plumbing for the fish tanks. We use them at night for electricity, but we also have kerosene lamps. It gets a little buggy around dusk, but the Canuks we bought the place from were kind enough to leave us insecticide bombs that we use almost every other night. Sleeping may be a little tight."

Mackey looked around to make sure no one was listening. "Hey, you hittin' that?" he asked, meaning Julia.

Cascaes smiled. "Hey, man, I don't kiss and tell."

"But if you *did* tell?" asked Mackey, who had met Julia at the same time as Cascaes and also found her to be drop-dead gorgeous.

"If I *did* tell, I'd tell you that she is everything you could possibly imagine," Cascaes said with a big smile.

"Uh, oh," said Mackey. "This doesn't sound like a guy getting laid. You are in *love*, my man?"

"Big time," said Cascaes.

"Holy shit," said Mackey. "I'm gonna' have to pick a fight with the Chinese just to keep you focused."

Cascaes laughed. "What about you? You getting laid?"

"Shit," said Mackey dramatically, "It's been so long for me, the last woman I was inside of was the Statue of Liberty."

✦

Shen Xun-jun stood at the head of the parade ground inside the aid station. He was not one to make sarcastic comments or jokes. Mr. Shen was an immensely intimidating figure, far beyond what would be expected of his five foot six and 120-pound stature. The man was perhaps sixty, but with his tight oriental complexion, looked younger. His face was a permanent scowl, and when he put his hands on his hips and stood with his stiff posture, people walked on eggshells around him. He didn't speak, really—it was more of a bark. He would shout short orders at the men that worked for him, who in turn would snap salutes and run to do whatever he had instructed. Their obvious fear of Shen Xun-jun was contagious. When Shen Xun-jun snapped at them in Chinese, they would in turn scream orders in French to the PAC soldiers, who complied immediately. The African soldiers figured if these Chinese officers were afraid of him, there must be a reason. And there was.

Shen Xun-jun did not wear the uniform of a Chinese "shao jiang,"—equivalent to an American major general—although that is what he was. He wore the khaki style reminiscent of the Japanese uniforms of early World War Two, right down the balloon pants and leggings. It bore no markings, other than a small red star on the short billed khaki cap. The same was true of his nine officers, who ranged in rank from sergeant major (liu ji shi guan) to colonel (shang xiao).

While none of the officers wore rank insignias, the PAC soldiers addressed Shen Xun-jun as "shao jiang" and the rest of the officers as "xiao." While xiao was a shortened form of several different ranks mixed into one, (shang xiao, zhong xiao, shao xiao) the PAC soldiers couldn't keep them straight and lumped the officer's ranks together. The Chinese, who had no respect for the PAC soldiers, could have cared less *what* they called them as long as they did as they were told.

Shen Xun-jun had started his army career twenty years earlier, and half way through his career had ended up in Army Intelligence. Now a special officer in the CELD (Central External Liaison Department), he had been given the assignment of putting together a force of Congolese rebels large enough to take down the current regime. With only nine officers and endless amounts of cash, food and weapons, Shen Xun-jun had exceeded the CELD's expectations. While they had anticipated a minimum of ten months to a year to put together an operation of this magnitude, Shen Xun-jun had an army training and hungry to fight in less than five months. Because his operation was so heavily supported with food, flown in almost weekly, his army had swelled to almost ten thousand around the country, including over six thousand in his central training center which was very thinly disguised as an aid station. Perhaps the most heavily guarded one on the planet.

As Shen Xun-jun stood on the parade ground in the hot African sun, he watched companies of soldiers training around his camp. They ran in formation around the perimeter, carrying brand new Chinese machine guns. Many of them had taken off their shiny new black boots because they had never worn shoes before, and they were constantly tripping. The Chinese let it go, so long as they kept their berets on and kept their weapons spotless.

They were a primitive bunch, in Shen Xun-jun's opinion, but certainly capable of deposing the shaky regime that currently ran the country. As long as the other African nations stayed out of the fight, which they most likely *would* since they had their *own* problems, the revolution had a great chance of success. The leader of the PAC, an educated man named Mboto Kangani, had promised the Chinese government carte-blanche once they controlled the country. With a puppet government running what would become "The People's Republic of Congo," China would have complete access to all of the nation's vast natural resources.

Back in China, government officials were already discussing the construction of a nuclear power plant in the new PRC. It would bring the poor nation out of the dark ages, and produce weapon's grade plutonium in the process for China's own agenda. Of course, a nation of mostly illiterate people would need lots of assistance from China, who was more than willing to help.

CHAPTER 10

It ended up being almost four hours back to Kalemie. By the time they arrived, the charm of sitting out on the open railcar had ended. Everyone was jet lagged, tired, hungry, and pretty much fed up with traveling. Unfortunately, Kalemie wasn't where they would be living. The fish farm was located further south, back towards the direction they had just come from, but there was no direct route from Lubumbashi.

The team unloaded the cargo boxes from the train and Mackey spoke with a young man at the station. The man disappeared, then returned with three other men. Mackey spoke his bad French with them for a bit, and then they hustled off to get the trucks. These men were truck drivers that the old Canadian company had employed for several years to transport the live fish from their village to Luano Airport at Lubumbashi. Today they would be transporting the team from Kalemie to a tiny little village called Buwali, about halfway between Kalemie and Lubunduye. The population of Buwali was less than 400 people, almost all of whom were fishermen.

Buwali consisted of mud huts with thatched roofs, and some primitive corrals that kept the few cattle and goats from wandering off. Small children tended the livestock, while the older ones worked with their parents on the Lake. Lake Tanganyika is one of Africa's largest and deepest lakes, and to stand on its shore, you would think you were at the ocean. Except, of course, one doesn't usually find crocodiles sunning themselves at the ocean.

The inhabitants of Buwali had been very upset when they found out that the fishery was being sold. For them, it was their major source of revenue. Most of the fish caught by the villagers was by hook for eating, and stayed in the village. But the live fish that they caught by gill net and delivered to the fish farm were sold for *cash*. That cash was just about the only money the village ever saw. Any other fishing, farming, livestock trading, etc. was just bartered in the village for day to day survival. The live fish they sold to the Canadians was their only real "industry" that enabled them to earn cash for purchasing items from the nearby cities. When Mackey showed up the week prior and word spread that another white man was working the lake, the fishermen began showing up with nets-full of live fish.

Mackey tried his best to explain that the fish farm wouldn't be open for another few weeks, but the men of the village knew the operation inside out, and without even asking or waiting for the farm to reopen, they happily began stocking the outside holding tanks with Frontosas, Benthochromis Tricotis, Leleupis, and other colorful Tanganyikan cichlids. The original Canadians had been from Quebec, and French was their first language. The Buwali people also spoke French, along with their own dialect, Swahili, and Kikongo. They had heard very little English, and used English words mixed with their creole style French for names of things that had no name in their own language. A Coca-Cola in Kikongo or Swahili was still a Coca-Cola.

Mackey's French was decent, but he struggled with the local French, which almost sounded like Patois, the Creole French on some Caribbean islands. When Julia told Mackey she spoke fluent French, he wanted to kiss her—more so than he already did—but he had conceded that to Cascaes. Julia, who spoke fluent Spanish as well as the Guarani language of the Paraguayan tribes, was a natural at picking up the sing-song French of the locals.

The team had arrived at the fishing village appropriately packed like sardines in three trucks along with their equipment. The drive had taken over an hour, following a worn path through the grass—nothing you would call an actual road. Had there *been* a road, they could have made it in fifteen or twenty minutes. The trucks pulled up in front of the small compound that was their new fish farm. Locals were standing around cheering their arrival. The villagers had brought gifts of local fruit and dried salted fish, one of their staple foods.

The team climbed down off of the trucks, now completely exhausted and so jet lagged they were almost hallucinating, but smiled and tried to communicate "hellos" to their new neighbors. Julia was quick to jump in with her French, and as soon as the villagers realized she could speak fluently, they surrounded her and started speaking a hundred miles an hour to welcome them to Buwali. She thanked them for the food and warm welcome, and explained that they would need a few days to get organized. Of course, there were dozens of offers of help with everything from cleaning, to cooking, to bringing more fish. They took her by the hand and led her down to the holding tanks. The holding tanks were 500-gallon plastic tubs with water being exchanged directly from the lake through an extensive plumbing system devised by the previous fish farmers. The villagers were proud to show her all of the fish they had caught.

While she spoke with the villagers and looked at all of the fish, Mackey gave Cascaes and the rest of the team a tour of the buildings. There were several huts that would serve as their new homes. The huts had thick mud walls and thatched roofs, with several windows that had no glass, but did have wooden shutters that could be opened and closed. The floor was dirt, but had woven mats that covered most of it. A large clay fireplace in one corner served as a cooking stove, and provided light and heat. The men looked at each other and laughed. It was going to take some getting used to.

Jon and his three men went down to the main building where the fish packing supplies and other holding tanks were located. They had been fully trained to run the operation as a legitimate business, and were happy to find the generators filled with gas and operational. The generators ran several overhead lights, as well as UV sterilizers to treat the water before packing the fish and shipping them off. All in all, it was a well-organized place, and it was obvious the people there before them had known what they were doing when they designed the place.

By the time the team finished unpacking their equipment, it was near six at night, local time, and all of them were famished. The villagers made a wood fire and speared some fish they had caught that morning and barbequed them over the fire. The villagers were nothing short of amazed at how much the group could eat. They laughed and kept cooking until finally the bottomless pits had been filled. After dinner, the villagers headed back to their own homes, promising to return early tomorrow. Julia was having a hard time curbing their enthusiasm, and like the rest of the group, she just wanted to lie down and sleep.

The team split into three groups and headed off to their huts to sleep. Mackey, Cascaes, Moose, Theresa, and Julia would be sharing a hut. No one ever mentioned it, but the group was well aware that Moose and Theresa and Cascaes and Julia had something going on. Mackey came right out and asked if he was allowed in the honeymoon hut. Everyone laughed it off, but the four lovebirds really did wish they had their own little place. With the exception of Lance Woods, who drew first watch, the entire group was sound asleep in ten minutes. Lance sat outside by the small fire and watched his first African sunset, smiling as he watched the red fireball drop behind the mountains in the distance.

CHAPTER 11

The haunting singing of a lone African voice carrying through the village woke up the group. They were still somewhat comatose from their long journey, and had crashed hard that night. When they each opened their eyes and looked around, they had to remember what planet they were on. The single bass voice was joined by another dozen or so voices all returning his song. One by one, the members of the group sat up and walked outside. There were a dozen fishing boats, large canoes really, out on the lake, and the fishermen were singing their song to the fish. While the team couldn't understand the words and had no idea why the men were singing, the group stood outside and enjoyed the beautiful sounds of the rich African voices in the otherwise silent morning.

Unlike an American morning, there were no car noises, no televisions or radios making background noise, not even a plane overhead. The quiet took getting used to, but the voices carrying across the lake were beautiful and something the members of the team would never forget. Once outside in the sun, the team realized it was time to start their day.

There was an outside latrine, which the men allowed the ladies to use first. There was a fifty-gallon drum that had been cut in half and filled with Lake water, then heavily chlorinated which was the 'sink' that they used to wash up with. The Canadians had devised a shower, but no one had heated up the water yet, which was done via the generator that had yet to be turned on.

Breakfast consisted of MREs and strong coffee made with water that had been boiled and treated with tablets brought from home. The team sat together outside on benches that were left over from the previous owners. The table was made out of wood, and looked to be about a thousand years old. The ants and termites had taken turns on it between insecticide sprayings.

Cascaes called Jon to sit with him, and they discussed what needed to be done to look like a fish farm. After their meeting, Cascaes had Moose and Ripper help prepare the SCUBA gear, including starting the generator which ran the compressor to fill their SCUBA tanks. After they finished their breakfast, Jon took his crew down to the building now dubbed "fish central," and began cleaning and filling holding tanks. They would follow the same process as the previous owners: the fish would be caught by net, brought to the farm and separated by species and variety, then held and fed for a few days to reduce stress. When enough fish of a particular variety was collected, they'd be put in large clear plastic bags with chemically treated water, and then the bag was filled with pure oxygen, sealed, boxed, secured, put in an outer box, and then put in the back of the trucks to be transported to Luano Airport in Lubumbashi. None of them would ever look at a fish in a pet store again quite the same way.

While the four of them did actual work on the fish farm, Mackey and Cascaes set up shop in their small mud house. They had batteries for all of their computer and communication equipment that were rechargeable via the gas generators at fish central. Neither their compound nor the village of Buwali had any electricity.

Mackey, Cascaes, Julia, and Smitty (Joe Smith, who had been CIA for almost ten years) set up satellite phones and laptops and created a miniature secure office that could communicate with Dex Murphy and Darren Davis back in Langley via burst transmissions or secure encrypted phone.

They could pull up satellite photos, maps and the most recent intelligence available through CIA right there in their mud hut. From outside the building, no one could see anything—there were no visible dishes or antennas.

The rest of the team used their first morning at their new home to clean and organize. They scrubbed, sprayed, and swept everything as best they could, then unpacked their gear while inside one of the small houses. They uncrated the weapons and ammo, assembled and loaded their weapons, and then repacked them in locked boxes that would be easier to get to than the double walled crates. Each of the mud huts would have a store of weapons and ammo. While inside the compound, no one carried a weapon. They were wearing shorts and were supposed to be civilians—with the locals dropping in all the time, they couldn't risk raising suspicion. Night time was a different story. After dark, when everyone went to bed down for the night, everyone had a weapon within arm's reach.

Mackey sent Dex Murphy an encrypted email, since it was five hours earlier in Langley, advising him that they were fully operational and preparing to start gathering information. The first orders of business would be to start building relationships with the local fishermen, and then a visit to nearby Buwali to meet the neighbors. As soon as it was practical, they would start snooping around to find the PAC and any leads on Nigel.

By noon, local time, they were all ready to eat again. Julia, having heard comments and rumbling stomachs, walked out to the shoreline of the lake and started screaming in French to the fishermen. They waved back and started heading in towards her. Cascaes followed her down and asked her what she was doing.

"We have a choice. Plastic meat-product in a sealed foil packet that requires hot water and Alka-seltzer, *or*, fresh fish right out of the lake. What sounds better to you?"

Cascaes laughed. "You *know*, the way to a man's heart is through..."

She interrupted him. "That's not how I got to *yours*," she said and then quickly smacked his butt.

He turned red and looked around, praying no one saw that, and luckily they were alone.

"I can have you charged with striking an officer," he said quietly, with a big grin.

"What if I let you spank me back?" she said in her sexiest voice. They started moving closer, dying to kiss each other, when the fishermen began calling out to them. Julia laughed.

"Just in time," she said, and then began yelling back in French. They stood together, wanting to hold hands or something, but behaved, and waited for the boats to arrive with fresh caught fish. It was a nice moment, standing by the lake with a cool breeze blowing away the heat of the day, watching the boats come in silently. The men rowed to shore, holding up dozens of fish that were strung together. They were the blackest men either of them had ever seen, from years of working outside in the African sun. The men smiled, their missing teeth showing in the sun.

When the boats were close enough to the gravel shore, the men hopped out of their boats and pulled them in, walking to Chris and Julia with their fish in one hand, and the rope to hold the boat in the other. They were all speaking to Julia, each of them telling her how good his fish were. They chatted for a while, the fishermen's good nature showing through their big smiles. They were obviously thrilled to have customers for their fish, and their smiles were contagious.

The three of them each gave Cascaes huge strings of fish, between twenty and thirty on each, with each fish being almost a foot and a half long. Julia spoke to them for a while and then they waved and hopped back in their boats to continue fishing out in the Lake.

"Don't we have to pay for them?" asked Cascaes.

"Yes, but we have a 'house account' evidently. They said they'd be by every day and then come to see us one day for what sounded like a picnic."

"A picnic?"

"I'm not really sure. It wasn't exactly French, but it sounds like they are planning a party or something. Whatever it is going to cost, trust me, we can swing it. I think these people make fifty dollars a year."

Chris and Julia walked back to the compound with the fish, stopping once for a quick check to make sure no one was around, and then sneaking a long kiss. Julia whispered, "Can't you find a secret mission for Moose, Theresa, and Mac tonight that would get them the hell out of the house for a couple of hours?"

Chris laughed. "Yeah, well, actually, I think Mac is going out tonight. Unfortunately, I'll be going with him."

CHAPTER 12

It had been a busy day, breaking once for fish roasted over the fire for lunch, and then again for a dinner of MREs. They all sat around the big campfire together to have dinner and relax. Everyone agreed they'd rather eat the same kind fish every day for a year rather than the MREs.

Mackey laughed when they complained about the MREs. "Oh, quit your bitching. When I was in Vietnam and you either weren't born yet or were still poopin' in your diapers, we had to eat C-rations. I swear to God, they were left over cans from the Korean War. If you think vacuum-packed steak is lousy, try eating twenty-year-old shit on a shingle. We ate the dead dogs we found rather than *that* shit."

"Oh *nice*," said Theresa.

"You think I'm kidding? We used to go down to the river and pick up the dead dogs after the river boats had gone by and wiped out the shoreline. Then we'd bring them over to Mama-san and she'd cook 'em up with these little bottles of hooch she made. She'd bring us these little green coke bottles filled up with some kind of sake or something that would take the paint off the trucks, and we'd eat the dogs and drink until we passed out. The dog was better than the C-rats, trust me."

"Oh man, that's just *wrong*, dude," said Earl Jones with a groan.

"No, man—I'll tell you what was *wrong*. I was in a little shop near Saigon once buying some food that was actually edible. So I go in, and there's a little old lady sitting with a puppy in her lap in the front of the store. I made the mistake of telling her I liked her dog on the way in. By the time I was walking out, the dog had been skinned, filleted, butchered and put into brown paper for me to take home. *That* was wrong, man."

The entire group was silent. Finally Theresa said, "Please tell us you're kidding."

"I wish I was," said Mackey.

"Well there goes *my* appetite," said Theresa.

"Yeah, well you already ate about ten fish anyway," said Moose with a laugh, which got him a shot in the ribs from Theresa.

The group continued to swap stories and enjoy a moment of relaxation together until Mackey put on his game face. He leaned closer and lowered his voice, and everyone immediately stopped speaking.

"Tonight, after dark, we're doing a little recon. About four miles back towards Kalemie the Chinese have set up an 'aid station'—more like a large military base. The place is guarded by a few thousand PAC guerrillas being trained by Chinese advisors. Of course, they'll tell you that they are just security guards for the food being shipped in by the Chinese, but that's a crock of shit. They have brand new uniforms and Chinese automatic weapons."

"Don't forget about the cute yellow berets," added Cascaes.

"Right," said Mack. "So at least you can spot them easily. There is a very minor possibility that Nigel may still be alive. If he is, and he's still in Africa, that's most likely where he's being held. We'll take a midnight stroll tonight and check it out. Everybody carries heavy, but we are recon only tonight. Get some sleep. We're up at midnight and traveling on foot.

"It will take an hour to get there. I figure we snoop from one to three and get back by four. We'll break up into smaller teams once we get there. Jon, you'll stay with your dive buddies—McCoy, Jensen and O'Conner plus Woods and Koches. I'll take Moose, Ripper, Hodges, Stewart, and Theresa. Chris, you take Jones, Jules, Smitty, and Ernie P. I don't want any contact tonight, but if something goes wrong and you have to take somebody out, do it silently and bring the body out with you. Somebody goes missing, they'll probably assume it was a deserter. They find a body and we'll have a war started out here. Any questions?"

There were none, so everyone finished eating and headed back to their huts to grab some sleep. Mackey, Cascaes, and Cohen went back to the "command hut" (Mackey and Cascaes's residence) and opened a laptop. Mackey had already marked the location on the GPS map, and they pulled up a satellite photo of the area. With the photo zoomed up tight, they could make out rows of long cabins with a fence around the rectangular camp that included towers in the corners.

Cascaes laughed at the picture. "Yeah, looks just like an aid station. And the government doesn't do *anything* about this?"

"They can't unless they are prepared to commit to a full scale war, which they can't afford. They've been begging the UN, but the UN says there are no reports of hostilities, which is true. There never are—right up until the genocide begins. This government is pretty broke. Their entire army isn't much bigger than the PAC, and their weapons aren't new. I saw border guards carrying bolt action rifles that were older than me—probably from the *first* Congo War. They wouldn't fare so well against the latest Chinese Type-81 assault rifles."

Mackey explained their approach through a grassy area where they'd have to watch out not only for sentries, but for cheetahs and other animals that might want to eat them. They would get close enough to look at the camp from all sides, taking pictures and gathering whatever information they could, and then reassemble and leave the same way they had come.

When they were satisfied that they knew their way around the camp as well as their route from their home base to the target location, they called it quits. Jon returned to his hut, and Mac and Cascaes lay down on their sleeping bags and tried to sleep.

CHAPTER 13

Mac's alarm went off on his watch a few minutes before midnight. They were up and dressed in camouflage fatigues within five minutes, then used black and dark green grease paint on their faces and hands. Weapons were checked and loaded, and they walked outside to gather with the rest of the team. Moose handed out coffee that he had been kind enough to make a few minutes before everyone else was awake.

Mac raised his tin cup and toasted his crew. "Okay—let's gas up and go," he said, then drank down the strong coffee. They walked out of the village in the dark of night, using night vision goggles. The moon provided some light, but it would have been almost impossible to travel without the night vision equipment. They were traveling fairly light, with only their weapons, some water, and the small computers for navigating through the grass and scrub land.

For the most part, the terrain from their camp to their target was hilly and open, with stands of trees and occasional small forests. They were traveling north by northwest, basically due west of Buwali, the closest village. They were about halfway through their hike when Ripper, on point, held up his hand and squatted down into the tall grass and shrubs. All of the team members were wearing throat mics and ear pieces, and could communicate quietly with each other.

They stayed silent and waited, watching the green world of their night vision goggles. Finally, they could see what Ripper had seen—people moving quietly up ahead of them in the stand of trees. They all went prone in the grass and froze. The group ahead of them was fairly close, and they could occasionally see a pair of eyes light up in their night vision.

Ripper spoke quietly into his mic. "Boss, I can't see much, looks like quite a few of them. They don't see us. Wait one." Ripper belly crawled closer to the group ahead of them moving slowly and silently through the grass. When his voice finally came back over the headset, he sounded like he was fighting back laughter.

"Uh, Skipper, you might want to move up and see this," said Ripper.

"What is it?" asked Mackey.

"Fucking *chimps*!" he said, finally laughing out loud. His laughter startled the group of chimpanzees, which had made large nests in the low trees. They started grunting and moving around faster.

Mackey told Ripper to move back. They'd go around the group of chimpanzees and give them a wide berth rather then get them riled up and noisy. While the chimps would most likely not get aggressive towards a large group of humans, now was not the time to find out. The team moved quickly and quietly around the chimps and continued northwest towards the PAC headquarters.

At almost oh-one hundred hours, they could make out the camp in the distance. There was no apparent activity, but that didn't mean that no one was patrolling. They broke into the preassigned groups and fanned out as they moved closer to the camp. Generators had been set up to run lights along the perimeter fence, although they were fairly dim and spaced far enough apart that an elephant could probably walk through the fence without being seen.

Jon and his group moved silently to the right, while Mackey and his group went left. Cascaes took out his night vision binoculars and crawled closer to the fence until he was about a hundred yards out. He lay on his belly with his high-powered night vision binoculars on a very small tripod and zoomed in tight. There were a few sleepy looking Africans up in the towers half dozing, and the camp was completely dark.

They spent the next two hours comparing the buildings to their satellite photos, making notes on which buildings were most likely sleeping quarters, and which appeared to have electricity and could possibly be communication buildings. There was nothing that could link anything they were looking at to China, other than a large sign in French that read *China aid station*. Some buildings appeared to be warehouses where food or medicine might be stored, but they could just as easily house a few thousand rounds of ammunition.

By two am, Mackey recalled his group and they silently melted away from the compound. They regrouped a quarter mile away and began their walk back home. Occasionally, an animal would stir from sleep and run through the scrub, causing everyone to drop and grab weapons, but other than that, the trip home was uneventful. By three fifteen, they were back in their compound changing clothes and washing up. They would be getting about three hours of sleep before the sun came up. Just another day at the office.

CHAPTER 14

The singing from the lake sounded sweeter than a rooster crowing, but only barely. The men and women of the team groaned and bitched as they woke up to fisherman calling up the fish from Lake Tanganyika, their deep voices echoing throughout the camp. On a different morning, it would have been charming, but today, on three and a half hours sleep, it was plain old annoying.

As the team assembled at their usual spot around the fire, they were greeted by Jon Cohen, who looked pretty darn chipper all things considered.

Moose took a cup of coffee from him and asked, "What are you so happy about?"

"We're going diving this morning. I'll finally get to see what's in the lake," he answered, sounding genuinely happy.

"Alligators," said Moose.

"Crocodiles, actually, but not around here. They're further south. We should be pretty free from large things that want to eat us up here."

"Well you have a good time, Jon. Personally, I'm planning a nap," mumbled Moose.

Jon laughed and sat down with Pete McCoy, Ray Jensen and Ryan O'Conner. The four of them would be diving the Lake together. As soon as they had eaten powdered eggs and some plastic looking thing that was supposed to be bacon out of a foil pouch, they headed down to Fish Central. With Hodges and Jones helping, they loaded their wooden dive boat, purchased from the previous owners, and headed out.

Hodges and Jones waved goodbye from the shore, and as the boat chugged away with its single outboard motor, Jones shook his head. "Man, those SEALs are crazy muthafuckers. Would you go diving in that water? There's fucking crocodiles and sharks and shit in there."

Hodges laughed. "You weren't paying attention in class, young man. There are no sharks in there—it's freshwater. And Jon said the crocs are further south or something. The fish they're catching are little. They'll be fine."

Jones rolled his eyes. "Yeah, well, my ass is staying right here on the land. I'll fight a thousand of those PAC mutherfuckers before I go swimming around in that shit. You remember Paraguay? Fucking piranhas, man! No way—uh-uh. This marine ain't getting wet this trip."

Hodges laughed. "Yeah, well, we'll see about that."

⊕

General Shen Xun-jun was observing the firing line where twenty-five PAC soldiers were target shooting at the far end of the compound. For the first two months, the soldiers had trained carrying spears and poles and whatever else they could use for "rifles." When the Chinese weapons arrived inside a huge shipment of rice—enough to fill two rail cars—the soldiers finally were issued real guns.

While many of them had fired weapons before, and some of them had fought in the Second Congo War, none of them had ever seen a Chinese made assault rifle. The Chinese Type-81 Assault Rifle offered the reliability of the Russian AK-47, with accuracy closer to an American M-16. In the right hands, it was a formidable infantry weapon. Just not in *these* hands.

Shen Xun-jun cursed and screamed at his officers as he watched the Africans firing long bursts and wasting ammunition. Most of the rounds they fired were nowhere close to where they were aiming. The soldiers that *did* have combat experience had for the most part had fired either ancient rifles, or AK-47s at very close range. Usually while slaughtering enemy women and children. These new Chinese weapons required much more finesse, and they sprayed everywhere in nervous and excited hands.

Shen Xun-jun's officers relayed the screaming back at the firing line in French, and the shooting stopped. The Chinese officers moved the men twenty-five yards closer to the targets, cutting the distance almost in half. One of the Chinese officers picked up a weapon, fired five short bursts, all of which were dead-on the target, and handed it back to the PAC soldier. He screamed in French for the men to slow down and fire single shots. The Type-81 had an effective range of four hundred meters. With the PAC forces, it was well under one hundred.

Shen Xun-jun watched for another ten minutes, and then ordered his men to unpack the bayonets. If they couldn't shoot straight, they would at least learn to assault using the working end of a bayonet.

CHAPTER 15

Jon Cohen, Pete McCoy, Ray Jensen, and Ryan O'Conner were sitting in the large open wooden boat. According to their fish-finder, they were in sixty-five feet of water, over a rocky bottom.

"Figure your weights about the same as saltwater," said Jon, referring to buoyancy weights divers used to remain "neutral" underwater. "The lake water is so hard it should be pretty close." The team already had their BCD vests and fins on, and were just adding weights to the vest pockets of the BCDs to adjust their buoyancy. They were wearing "two millimeter shorties," short-sleeve wet suits designed for warmer water.

McCoy checked his o-ring and attached his tank to his regulator. "I'm looking forward to getting wet," he said with a smile. "Man, I haven't been underwater in almost two months—that might be a record in the last six years."

"Yeah, I hear ya'," said Jensen. "And I can't even remember the last time I was diving just for fun."

Jon laughed. "Hey man! This isn't for fun! We're *working*." He threw a very large net attached to a wooden pole at Jensen. "Now catch me some fish!" Ray laughed and caught the net.

"Aye, aye, Skipper!" he said sarcastically, and snapped a salute.

The four of them finished getting ready, and then made sure their anchor was secure at the bottom of the lake. Once they were secured, they pulled their tanks on, held their hands over their masks, and did a giant stride entry off the back of the boat. They descended slowly, pleasantly surprised by the numbers of fish. As they descended, a school of *Cyprichromis leptosoma*, commonly called "Cyps," engulfed them. The small fish, about the size of sardines, numbered in the thousands. While the females were a fairly plain-looking grayish-brown, the males glowed blue orange and yellow and flashed their fins at the females, trying to find mates.

At first, the divers just stopped and watched as the thousands of fish swarmed all around them. They appeared to go on forever, in a giant moving wall that changed shape as the fish moved together through the water. It was McCoy who was the first to remember they were supposed to be *catching* the fish. He laughed underwater as he opened his net and watched as dozens of fish swam right into it.

"Not the brightest creatures on the planet," he thought to himself as they swam right into his giant net. The others saw what he was doing and opened their nets to allow the fish to swim right into them. They had thought it would take hours to catch fish—instead, their nets were full of hundreds of fish and they hadn't been in the water for five minutes. Jon gave a "thumbs-up" signal to ascend, and the group closed off their nets and began surfacing. Jon broke the surface first and swam to the boat, where he took off his tank while still in the water and gave it to McCoy to hold. He climbed aboard and dumped his net full of fish into one of the large drums of water on the boat. The others handed up their nets one at a time until the drum was full of Cyps, oblivious to being inside a container, and still trying to mate.

Jon stepped back into the water, pulled his tank back on and told the others to ignore the fish until they got to the bottom. He was curious about the lake's bottom and what types of life he would find down there. They descended again, the Cyps now gone from their location, and dropped slowly towards the bottom. A few larger fish swam by, obviously predators by their large mouths, but the deeper part of the water column seemed "calmer."

When they reached the bottom, they adjusted their buoyancy until they were all neutral, and slowly swam a large circle under their boat. The bottom was sand and rocks, with some sponges, snails, crabs and an occasional eel. They stopped when they reached a large sand pyramid where a pair of fish was doing their courtship dance. The four divers watched for almost five full minutes as the male flashed his beautiful colors and put on quite a show for his female, who eventually began laying eggs. She picked them up in her mouth as he fertilized them. Instead of having the same crude thoughts that they had made in Langley, now they watched in awe at one of nature's marvels. The female would hold her brood in her mouth for almost three weeks, not eating in that time period in order to give her young a chance at life. It was pretty amazing to watch.

Jon finally signaled the group to move on, and they were fortunate enough to come upon a group of Frontosas. "Fronts," as they were called in the hobby, were known for the large nuchal hump on top of their heads. They were a light bodied fish with five wide dark purple stripes. Their faces and long ventral fins were a bright powder blue. At over a foot long and half as high, they were powerful fish, although very slow moving unless startled. They were most active at dawn and dusk, when they tended to feed on the large schools of Cyprichromis. Having just eaten, they were now being lazy on the bottom, watching the divers as they approached.

Jon signaled the others to prepare their nets, and they slowly moved around the colony of fish. Frontosas didn't live in large schools, but rather small colonies. The divers circled around the fish, as if practicing an ambush, and then very slowly opened their nets. The large fish could easily have scattered and out-swam the divers, but they had never seen humans before and naively watched as the men approached and opened the large nets. By the time the "fight or flight" mechanism in their tiny brains triggered the "swim like hell" signal, they were already inside the nets. The divers surfaced slowly and repeated the process of loading the fish into the drums.

The Fronts were so big that they filled the other two drums. The group called it a day and stripped off their wetsuits to warm up in the late morning sun.

"I tell ya' man, I could get used to this," said McCoy, lying back on the side bench of the boat to warm up.

"A whole new way to fish," said Jensen with a laugh. "I think it's cheatin'."

They enjoyed another thirty minutes of relaxing conversation and then headed for the fish farm, feeling like real fish farmers.

CHAPTER 16

Shen Xun-jun was drinking a cup of hot tea, missing China, as he sat in a small chair watching a few hundred soldiers attack straw dummies with bayonets. The PAC soldiers had a warrior spirit, and appeared to have a good attitude so far in training, but nonetheless, they were terrible marksmen. The only thing that kept Shen Xun-jun from feeling totally despondent was the possibility that the DRC soldiers couldn't shoot any better than his own. In any case, at least *his* soldiers would have Chinese machine guns. At the very least, they could "spray and pray" when they got close enough to the enemy.

As he sat watching the Africans mercilessly attack bags of straw, Major Wu Liling approached him and saluted. The general returned the salute and grunted from his seat.

"I have received word on the heavy shipment, General," said Shang Xiao Wu.

The "heavy shipment" was a delivery of high explosives, anti-tank weapons, RPGs, and heavy machine guns they had been waiting for. Before they could make a move against the capital, they would have to be prepared to take on armor. While the DRC owned very few operable tanks or armored personnel carriers, even a few was too many when you had poorly trained infantry and no air or artillery support.

"And what is the status, Mr. Wu?" asked the general.

"It is being flown in, Shao Jiang. Beijing was concerned about transporting it by ship through the port city of Banana for fear of the shipment being stolen or discovered along the long rail route to our camp. Instead, the shipment will arrive in two large transport aircraft."

"They are flying into Lubumbashi?" asked Shen Xun-jun, surprised that they would risk such a shipment to the DRC's largest airport.

"No, sir. They are flying *here*."

The general didn't understand for a moment. "*Here*? They are going to try and land *here*?"

"Yes, sir. We have been instructed to provide an adequate landing strip here at the compound. We have one week."

They stared at each other. Shen Xun-jun was dumbstruck. Two large military transports heavily loaded with cargo of that magnitude would need a large runway. They had no equipment to clear the land and make a runway—this in a part of the country that didn't even have a real road.

Shen Xun-jun stood up and put his hands on his hips, his usual pose when he was very serious. He looked back at his colonel. "We built the great wall. We can build a flat piece of dirt. Assemble the entire camp on the parade ground. Cancel whatever else is planned for the week."

The colonel snapped a salute and ran off to inform his sergeant major, the "liu ji shi guan" of the change in plans. Shen Xun-jun finished his tea and lit a cigarette. He felt cursed. Perhaps he would feel better when his heavy weapons arrived.

By the time the general had finished his cigarette, the camp was in total chaos. Thousands of PAC soldiers were trying to assemble at the same time on the parade ground, with only nine Chinese officers there to organize them. The handful of Africans that had been made "sergeants," designated by a white star with crossed rifles on their shoulders, tried desperately to get their platoons into neat rows, but it was a mess.

Shen Xun-jun watched, disgusted, and lit a second cigarette. One company of Chinese infantry could annihilate this whole army. He shook his head and smoked, trying not to listen to the screaming of his officers. When he finished the second cigarette, he walked to the front of the assembled men. There were almost 6,000 men now assembled at the open end of the camp. While the rows and spacing were not to his standards, at least they had finally shut up.

The general stood, hand on his hips, and screamed a salutation to his army. "People's Army of the Congo!" His colonel, speaking through a megaphone, translated into French. When he did, the 6,000 men began cheering. (It seemed like the right thing to do.) "Our army grows stronger every day!" After translation, this was also met with a great cheer. "We have great weapons coming to defeat the worthless regime that is destroying your country." Another cheer. "We have two planes coming in seven days, and you will make a road for them to land on." No cheering, just confusion. Many of them had never seen a plane up close.

Shen Xun-jun walked back and forth, very agitated. "Tonight, we will have a great feast to celebrate. And then tomorrow we will begin working. Anyone who works on this road will get double rations. That includes your families. They may work as well. We need lots of workers." This translation took a few minutes to sink in. One of the Africans screamed out that they could bring their families to work, and they would all get double rations—this led to the loudest cheer yet. Shen Xun-jun grunted. Perhaps this would work after all.

Shen Xun-jun stormed off the parade ground to his cabin to pick the best location for the airstrip. The ground was fairly flat around the camp, which was good, but it was also covered with large rocks, stands of trees and underbrush that would all have to be cleared. He walked into the large cabin that housed himself and all of his officers, and sat at a large table across from Nigel Ufume.

CHAPTER 17

Jon and his dive team chugged back to the fish farm wearing big smiles. Their first day of fishing had proven to be very successful, and they had thoroughly enjoyed the dive. As they slowly pulled in next to the rickety wooden dock by Fish Central, a few of the others walked out to meet them. Most of the team was sitting around the fire eating lunch together.

Eric Hodges and Earl Jones, the two marine recondos, helped secure the boat and tie it off.

"So how was it?" asked Hodges. "See any crocs?"

Jon laughed. "No, man, no crocs. But we caught a ton of fish. We might actually have a good little business going here."

They bantered back and forth for a while, and then began the process of unloading the live fish. The Canadians that had run the farm before them had devised an ingenious way of unloading the fish without having to remove the fifty-gallon drums from the boat. At almost nine pounds per gallon, a fifty-gallon drum was pretty darn heavy when it was full of water and fish. Instead of unloading the drum, a large open pipe was extended from the "fish corral" to the boat. The pipe, or half-pipe, really, was full of water. The men merely re-netted the fish, dropped them into the half pipe, and let them swim to the large holding tub at the other end. Any fish that were reluctant to move along the pipe were merely "shooed" along by hand. In less than an hour, all three drums were emptied of fish, drained, and then refilled with fresh lake water for the next day.

Jon was supervising the men when two boats paddled into the dock. One small canoe was manned by a single fisherman; the other older man had brought his son with him. As they tied to the dock, they began speaking in French to Jon, who began waving frantically to Julia to come and translate. She was sitting with Chris Cascaes and the others back at the campfire.

The men pulled up large nets that were full of live fish, being towed behind their canoes, and began emptying the fish into the half pipe. They had obviously done this many times before with the old Canadian crew that was here before. They were finishing up when Julia arrived with Cascaes. She greeted them, and received giant smiles and two men speaking at once, obviously excited to see the woman who spoke French again. They chatted for a while and then the men waved and said goodbye, rowing off towards Buwali again.

Julia looked over at Jon and said, "Well, bwana, looks like you are officially a fisherman."

"The drivers from Kalemie will be here in another day or two to transport the fish to Luano Airport," said Cascaes. "Good job. You look like you've been doing this for years, which is exactly what we were hoping for."

Jon thanked him and told him a little bit about the dive, and then the four divers unloaded and cleaned off their gear. They brought the tanks back to the compressor at Fish Central to be refilled for tomorrow's dive. Cascaes told Julia to get in the dive boat. He wanted to take a quick scout up north towards Buwali to see what the coast looked like. Jensen offered to drive the boat again, but Chris told him to finish up here, and he'd be fine.

Julia hopped in and cleared the lines while Chris cranked up the outboard. They chugged off out into the lake turning north. Chris stood at the center console of the open boat and Julia walked up behind him. When they were out of sight of the fish farm, she put her arms around his waist and rested her head against him. Neither of them spoke for a while as they enjoyed each other's company and beautiful scenery of the giant lake. The water was smooth and there was barely a breeze.

"Where are we going?" Julia finally asked.

"Nowhere," said Chris, smiling, as he turned the throttle down to its lowest speed and turned the boat out towards open water. He turned around and started doing what he had wanted to do since arriving in Africa a few days earlier. Julia was just as anxious as he was, and it wasn't more than a minute before both sets of clothes were on the floor of the boat, beneath the bench seat where they were entwined. The rocking of the boat was not from the waves.

CHAPTER 18

Shen Xun-jun sat across from Nigel Ufume and pulled out his cigarettes. Although he couldn't speak French, Shen Xun-jun's English was excellent.

"We have a new challenge, Mr. Nigel," said Shen Xun-jun.

"And what is that, general?" asked Nigel.

"Our shipment of heavy weapons will be arriving here by plane. We need to construct an airstrip big enough for large transports to land."

"You have over 6,000 men here. It doesn't sound like too big a problem."

Shen Xun-jun exhaled a blue smoke ring. "We will have our soldiers bring their families here. We will have 10,000 laborers here by the day after tomorrow. Even without tools, they will be able to provide a runway for our planes."

Nigel reached for his own cigarettes. "What are they sending?"

"Not enough, I'm afraid," said Shen Xun-jun. He was being uncommonly candid with his newest ally in the PAC rebellion. "The present government does not have much of an army, but they do have some light tanks and armored personnel carriers. We have no air support, no artillery, and a few thousand soldiers who can't shoot very well. Unless we are able to take Kinshasa with total surprise, we will have a problem."

Ufume exhaled his cigarette and leaned closer to the general. "If the PAC fails to take out President Kuwali and Prime Minister Gugunga we're all dead men. The cabinet ministers are weak. They will flee or sign on with us, but Kuwali and

Gugunga have loyal supporters. They must be killed the first day of fighting or everything we have worked for will fall apart."

Shen Xun-jun sat back and crossed his legs, eyeing the Congo-born American. "Then I suggest you make sure it happens."

Ufume scowled. "It will be difficult. I will need to move on the president's residence at night. If one of your officers will lead another force at the same time and take out the prime minister, we can take the capital in one day. If we televise our new government the next morning with our army in the streets, Kuwali's army will disappear instantly."

The general pondered that and spoke quietly, "And you are sure that these Africans have no attack aircraft anymore? Our intelligence reports indicated MiGs."

"Whatever aircraft they had are either scrapped or aren't in flying condition. Not in almost five years. They have half a dozen transports and a few helicopters, but they are not armed. Our biggest problem will be their tanks, which are ancient, but still effective against light infantry. That's why I need your officers to lead a few platoons against the prime minister's residence at the same time I take out President Kuwali. With both the president and prime minister taken out, the army won't move against a large force in Kinshasa—not even with tanks. They'll fold."

"You are betting our lives on that, Mr. Ufume."

"Will you give me some of your officers to lead the other platoon?" asked Nigel, growing impatient. He was already growing tired of this Chinaman, and was second-guessing his ability to work with them once the government was changed.

The general looked into Nigel's eyes and finally agreed. "I will have Major Wu lead the second attack platoon against the prime minister. He will bring Sergeant Major Han as his executive officer. You will coordinate with them at the appropriate time." He drummed his fingers against the desk. "Beijing was very specific about not wanting Chinese participation in military action. My men will be advisors only, although they will be armed for self-defense."

"I understand," said Nigel. *In other words*, he thought to himself, *if anything goes south, they are outta' here.*

"And when will you want to begin military operations? These Congolese soldiers still need much training," said the general.

"As soon as the weapons arrive, I would like to attack. The longer we wait, the more chance there is of American intervention. The UN will do nothing, but I'm sure the Americans are already here looking for me. And you," added Nigel, to remind the general that they were in this together. "It won't take the Americans long to find this compound. You can't hide a few thousand soldiers from their satellites."

The general smiled. "You speak like you are no longer an American," he said, suspiciously.

"I stopped being an American the minute I decided to join the PAC revolution. I'm in up to my eyeballs now, general. I will either help my people rebuild this country and become a first world nation, or I will be dead right alongside *you*."

The general looked surprised. "*Your* people, Mr. Ufume? You consider yourself a Congolese?"

Nigel scowled, annoyed at the man's accent.

"I *am* Congolese, general. My parents went to America after I was born. But I am home now. There's no excuse for what I see when I look around this country. The Americans say they support this government and the people—but nothing improves. Perhaps a communist government is what these people need. The current democracy is a joke. It's corrupt and does nothing for these people."

"Well, Mr. Ufume, China will be a good trading partner with the new People's Republic. We will pay fairly for the raw materials we need, and with your help, the new government will rebuild this country's infrastructure."

Nigel laughed, and the general gave him a quizzical look.

"We will not be "rebuilding." We will be starting from scratch. There is very little here worth keeping. We will build a modern nation. It is time for the mud huts to go away. There's no excuse for not having running water that's safe to drink, or electricity in every village."

The general smiled as he thought about his own native China—the world's largest superpower—that still had many villages that didn't have electricity or running water. In fact, the issue of water pollution was reaching epidemic proportions all over China. Most of China's rivers around the cities were so polluted, not only was the water unfit for drinking, but even for watering crops. Shen Xun-jun stood up and walked to a desk where he pulled out a topographical map that showed their compound.

"We will find the most level field and construct the landing strip according to the prevailing wind. These transport planes are very large and heavy and will require extra-long runways. They will also need the wind in their nose to take off." The general rolled up the large map. "Come, Mr. Ufume. We will find a place for our new airport."

CHAPTER 19

Julia and Chris were still naked, curled up in the hot sun on one of the side benches of the dive boat. She was lying in front of him, using his arm as a headrest. They were both smiling and soaked with sweat.

"Twice in thirty minutes—how old did you say you were?" she asked playfully.

"I'm a SEAL. We train very hard," he joked.

"Yes, key word 'hard,'" she said still smiling. She rolled over and crawled on top of him, kissing him for a long time.

"Careful or I'm going to try for three," he said.

"I dare you," she said with a smile, and started kissing him again. She *was* a pretty darn good kisser. She felt him responding under her and started laughing out loud. "I think I'm going to lose the dare, huh?"

"I'm pretty sure," he whispered as he started kissing her neck. "I've been looking at you without touching for over a week. I have to make up for lost time."

She moaned softly as he kissed her neck and reached down to make sure she lost the dare.

Back at the fish farm, Mackey was in his mud house on the phone with Dexter Murphy back in Langley. They spoke via secure satellite uplink phone, and all things considered, the sound wasn't bad.

"The Marines are off the coast of Tanzania, but they have no orders. They are currently being told to sit tight. They have helicopter transports, but it would take hours of ferrying them in to have an effective force in-country, which means they can't be dumped in the middle of a hot spot. While President Kuwali has repeatedly asked for our help in putting the PAC out of business before anything happens, there have been no reports of violence yet, and so far there is no support for sending in the Marines. What are you hearing over there?"

"So far, nothing. We did a little recon and took a look at the PAC base. There appears to be a sizeable force there. Definitely too large a force for us to go toe to toe with unless we have the Marines," said Mackey. "We're still feeling our way around here. We'll head out to some of the villages and see how active the PAC has been with recruiting. I'm not sure where public sentiment is around here. These places change governments like you change underwear."

"No sign of Nigel?" asked Dex.

"Negative. We'll start digging today and tomorrow. So far, we've been taking it slow, trying to look like fishermen and maybe make some friends at the next village. 'Buwali.'"

"Okay, Mac. Be careful. The PAC may have ears everywhere. If anything changes on the political scene over here, I'll let you know. I'll wait to hear from you. Out."

Mac ended the call and put the phone back into its small case in his pack. He walked outside and found Moose. "Where's Cascaes?"

"He went north to take a look around. Took the boat with Julia."

Mac and Moose looked at each other for a few seconds. Finally Mac cracked a smile. Moose leaned closer and spoke quietly, "Maybe I could take Theresa and check south later," he said.

"Jesus fuckin' Christ. How are we supposed to stop a fucking revolution with half my team trying to get laid?" He laughed and shook his head. "Make sure you put gas in it when you're done."

Moose held back his grin. "You wanted something else?"

"Yeah, in between everyone getting laid, perhaps we can take a drive over to Buwali and meet our neighbors. I'd like Cascaes and Julia with me when I go. He bring a radio?"

Moose fought the urge to grin. "I don't think so, sir."

"Oh great, his highness doesn't wish to be disturbed. When he gets back, have him get his ass over here."

Chris dove into the lake, still naked, followed by Julia. They splashed around for a few minutes to cool off and take their "post-marathon" bath, then kissed for a while before climbing back up onto the boat.

"We better get back," said Cascaes. "Mac is gonna be pissed. I wasn't counting on being gone so long."

"Just a quickie, huh? That all I'm good for?" asked Julia as she punched his arm.

He laughed. "Only the first one was a quickie," he answered as he pulled his shorts on. He revved up the outboard and headed back towards the fish farm at full speed. Julia sat towards the bow, allowing the wind to dry her hair. Chris watched her from the center console, still smiling, and decided he would have to marry that woman one of these days.

They slid into the dock, surprised to see Moose standing there waiting for them. Moose threw Julia a line and helped them tie off the boat as Chris killed the engine. Moose helped her off the boat then spoke quietly to Chris.

"Hey, Skipper, Mac wants you up at the hut ASAP. I think he's a little pissed."

Cascaes said, "Oh, great," under his breath and hopped onto the dock.

Moose added, "And he said to bring Julia. I think you guys are heading out to meet the neighbors."

Chris and Julia walked quickly up to the huts, where Mac was sitting outside drinking coffee. Mac looked at them, but refrained from lacing into them. Instead, he just said, "I'm glad you two are back. We're going to take a drive to Buwali and I need your language skills, Julia. Grab sidearms and keep them concealed. As soon as you are good to go, we're out of here. By truck, Buwali is at least twenty minutes." Mac cupped his hands and screamed over to Jones and Koches, "Yo! Koches! Jones! On me!"

They dropped the firewood they were gathering and jogged over to Mac.

"What's up, boss?" asked Koches, with Jones right behind him.

"Grab sidearms you can conceal and a sack of rice." The sacks were thirty pounds each, and were left over from the Canadians. "We're taking a drive to Buwali."

The five of them met at the old pickup truck five minutes later. Julia's hair was still damp, and both she and Cascaes had that "just-fucked-look." Mac hopped behind the wheel and Cascaes rode shotgun—with a shotgun. Behind him, Julia sat next to Koches. Jones was seated in the back of the pickup on top of the large sack of rice.

Jones, the only black man on this trip, couldn't help himself. "Yeah—don't think I don't see what's goin' on here, man. The brutha' gotta' sit in the back of the bus while the *man* sits up front!" He was joking, of course, and Mac honked his horn and yelled at him. "You're just lucky I'm not making you jog alongside the truck!"

They drove north along a path in the foot-high dry grass. The path was probably a few hundred years old, worn into the ground by thousands of feet, some horses and wagons, and now cars. It was twenty-five minutes later, and a thousand years back in time, when they arrived at the village of Buwali. Theirs was the only vehicle in the entire village, except for an ancient pickup truck that sat in the center of the village with no tires, glass, seats, or anything else. It had been stripped over the years, and only its rusted frame was a reminder that it used to be an automobile of some kind.

By the time they stopped in the center of the village, almost everyone had followed them, and surrounded the car waving and smiling and speaking in French and their tribal language. Visitors to the village were a special event, and the children smiled and cheered. Mac and his crew got out of the truck and smiled and waved and said "bonjour" about a hundred times—about as much French as most of them could muster.

The village elders walked out to greet their visitors and gave hearty two-handed handshakes and formal welcomes. Julia spoke to them in her fluent French and they were very excited to hear that their friends from Canada would be operating the farm again. Mac told the elders that he had brought them a payment for some of the fish they had brought so far—a large sack of rice. This brought giant smiles from the three old men who patted their hands and arms and thanked them profusely.

Jones unloaded the huge sack, threw it over his shoulder and walked it to them. "Where do they want it?" he asked Julia, who translated into French. The elders led them to the center of the village, where a large cook-pot was suspended over a fire. While each family had their own food, they all did share some of it in the town center each day at their large evening meal. Julia spoke with them for a long time, and then the elders spoke to some of the children who ran off to get water from the lake. They would boil the water and make the rice, and then the fishermen would add some fish and some of the women would add some local vegetables, and pretty soon, there would be a giant pot of food for everyone to share.

Mac and his crew watched as the villagers worked together, singing and smiling, and evidently very happy for the rice and visitors. They smiled at the simplicity of this village life—everyone very content just to know where the next meal was coming from.

Mac whispered to Cascaes, "If the PAC came in here with food, clothes, and medicine; how hard would it be to bring the whole village into their fold?"

"I hear ya," said Cascaes. "But seriously, do these people look like soldiers to you?"

"Put a Chinese Type-81 into their hands and they all look like soldiers to me," said Mac. "But remember, I'm an old fucker—I was in small villages like this in Vietnam. The skin color was different, but it was the same shit. Smile by day, kill us at night."

"That's a pretty big leap," said Cascaes.

"Yeah? Was it different in Iraq? Villagers smiling and waving during the day and planting IEDs at night when they were finished mortaring our base?

"Come on, Mac. Don't get so cynical. Let's go win some heart and minds."

Julia interrupted their conversation. "The old man with the white beard is the chief. His name is Ma-fafe. He says you would honor them if you would eat with them. The rice was a pretty big deal."

Mac looked at Cascaes. "I can almost feel the diarrhea already," he said quietly.

"The water is right out of the lake, Mac. Seriously—we better pass," said Cascaes quietly.

Mac looked at Julia and was quick on his feet. "Tell him we just ate, maybe next time. Ask him if we can talk somewhere." Julia translated, and Chief Ma-fafe smiled and took his hand and led him to his small thatched hut. He sat on the woven mat floor with Julia and Cascaes and Mackey while Jones and Koches stayed outside and tried to communicate with the children, who found them most entertaining. Jones was trying his best to teach a small boy how to say "muthafucker," which he found absolutely hilarious. Each time the child would repeat it, Jones would scream in fits of laughter, which only encouraged the boy to do it again. By the time Koches found Jones, Jones was on his back hysterical with a small boy standing over him saying "muthafucker" over and over again. It wasn't long before Koches was on his knees laughing hysterically next to them.

Inside, Julia was translating for Mackey. She asked the chief how things were in the village, and the chief smiled and said the weather had been a blessing this year. There were good crops, plenty of fish, many cows and goats had been born this year, and the village had grown by twenty-two people. Evidently, population was one way to know how things were going. If more died than were born, things weren't going so well.

The chief reiterated how happy he was to have them as neighbors again, and that his fishermen were the best in the world. Cascaes smiled and thought about the old man he used to call Pop—he was a helluva fisherman and might have taken issue with that claim. After they spoke for almost twenty minutes, Mac began asking more specific questions.

He asked the chief if he had ever heard of the PAC or People's Army of Congo. The chief said no, and told them they were safe. The war had ended years ago, and he didn't want them to get frightened and leave. Mackey took a picture of Nigel Ufume out of his pocket and showed it to the old man. Julia asked him if he knew this man. The chief smiled and said yes, it was his friend. Then the chief asked Mackey where the man called Ufume had gone. Mackey explained through Julia that he was hoping the *chief* would answer that question.

They spoke for a while longer, but it was apparent that this isolated village had no idea what the PAC was, and while Nigel had been here before a few times, he was gone now and the chief had no idea where. Either that, or the chief was a really good liar.

CHAPTER 20

The early morning hours brought chaotic activity to the PAC "aid station." The word was out that anyone who showed up would be guaranteed work building a road and entire nearby villages were showing up. Men, women and children arrived with primitive tools or nothing at all, anxious for a chance to earn "double rations," as it had been explained to them.

The PAC soldiers helped organize the huge crowd into smaller work groups that would be led by either village elders or PAC soldiers. Shen Xun-jun and two of his officers had informally surveyed the fields around the base the night before. They had chosen the flattest ground and aligned the runway with the prevailing winds as best they could. Using diesel for the generators, they had torched the area in the morning and burned off as much of the brush, grass and trees as possible. With the thousands of workers they now had, leveling and clearing what amounted to a quarter mile road wouldn't be an enormous undertaking. It also provided the PAC with another recruiting opportunity.

Shen Xun-jun was driven out to the huge crowd by Sergeant Major Han. When they had arrived near the center of the chaos, the general stepped out of the car and handed his bullhorn to Sergeant Major Han, who would translate into French. The thousands of Africans would in turn retranslate into another half dozen tribal languages—Swahili, Kongo, Lingala, Kingwana, Kikongo, and Tshiluba.

Shen Xun-jun put his hands on his hips and walked stiffly as he addressed the huge crowd, looking more like Hitler than

a Chinese officer. "People of the Democratic Republic of
Congo! The People's Army of Congo is here to help rebuild
your country. We will build an airport and bring in food
and medicine for your children! We will build hospitals and
schools and end the government corruption! Today, you will
build a runway for relief planes to bring your people the help
you need! Work hard! Work to rebuild your country!"

The people cheered and clapped, although a bit half-hearted.
Many of them were still trying to translate from the sergeant
major's poor French. They understood "work," "food," and
"medicine," and that was enough for most of them. Sergeant
Major Han then began barking out orders to the PAC soldiers,
who quickly began shouting at the huge crowd. Within
moments, thousands of men, women and children began
digging out rocks and stumps to clear the long runway.

The PAC soldiers had the huge crowd spaced out along one
long end of the runway, and basically had the crowd work their
way across the marked out area. Children pulled out small
rocks and burnt wood while men and women worked like
animals digging out rocks, some of which weighed hundreds
of pounds. The most interesting obstacle was a seven-foot
termite mound. Its hardened shell required dozens of strong
men using hammers, sticks, and rocks to break it apart. As
the termites swarmed, women and children eagerly picked
them up and collected them for later—they would add to the
evening's dinner—a local delicacy.

By noon, the temperature was over eighty degrees, and
the villagers had stripped down to shorts or loincloths. The
PAC soldiers wore their uniform pants and boots, something
new for most of them, and they were having a hard time with
the heat because of the extra clothes. The smallest children
were used as water porters, and they moved through the huge
crowd bringing water from a well the Chinese had drilled. For
themselves, the Chinese treated the water; for the Africans, it
was drawn and served right out of the ground, but it was a deep

well, and the water was cleaner than what the villagers drank from the lake.

The workers sang African songs and worked cheerfully, even though the sweat ran down to their feet. The soldiers wearing boots sloshed in their wet socks. General Shen marveled at how fast they were working—as good as any Chinese work crew he had ever seen—and thought they would make good workers at their new uranium mines in the coming months. Shen Xun-jun walked to his truck and barked at Sergeant Major Han to drive him back to his office. Once there, he instructed Sergeant Major Han to take some PAC soldiers and a truck and drive out to one of the lake with some villagers to get some fish. He would feed these people well, and continue to build his army.

Sergeant Major Han snapped a salute and ran to find a few reliable PAC soldiers and a large truck. They would drive out to one of the larger villages on the lake, a place called Buwali.

CHAPTER 21

While Mac, Cascaes, and the others sat around the morning campfire back at the fish farm discussing their next move, a Chinese Army transport vehicle rumbled into Buwali. Two Chinese soldiers and two PAC soldiers stepped out in the center of the village. Unlike the "Canadian" fish farmers, these men made no bones about showing off their new Chinese machine guns. The Chinese officers, in particular, looked about as much like relief workers as Nazi storm troopers.

Sergeant Major Han spoke to his PAC soldiers in French. "Tell them we need as much fish as they can provide. We have rice, corn, flour, and powdered milk. We also have Congolese francs if they want cash. We will buy their cattle, too, if they will sell them."

The PAC soldier translated to one of the village elders who had come out to speak with them. The old man was more cautious with these men than he had been with the Canadians. These men were armed, and the village elder vividly remembered the last Congo war. The armed Africans were scarier to him than the Asians. The old man smiled and told him their fishermen would love to sell them fish. He didn't mention Canadians visiting the day before.

The chief of the village, Ma-fafe, approached the men with a cautious smile. He too, saw the weapons and was worried. Whole villages had disappeared during the last war between the Hutus and Tutsis, and men with weapons were a scary sight in Africa. Ma-fafe greeted the guests and spoke with the other elders about their request to buy fish. The chief was very

94

pleased—two new customers in the same week, this was big. He asked how much they needed, and through the translators was told "all they could catch, as fast as possible." The chief tried to explain that there were more fish in the lake than would fit in the truck, but the Chinese man in charge said they would get more trucks if needed. They had many mouths to feed.

The chief asked when he wanted the fish and was told "now." He smiled and started speaking out loudly to his people. Word traveled fast, and within moments, every able-bodied person in the village was getting into a boat. The entire village was singing and preparing to fish while the PAC soldiers were unloading the bags of supplies. Buwali was a busy place.

Jon Cohen and his three divers were north of their fish farm looking for Frontosas. While it really didn't matter what kind of fish they caught, after all, this was just a cover story, Jon really liked the big striped fish with the huge bumps on their heads. They hadn't traveled this far north before, and were surprised by the number of fishing boats.

"Looks like the whole village is out today," said McCoy.

"Yeah, I was just thinking the same thing," said Jon. As they moved further north, more and more of the small boats appeared until there were hundreds out on the lake.

"Damn, man. I didn't think there were that many people in the whole *village*!" exclaimed O'Conner.

Jon watched and turned his boat towards the fishermen. Buwali was off in the distance, visible along the dry rocky shoreline less than a kilometer away.

"You going to the village?" asked McCoy.

"Let's just go check it out," said Jon. "If these guys bring us all these fish, we're screwed. We can't handle this kind of quantity."

Jon revved the outboard and skipped over the small chop towards the old village, fishermen waving as they cruised by. As they neared the village, they had to slow down to avoid upsetting the small canoes that were everywhere. Villagers used nets as well as hand lines and were pulling up fish everywhere. As they passed one small dugout canoe, a young boy held up a giant carp almost as big as he was. The men slowed down and applauded the boy, who was smiling ear-to-ear and puffing out his chest proudly. He was maybe eight years old.

Jon slowly maneuvered their boat through the canoes as they approached the shoreline. It wasn't a sand beach, more like gravel and hardened earth and rock. McCoy hopped off the bow into the water and grabbed the bowline to lead the boat into the shallow water as Jon killed the engine and raised the outboard.

Jensen was the first to see them. "Hey, Skipper—be cool, but there are two guys up there with machine guns. Shit—make that four. Two Chinese with the Africans."

Jon's stomach dropped. "Shit," was all he could muster. "We can't split without raising suspicion. We're Canadian fishermen here to buy some fish for our camp, that's all. Try not to talk too much. O'Conner, your French is better than mine, you do the talking."

All four of the men were trying to be cool, but none of them had weapons, unless you counted fishing nets. McCoy pulled the boat in until the bow brushed the grassy bottom, and then he threw the anchor off into the water and pulled it tight into some rocks. The other three hopped into the water, wearing only shorts and swim shoes, and walked up the shoreline to where dozens of women cleaned hundreds of fish of every shape and size. The fish guts and scales were collected by small children for use as fertilizer in their small home gardens. The cloud of flies that followed them was proof of the wonderful aroma.

The four men walked up towards the village and saw Chief Ma-fafe walking towards them. He looked a little nervous, but smiled and greeted his friends from Canada.

O'Conner tried his best. *"Bonjour, je voudrais acheter les poissons."*

Jensen looked at McCoy. "What did he say?"

"I think he tried to ask him to buy some fish," he whispered back.

The chief spoke too quickly for O'Conner to understand, but he was pointing at the Chinese men up the hill and sadly shaking his head at the request. O'Conner listened for a while and finally turned to Jon and said, "I think the Chinese guys are buying all the fish. Sounds like he already has a deal to sell them and can't spare any. But honestly, Jon, my French is so bad he might have just asked to marry your sister."

Jon laughed. "Which one?" he asked. Jon smiled at the chief and said goodbye, then started to move backwards towards the boats, but it was too late. The Chinese officers and their two PAC goons approached them with their weapons slung under their arms. The uglier of the two Chinese men spoke first to the four white men, first in French, and then, when they gave no sign of understanding, in English.

"What you doing here, American?" asked the pug faced man.

Jon smiled and extended his hand. "I'm Canadian, actually. Name is John Murphy. You speak *Engrish*?"

The Chinese man didn't shake his hand.

"We run the fish farm down the river. We export tropical fish. Live fish, not the kind you eat."

"What you do *here*?" he repeated, sounding more than slightly menacing.

"We were trying to buy some fish for dinner," said Jon, dropping his hand.

"You said you fisherman. Why you come here buy fish?"

"Like I said," repeated Jon, "We catch tropical fish to export *alive* as *pets*. We don't have fishing hooks and gear for larger *food* fish."

The two Chinese men spoke to each other quickly in Chinese, perhaps deciding whether or not to make fish food out of the four visitors, while the four SEALs stood, feeling helpless in front of the men with the assault rifles.

"Well, if you guys need all the fish, I guess we'll try and figure out something else," said Jon. He turned his back and started walking back to the boat waiting for bullets in his spine.

The Chinese men continued speaking to each other and ignored the dive team as they went back to their boat. They ordered the villagers to just throw the fish into the trucks without bothering to clean them. They were in a hurry. McCoy walked quickly next to Jensen and O'Conner and whispered, "Just keep moving…"

CHAPTER 22

The dive team did twenty-eight knots—top speed—for the entire trip back to the fish farm.

"Last time we go anywhere without packin,'" said Jensen. "I hated standing there while those fuckers decided whether or not to kill us."

"I hear ya," said Cohen. "We'll run it past Mackey."

They arrived back at the farm in almost half the time of the trip out and tied off at the rickety wooden dock. The four of them jogged up the small hill to where the campfire was usually burning. Sure enough, Mackey and Cascaes were chatting by the fire. They spotted the foursome running up the hill and stood. *Something* was up.

Jon spoke first. "Hey, Skipper—we made contact with the PAC today. By accident."

Mackey raised his eyebrows. "What happened? Where?"

"We went north to fish and saw hundreds of little fishing boats out of Buwali—"

Mackey interrupted him. "Hundreds? Slight exaggeration?"

"No, sir. Hundreds. I think the villagers had everything that could float out on Lake Tanganyika. So we went to Buwali to see what was up. The Chinese are what was up. Two dinks, maybe officers—they had that sort of look, and two Africans, PAC, I assume. All four were carrying Type-81 Assault rifles."

"And they saw you?" asked Cascaes.

"Hell yeah. We talked to them. We went into the village and saw the chief. We were going to ask him what was up when these four thugs come down with guns out. The head Chinaman wanted to know what we were doing there…assumed we were Americans, but we stayed with our story. Anyway, it was hairy for a couple of minutes. We weren't armed."

"But we will be next time," said Jensen, still looking pissed.

"Easy there, Sergeant Rock," said Mackey. "You are a Canadian dive team catching fish, not American SEALs, remember?" He looked back at Jon. "So what happened?"

"Well, after we insisted we were just there to buy fish, they told us they needed all of the fish for themselves, and we split."

"They know where you were coming from?" asked Cascaes.

Jon grimaced. "Yeah, we had to stick to our story, so I played it like a regular event, ya' know? Like it was no big deal, but yeah, they know where to find us now."

Cascaes nodded. "Okay, you did the right thing, but we have to rethink what we're going to do now. We're not set up to defend this position against a few thousand armed guerrillas."

Mackey made a face. "You think they bought your story, Jon?" he asked.

"I have no idea, Skipper. They didn't shoot us, which they could have done, but I guess that would have tipped off the villagers that they aren't 'the knights in shining armor here to save the country' that they say they are."

"Damn," said Mackey under his breath. "If we split, they'll know something is up. If we stay, they have the option of killing us whenever they want. Here's what we do: starting now, the fish farm is run by you four. They saw you guys, but that's all they saw. As long as the villagers don't go blabbing, they won't know about the rest of us. Hell, if they were to come here and ask about us, you could just say we were bringing fish to Luano Airport in Lubumbashi. We'll set up defensive perimeters and begin night watches from outside the compound. Sorry to say, you four get to stay as cannon fodder."

Jon nodded. "No problem, Skipper. What do you think if we sleep out by the dock? If the shit hits the fan, we can always boogie to Tanzania or something."

Mackey looked at Cascaes. "Not a bad idea. Okay, fine. You guys can set up down at the lake, keep plenty of extra ammo down with you and make sure the boat stays gassed up with extra fuel, secure coms and weapons on board. We'll be camping out in the bush outside the compound and setting motion detectors for night time security. Everybody takes turns on watch—two hours intervals. We'll take another poke around Buwali and see if the PAC is staying there, or just looking for food. Maybe their MREs suck as bad as ours do."

Cascaes laughed. "Hard to fuck up rice."

"You never tasted my ex's cooking. She could fuck up water," said Mackey. "Okay, get everybody to the campfire and we'll brief the rest of the crew. I liked this better when they didn't know we were here yet."

"Sorry, boss," said Jon, "My fault."

"No, it's okay. I would have gone to the village if I was there with you. Don't sweat it. All you did was push our schedule up a day or two. They would have found out we were here, anyway. Let's just hope they bought the story and are busy with other things."

"I wouldn't count on it," said Cascaes.

⊕

Sergeant Major Han watched as the endless line of Africans filled the back of their truck with fish, some of which were still gasping. Major Wu, not an officer to usually ask the opinions of NCOs, walked over to his sergeant major and spoke quietly.

"Sergeant Major Han—do you think they were Canadians or Americans?"

The sergeant major, surprised to be asked for his opinion, bowed politely and thought about his response for a moment.

"Would not Americans have been armed, Shao Xiao?" he asked. "They looked frightened, not cocky like the Americans I have seen on television."

The major scowled and thought it over. "I will report this to General Shen. Perhaps the local chief can tell us something."

The sergeant major bowed, snapped a salute, and ran off to find Ma-fafe with his two PAC soldiers right behind him. Ma-fafe wasn't far away, watching his people unload basket after basket of fish. The village would be very rich if this customer returned regularly.

Sergeant Major Han approached the chief and asked him in French if he knew the white men. The chief said, yes, and explained they ran the fish farm down the lake. His men brought them live fish for pets in Canada, not the big fish for eating. Sergeant Major Han thought about it for a moment and asked how long the fish farm had been there. When the chief, not fully understanding what he was being asked, responded that the farm had been there for many years, Sergeant Major Han felt relieved. He ran back to the major and spoke quickly.

"I am pleased to report that the men have been there for many years and do, in fact, run a fish farm for exporting fish back to Canada. They are fish the Canadians keep as pets, not food."

Major Wu smiled, something rather out of character for 'His Grouchiness.' "Good. We can continue our work without interference for the time being. Get these fish loaded and we will return to base."

Sergeant Major Han watched as the endless line of Africans filled the back of their truck with fish, and smiled.

CHAPTER 23

Shen Xun-jun sat in a chair sipping tea, watching thousands of Africans clear a long stretch of ground that would be his runway. Nigel Ufume sat next to him drinking a gin and tonic.

"You should try one, general," he said, feeling slightly buzzed. "The quinine in the tonic fights the malaria. The Brits figured this out a couple of hundred years ago. And if it doesn't, who cares? It tastes better than tea."

The general looked at the American traitor with disgust. As soon as his usefulness was gone, he would be disposed of. "Tea is an honorable drink. It doesn't cloud one's mind like alcohol, Mr. Nigel. There is work to be done. It is not the time for drunkenness."

Nigel got pissed. "General, lemme tell you something—unlike the Chinese, Americans can drink without getting all fucked up. You want tea? Drink your fucking tea. I'll stick to my Tanq and Tonic, thank you very much." He was slurring slightly. "I'm gonna' help you build this country into a modern nation. China is gonna' make us rich, and the world is gonna' stop shittin' on Africa."

The general was growing impatient, and would have been very happy to put a round through Nigel's forehead, but grimaced and held his tongue. The black man would be needed in the months ahead as they rebuilt the Congolese government—a Chinese satellite that would provide the resource-hungry mainland with so much of what it needed to continue on its path towards world dominance economically, politically, and militarily. As the general looked at his traitor ally, he thought it appropriate that an American would be the one to help China become the next supreme superpower.

Shen Xun-jun stood up and called out to the PAC soldier that stood guard by Shen Xun-jun's truck. He would rather stand in the heat and dust than sit with this drunken fool another minute.

The soldier ran to Shen Xun-jun and saluted. He spoke no Chinese and Shen Xun-jun spoke almost no French. Instead, Shen Xun-jun merely pointed to the truck and the soldier ran and opened the rear door for Shen Xun-jun to sit in the back. The general sat and pointed to the workers, and the soldier drove him out to inspect the progress. Back on the porch, Nigel raised his glass to the departing general.

"Here's to you, you fucking chink. You are gonna' make me rich—king of this fucking shithole. And the minute you fuck with us, we are gonna' throw your asses out of here." Nigel poured another couple of shots into his glass, spilling some on his hand, which he licked off. His heavy drinking had started shortly after he arrived back in Africa and saw the living conditions of people who all could have easily been him.

As Shen Xun-jun pulled out of the compound towards the workers, the truck rumbled in from Buwali with Sergeant Major Han behind the wheel and Major Wu in the front seat next to him. Two PAC soldiers stood in the back, literally up to their waists in fish. Between the supplies on hand and the fish, Shen Xun-jun would easily feed his army and keep it loyal to him. It wasn't much different in the old Chinese army— provide food, shelter, clothing, discipline, and fear, and your army would do anything for its leaders. The Congo would be much better off under Chinese influence, of that, Shen Xun-jun was sure.

The truck squeaked to a stop in the center of the compound, near the large open tent where the cooking was done each day. Sergeant Major Han hopped out and started screaming in French to the nearest men he could find, who quickly ran to get wheelbarrows and begin the process of unloading several thousand pounds of fish. The two miserable PAC soldiers in the back were soaked with fish blood and skunked water, and trotted off to bathe in the lake and find new uniform trousers. Sergeant Major Han recruited several women and children from the other side of the compound who were performing other duties, and had them join in the daylong process of preparing fish for a meal. The cloud of flies surrounding the tremendous pile of fish guts and scales was so thick an hour into the cleaning process that Sergeant Major Han ordered holes dug and the mess buried as the people worked, rather than wait until the end of the chore. As Sergeant Major Han jogged off to find General Shen, he cursed this continent under his breath.

Shen Xun-jun was sitting on the hood of his truck watching the progress on his airstrip when Sergeant Major Han and Major Wu arrived on foot. They were both amazed at the number of workers and the amount that had been accomplished.

Major Wu snapped a salute. "Beg to report, General Shen, we have returned from Buwali with the fresh fish. The village can keep us supplied indefinitely. We did make contact with caucasians."

Shen Xun-jun's eyes narrowed. "Americans looking for us or Mr. Nigel?"

"We do not believe so, Shao Jiang. The locals in Buwali report that Canadian fish farmers have worked on the lake for several years. They catch fish to send back to Canada as pets. They supply fish for fish tanks, not for food. They were in the village trying to buy food fish, same as us. We sent them away."

Shen Xun-jun mulled it over. "And do you know where these men are located?"

Major Wu fudged his answer a bit. "We can easily locate them, Shao Jiang. They are not far from Buwali." Sergeant

Major Han was making a mental note to find the damn fish farm as he listened to Wu Liling answer the general.

Shen Xun-jun slid down from the hood of the car and walked towards the thousands of Africans, sweating under the bright orange sun.

"We will have an airstrip by tomorrow," said Shen Xun-jun quietly. "And then we will have our weapons." He turned back towards his men. "It doesn't matter if they are Canadians or Americans or Russians. In a week, China will be running this country. We will return home as national heroes and spend the rest of our careers on assignments anywhere we choose. That includes you, Sergeant Major Han."

The sergeant major bowed politely. "Thank you, Shao Jiang. You are most generous."

Cascaes was on his stomach next to Mackey, using an extra high-powered sniper scope. They were both invisible, wearing ghillie suits that made them both look like clumps of dried grass that mimicked everything around them.

"Road or airstrip?" asked Cascaes to Mackey.

"Airstrip. Think about it—they're working across the length of a finite piece. If it was a road, they'd be working towards some direction of travel from the compound. These guys are just making an airstrip. Even have it set up for wind direction."

Cascaes nodded. "Yeah—wind direction. I forget you're a pilot. Good catch—I would have missed that, too. Okay, so they are building an airstrip. What for? Bringing in Chinese troops? Moving PAC troops around the country? Any guesses?"

Mackey kept watching. "We should have brought Jon with us. He could have ID'd the guys from the village. Damn. Look at the little guy by the car. Bet ya the farm that he's the ring leader."

"Yeah. Look at how the others two bow and salute and shit. Aid-station my ass. They don't even try and hide it anymore. How many you figure they got recruited out there?"

"Been trying to count, but damn, there's a shit-load out there. Could make three regiments out of that mess easy enough. Langley predicted five or six thousand, but there has to be almost double that out there. And that's only *here*—what about in the rest of the country?"

"We better get the hell out of here. I only have about a hundred rounds. Definitely can't take the rest of them in hand to hand," said Cascaes dryly.

Mackey smiled. "I am way too old for hand to hand, brother. These days I prefer calling in an airstrike."

"Yeah, well don't get your hopes up. Like the man said in Virginia, we're out here without a safety net. The Marines offshore are not coming to bail us out. Come on, let's split."

Mackey and Cascaes, almost a mile out from the compound, packed up their scope and slowly crawled through the grass until they were in heavier vegetation. They worked on the assumption that someone in camp had a scope as well, and was trying to find them, so they moved methodically until they were comfortable that they would be concealed to even a heavy telescope. Once they were in the forest, they jogged back to their waiting truck, where they stripped off their suits and hid them along with their scopes, under some boards in the back of the truck. If they were stopped, they were merely Canadian fish farmers looking for game. They did have a shotgun in the cab.

Cascaes drove the truck back towards their fish farm, and Mackey called ahead to Moose on his radio.

"What's up, Skipper?" asked Moose from his end.

"Get our com equipment set up and ready to go. I want to call the company when we get back right away. Looks like our buddies are ahead of schedule. Out."

CHAPTER 24

By the time Cascaes and Mackey drove into the fish farm, the team had finished setting up motion sensors in a hundred yard perimeter around the compound. Weapons and ammo were concealed, but easy to reach, in Fish Central, the huts and the boat. The team had split into two-person teams and spread out to keep watch in all directions. They felt a little bit like George Armstrong Custer.

Mackey and Cascaes went right to their hut, where Moose was ready with the secure burst satellite phone. Mackey grunted a hello and called Langley, where Dex Murphy picked up on the third ring. It was early morning back in Virginia.

"Morning, Boss," said Mackey. "I bring you greetings from the Congo."

"Happy to hear your head isn't on a pole," said Murphy.

"No, that was the last assignment, remember?" said Mackey, thinking about his last gig in Paraguay where there actually *were* some cannibals.

"Yeah, I remember. What's going on out there? Any sign of our missing person?" he asked, concerned about Nigel.

"Not the first clue," said Mackey. "But I think our Chinese friends are way ahead of schedule. They're building an airstrip at the aid station and they have quite an army out there, boss. I'm guessing close to 10,000 of them now. And that's only at this location. Not sure how many other aid-stations the Chinese have out here."

"10,000? Damn. I'll send that up the chain. If they fly in more advisors or artillery support, the Congolese president is going to be out of a job real fast. They know you're out there yet?"

"Well, that's not a hundred percent clear yet. We've had contact with advisors and PAC soldiers at Buwali, but they may have bought the cover story. So far, they haven't come sniffing around, but we are preparing."

"Preparing *how*?" asked Murphy, sounding concerned.

"Well, they only know about four of us, as of right now. Those four are staying in the compound and the rest of us will be patrolling outside. If it gets ugly, we have a boat and will head east across Lake Tanganyika."

"That's fine. Remember, I'd rather you just split without shooting if you can. Stay with your cover story. We're waiting to see what political solutions can be tried before we start another Congo War."

"We aren't starting it, boss—we're trying to prevent it," said Mackey.

"Yeah, well if you get jammed up and United States Marines end up shooting at Chinese Nationals, we have World War Three on our hands."

"I thought you said the Marines wouldn't bail us out?" asked Mackey.

"I said don't count on them, but they're off the coast now, and the president has been taking a hard line at the UN. The chief has called on the General Assembly to step in and put down the PAC forces to assist the legitimate government of the DRC, and of course the UN says there are no reports of violence. China has been 'blocking US interference' and criticizing more US intervention around the world. Shocking, huh?"

"Yeah, great humanitarians, those Chinese."

"Anyway, the president has stated publicly that the United States will not allow guerrillas to overthrow the DRC, and has acknowledged US forces are offshore in the region. That went over real big with China at the UN, who came out and said it has humanitarian relief efforts going on in the DRC and will protect its people from any outside violence. To the UN, it sounded like protection against the PAC—to the president, it sounds like protection against us."

"And what about the Congolese president? What's he saying?"

"Both President Kuwali and Prime Minister Gugunga have made public statements that they believe the Chinese are meddling in the DRC's governmental affairs and said they would expel any Chinese supporting the PAC movement. Of course, they have no way of doing that unless they go to war with the PAC right now, which they aren't ready to do without foreign aid. So, as usual, everyone will watch and do nothing unless the president sends in the Marines. Interesting little powder keg you all are sitting on."

"No kidding," said Mackey. "Does President Kuwali know that the US has friendly forces here?"

"No," said Murphy. "You guys don't exist."

"Okay, so President Kuwali and Prime Minister Gugunga will keep begging for help from the UN that won't come, while the Chinese prepare to overthrow them and set up their own little government to have access to the raw materials they want, and we are going to sit back and do nothing?"

"As of this moment, I have no idea what we're going to do. Like I said, POTUS has announced to the world that the Marines are nearby. The problem is China may now move troops into the area to protect its 'relief workers.' We aren't sure how fast they'll do that, but if they move quickly, we'll have our marines looking down gun barrels at Chinese troops. That's a scenario that no one wants. Ever hear of the Korean War? For now, I think you guys should sit on that airstrip and see what's going on. We need to know what they're bringing in. We're realigning spy satellites to try and monitor the area, but it will take another couple of days. By then, they could have a tank division flown in."

"Roger that. Okay, we'll pull shifts and sit on the airstrip. We did ask about your missing agent in Buwali, but the folks there don't know what happened to him. He'd been there before—they ID'ed him, but they either don't know or they won't say where he is now."

"Poor bastard. If the Chinese have him, for his sake, I hope he's dead."

CHAPTER 25

Nigel Ufume was still on the porch of General Shen's cabin drinking gin and tonic when the general and his officers pulled up in the truck. Nigel was completely drunk and made no attempt to conceal it from the stuffy Chinese officers. General Shen walked over to Nigel and put his hands on his hips. He was not pleased with the glazed look in Nigel's eyes.

"The airstrip is finished. We will get these people fed and begin educating them," said Shen Xun-jun with disdain. "They must be willing to fight for the PAC—and for *us*. *You*, Mr. Nigel, *you* must talk to your people. It's why you're here. And you must be sober when you do it." With that, he smacked the bottle off the small table next to Nigel, sending it crashing off the porch.

Nigel would have protested, but General Shen was obviously angry about his drunkenness, and standing there with his officers behind him, he was not to be messed with.

Shen Xun-jun stared at him for a long moment, and then spoke quietly. "The Africans will be fed well tonight. And then you will address them. You *will* be properly dressed and sober, and you *will* gain their loyalty and respect. Or I don't need you."

The words "or I don't need you" were a shot across the bow for Nigel. The General had just told Nigel in no uncertain terms that Nigel would use the Congolese heritage to bond with "his people," or he would be feeding the jackals on the African plains. Shen Xun-jun walked into the cabin with his men, leaving Nigel alone on the porch. Nigel stood from the rickety chair, almost falling, and stumbled towards the camp mess tent. As one of the "officers" of the camp, he could take food whenever he wanted. He decided a small meal and lots of coffee would be the next thing on his "to do" list.

Inside the cabin, Shen Xun-jun sat at his desk with his officers seated around the room in front of him. Sergeant Major Han turned on their secure laptop and sent a message to Beijing informing their superiors of the airstrip's completion and asking for an exact delivery time. General Shen was surprised to hear that the planes were loaded and fueled, and would be leaving for the Democratic Republic of Congo within a few hours. The Intelligence officer spoke directly to Shen Xun-jun, asking him specifics of what they had planned and when. Shen Xun-jun explained that they would be moving on the capital city as soon as the heavy weapons arrived, and planned on taking out the president and prime minister within the first day of open hostilities. His plan was approved, and the phone went dead.

Shen Xun-jun turned to his sergeant major and told him to have his men begin the "feast and celebration" preparations.

CHAPTER 26

Ripper and Moose, who almost always worked together, whether on land or in the water, were wearing their ghillie suits and watching the aid station from a half-mile out. It was near eighteen hundred hours, and the pair had been hunkered down for almost two hours, babysitting the airstrip and camp. They took turns watching through powerful sniper/spotter scopes. Their mission was recon only, avoiding hostiles and leaving no trace of their visit. The team would be working in shifts, non-stop, keeping tabs on the airstrip and the camp.

"Little fuckers sure are busy tonight," said Ripper quietly. "Looks like a real party down there."

Moose was watching also. "Yeah. I was thinking…"

"I thought I smelled something burning," interrupted Ripper.

Moose ignored him. "*We* had a pretty good party the day *we* left to come here, right? I mean, lots of food and booze from the boss. A little 'send-off.'"

Ripper mulled that over. "You think something's up? They getting ready to make a move?"

Moose frowned. "I only have about 300 rounds. Think we can take 'em?"

"Abso-fuckin-lutely," answered Ripper dryly.

Moose smiled, because he knew Ripper was serious in his own mind.

"We better call this in," he said quietly, and then activated his earpiece and throat mic that transmitted to their fish farm.

"Hey boss, you on?" he asked quietly. It was so quiet where they were lying in the grass he felt like he was shouting.

"I read you," said Mackey's voice.

"Looks like something is up. Big party or something. Looks like everyone is eating and dancing and having a good ol' time down there. And there are a *shit-load* of 'em boss. Men, women, and children. Like a few villages worth," whispered Moose.

"What's your take?" asked Mackey.

"Not sure what to make of it. Maybe they do this every night, for all I know, but I was thinking it might be the big send-off before they get busy, know what I mean?"

"No planes, right?"

"Correct. Negative on the airstrip. Just a big cookout. Hey— wait one. Out." Moose cut his call off and watched closer as the crowd apparently stopped partying to stand up and gather at the open end of the camp. Chinese officers were walking out with an African. Ripper ID'd him first.

"Fuck! They got Nigel! He's still alive!"

The two of them watched in silence as the officers and Nigel Ufume stood at the end of the large parade ground and the thousands of Africans stood and gathered to listen. Moose tapped Ripper on the shoulder and started moving forward, cautiously but quickly, towards the camp. The two of them moved through the tall grass mindful of sensors and booby traps, but saw nothing other than scrub vegetation. They continued until they were only a few yards from the recently cleared airstrip, not more than a hundred yards from the wire fence that surrounded the camp. They froze and watched. To their amazement, Nigel did not appear to be a captive.

One of the Chinese officers began yelling through a bullhorn in French. Ripper and Moose looked at each other, not understanding a word.

"Boss, you on?" asked Moose.

"Roger that," said Mackey.

"Get Julia on the horn to translate. Some shit is going down, and I am looking at Nigel Ufume standing with the Chinks at the head of the class."

It took a second for Mackey to say it over in his head. "Confirm. You have Nigel Ufume ID'd?"

"One hundred percent, Skipper. And he does not appear to be a captive. They are addressing the crowd. Get Julia."

Mackey passed the headset to Julia, who was sitting next to Cascaes in their hut. "Translate!" he yelled as he handed her the headset.

Julia popped the headset on and closed her eyes, trying to concentrate on the voice in the distance. It was difficult, but she could make out some of it. First, a voice, speaking French, that had to be a Chinese officer. He was introducing someone that sounded important, but she was losing parts of it. Damn. The voice was so muffled and far away. She commented out loud about how hard it was to hear.

Mackey spoke into his mic. "Moose, can you get any closer? It's hard to hear."

Moose couldn't hear him, because he had taken his earpiece and throat mic which were connected by a wire, off, and was holding them up towards the camp. Ripper answered Mackey instead.

"Skipper, we're at the edge of the runway. If we try and get any closer we'll be in the open. We can move up a *little*, but not much. If we try and circle around, it will waste too much time. We might miss the whole thing. And there are guards up in the towers."

"Okay, be careful. You get spotted and we're cooked."

Ripper belly-crawled to the edge of the airstrip with Moose right next to him, holding up the mic towards the camp. They were voice activated unless you held down the button, so Moose had to hold the mic "open" and aim it at the camp, which was a bit awkward. Miles away, Julia strained to hear the speech. It was now another man, who spoke much better

French and did not sound Chinese. Ripper interrupted her thought.

"Skipper, that's Nigel—he's making a speech to the Africans."

"People of the Congo! It is time we took back our country! Together, we have worked to build an airstrip. We will have weapons soon that will make our army invincible. We will take back Kinshasa. We will arrest the traitor president and his prime minister, and we will restore good government to our country. These men have robbed our treasury! They have lied and cheated you out of what is yours! We are a great nation and the time for living in mud huts is over! Your children starve and the government does nothing! But tonight—did you not eat well?"

(The cheering was loud, even from far way.)

"Yes! You ate well! Our new army has been trained well! You have new weapons from China that are better than the government's, and you are ready to fight for your country! For your families! For your future! Fight with us, and never go hungry again! We will have medicine, doctors, schools, everything we need!"

(More cheering.)

Julia was trying to repeat what she heard each time Nigel waited for the crowd's cheers to settle down. Mackey and Cascaes were frowning as they listened. The shit was about to hit the proverbial fan.

They listened for almost another thirty minutes while Nigel whipped the crowd into a frenzy, ultimately ending up in dancing and singing and occasional gunfire as soldiers fired into the air and danced with their families. Shen Xun-jun almost cracked a smile as he congratulated himself for including Nigel in his plans. When Nigel was finished he walked out into the crowd, very pleased with himself and his sea of supporters. Shen Xun-jun watched with interest as Nigel shook hands and worked the crowd like a seasoned politician, smiling and complimenting the soldiers, women and children. The Congolese ate it up, smiling and praising him, patting his back, shaking his hands and chanting patriotic slogans about the People's Army of Congo.

Shen Xun-jun leaned over to Major Wu. "'President' Ufume apparently believes he will be running this new country."

The major smiled and bowed his head, understanding the general's amusement.

Back at the fish farm, Mackey, Julia and Cascaes sat on the woven mat that was their floor. "Unbelievable," said Mackey. "Fucking guy flipped on us."

"What if he is just trying to get in closer?" asked Cascaes. "You know, make it *look* like he's flipped…"

"*Bullshit*. He knows protocol. He would have called in. And if for some reason he couldn't, he would have gotten a message through his network out here. *And*, on top of that, the company sent another guy in here before me to try and find Nigel. He has apparently dropped off the face of the earth, too, and I'm now I'm thinking Nigel is responsible for *that*, too. This fucker is dirty. I'm calling it in."

Julia looked at Cascaes sadly. "I agree, Chris. Good agents get in close, but they follow protocols. He's been missing for *way* too long, and his speech sounded way too *good*. He sounded like he believed what he was saying."

Mackey had Dex Murphy on the secure phone. "Hi, Boss. I hope I'm interrupting something good."

"Actually, I am sitting with the Deirdre Gourlie at the A-Desk. We are waiting for new satellite pics to come online. Should be pretty soon."

"Oh, *good,*" said Mackey sarcastically. "You can zoom in and take a picture of Nigel while you're at it."

"You found him? Is he alive?" It was Deirdre's voice, sounding excited.

"Oh, yeah. He couldn't be better. I hope you're sitting down," said Mackey.

There was a brief pause, then Deirdre's voice again. "What's going on, Mac?"

"Nigel has gone to the dark side, no pun intended. We just heard his rousing speech to the PAC. He was standing with the Chinese 'peace corps.'"

A longer pause, then Murphy's voice. "Mac? You're saying that Nigel Ufume has doubled on us? You're sure on this?"

"Well, let's see. The guy that we were worried about being tortured and pumped for information—*that* guy, yeah, well, apparently he is pretty damn healthy. I have two of my men watching him right now. They are sitting on the airstrip waiting to see what 'Santa Kwong' is going to bring on his sled."

Mackey could almost hear Dex and Deirdre shaking their heads in disbelief.

"Sorry to be the bearer of bad news. Sounds like he is running for class president, by the way. Looks the Chinese and ol' Nigel have a little deal of their own worked out. They must pay better than you do."

"Everybody pays better than we do," said Dex and Deirdre in unison like they had rehearsed it.

"So now what? We can't take him out. He's in the middle of the camp with about 10,000 Africans."

"Just try and keep tabs on him," said Dex, sounding very tired all of a sudden. "Let us know the minute you see a plane. We need to know what they are doing over there. Satellite feed should go live pretty soon. We see anything important, we'll holler. Out."

Dex and Deirdre looked at each other and shared a collective, "Shit."

CHAPTER 27

Eric Hodges and Earl Jones quietly worked their way through the brush up behind Moose and Ripper's position, but stopped well shy of the airstrip. They would be on watch when the sun came up, and had to stay further out. Hodges quietly called in to Moose and Ripper over their throat mics to tell them of their arrival. Moose and Ripper quietly moved away from the strip and linked up with their replacements. It was almost one in the morning.

"We're happy to see you guys. Almost time for our naps. Oh, and by the way, there are about ten thousand Congolese on the other side of that fence, armed with brand new assault rifles. Have a nice day," said Moose as he quietly moved past the two replacements.

"Gee thanks, Moose," said Hodges.

"You goin' soft in your old age, Moose? We figured they would have surrendered to you by the time we got here. You turn into a pussy, man?" asked Jones with a broad smile.

"Actually, Ripper wanted to pick a fight, but the boss said recon only, so I had to hold him back. Besides, the plane didn't arrive yet—it wouldn't be a fair fight. When the reinforcements arrive, then we'll assault."

The four of them exchanged quick fist bumps, and Moose and Ripper slipped away into the dark. Jones and Hodges added more local grass and brush to their ghillie suits and lay down to set up their high-powered spotter scopes. Even in broad daylight, they would be invisible.

The camp had settled down several hours before. The Africans, having worked like animals on the airstrip, and then having eaten a huge meal, were all fast asleep. Jones and Hodges passed a very boring night, taking turns with one hour naps. The red sunrise at a little after oh-five hundred was the signal that naps were over. They lay in silence, watching the Africans waking up slowly. A very long line slowly formed at the mess tent as thousands of Africans waited patiently for their morning meal. The Chinese would keep them very well fed and happy before putting weapons in their hands and sending them out against the government troops.

The sound of a truck engine starting up was loud in the quiet African countryside. Both Jones and Hodges readjusted their scopes to find the source of the noise—a small Jeep filling up with Chinese officers.

"Small guy in the back. He must be 'the man,'" whispered Jones.

"Roger that," whispered Hodges. "They look a little excited, huh?"

Jones watched as the Chinese men seemed to wave their arms and speak frantically about something. The sound of aircraft approaching answered *that* question. Hodges was on the horn immediately.

"Boss, you awake?" whispered Hodges.

"It's me," said Cascaes. "Mac is asleep. Whatcha' got?"

"Aircraft. Three transports coming in. Big ones, Skipper."

"Okay, sit tight and watch carefully. Count personnel getting off or on and see if you can ID weapons systems. We'll be there soon. Out."

Hodges and Jones stayed motionless, watching as the three huge transports circled over the camp. The Jeep drove quickly alongside of the strip, and a Chinese officer lit oilcans that were alongside the runway to help the pilots lineup the dusty path.

"I'm so dumb," said Hodges. "I thought they were garbage cans."

Jones smiled, he hadn't even noticed them.

As soon as the cans were lit, the officer threw a green gas canister at one end of the runway to indicate wind direction, and the Jeep moved out of the way. Thousands of Africans from the camp began streaming out towards the runway, all eyes fixed overhead. Many of them had never seen a plane before up-close.

The lead transport dropped down and slowed its engines as it lined up the airstrip. It came in low and slow, its massive wings teetering up and down in the crosswinds. It was huge. As its nose gear touched down, dust and dirt flew high over the plane, making it disappear for a moment, until the plane bounced above the cloud, only to touch down again and again. It rumbled down the dirt runway, looking slightly out of control until it was able to brake and reverse its huge turbine engines and come to a stop at the very end of the path. The pilot drove off the runway and continued out of the way, turning his plane to face the camp so the nose of his plane could be raised to unload the mystery cargo inside.

The second plane came in like the first, also fighting the crosswinds and now had to contend with large "divots" in the runway left by the previous aircraft's huge tires. It bounced harder and higher than the first plane, also almost out of control. The pilot fought against the controls as his massive plane swerved all over the dirt. By the end of the runway, he was under control and slowed down enough to avoid the first plane, now raising its huge nose-cone.

The third and last plane came in slightly steeper than the first two. The pilot had been told of the difficulty and the crosswind, but was still having trouble lining up the dirt path, now partially hidden by the clouds of dust, dirt and smoke from the fires alongside that were supposed to be helping, not hindering. As the first pilot looked up at him, he called him on the radio, screaming for him to abort and pull up. It was too late. The third plane hit the runway much harder than the first two and bounced wildly, spinning to the left. When it touched down the second time, the tip of the long right wing smacked against the dirt runway and snapped, throwing debris hundreds of feet into the air, some of which was sucked through the giant turbine engines. The explosion was immediate, and the plane bounced a third and final time, this time completely out of control, with the tail coming up over the nose.

The third touchdown was directly on the roof of the pilot's cockpit, situated to the top rear of the deployable nose assembly. The pilot and crew were killed instantly as the weights of the cargo and aircraft drove through the front section of the plane in a few seconds. By the time the tail section was sliding through the nose, the plane exploded with such force that everyone in the camp was knocked off of their feet. Those Africans who could get back up did so, and ran as fast as they could in every direction. Jones and Hodges covered their heads and waited as the massive shock wave rolled over them.

It was several more seconds before they could hear again. Jones looked over at him and mouthed, "Holy shit."

Hodges called back to the fish farm, almost three miles away.

"Skipper, you there?" asked Hodges.

"What the fuck was that?" yelled Cascaes, having heard the massive explosion all the way back at the fish farm.

"You heard that?"

"Damn right! What the hell is going on? You guys under fire?"

"Negative, Skipper. The last of their three planes just crashed coming in. Wish we could take credit for it, but it wasn't us."

"Holy, shit," said Cascaes. "You guys okay?"

His answer was a series of secondary explosions as weapons and ammunition on board all started going off at the wreck site.

Hodges and Jones covered their heads and ears and waited for the long series of explosions to finish.

"Damn, Skip. I don't know what they were carrying, but whatever was on board, that aircraft is *cooked*. That's probably a good thing from the sounds of it."

"Roger that. Are you safe in your current position?" asked Cascaes.

"Not sure, Skipper. There are villagers running everywhere. They aren't on us yet, but I think we better boogie outta' here."

"Okay. Get your asses out of there. Either find a safer spot where you can still see, or just get your asses home. Satellite should be able to help us out now anyway. Stay low. Out."

Hodges and Jones crouched in the tall grass, looking like clumps of grass themselves, and moved quickly away from the camp towards the woods a few hundred yards away. Back at the camp, the Chinese officers regained their feet, and the two surviving planes moved slowly away from the fire, bouncing over the scrub floor of the African countryside to a safer location. The tail section of the second plane was severely damaged from flying debris, and would make a lovely addition to the African countryside, as its flying days were now over.

A voice whispered in the earpieces of Hodges and Jones. It was Moose. "You guys okay?"

"Roger that. What's your twenty?" asked Hodges.

"Coming up behind you in the woods I think. We heard the explosion—didn't know it was a plane until we ran back here. We were a mile away and that was still *loud*," said Moose.

"Yeah, plenty of secondary explosions. We're under the big, dead tree, meet us over here," said Hodges. The four of them met at the tree and then set up their high-powered scopes again. They watched as the Chinese officers tried to restore order amid the chaos of thousands of terrified villagers running in every direction. The wrecked plane continued to burn wildly, sending up thick black smoke that would be seen miles away—and that worried Shen Xun-jun. He screamed at his officers, who in turn relayed instructions to the Africans to begin unloading the other two planes, while others tried to throw dirt on the burning wreckage. Sergeant Major Han ran full speed to the command cabin to call Beijing and notify their superiors of the catastrophe with the third plane. They wouldn't know what was lost until they unloaded the first two and took some kind of inventory.

The PAC soldiers, more afraid of Shen Xun-jun than of the fire, calmed down and began making a long line from the open nose of plane one all the way back into the camp. Boxes were being unloaded and passed along the long line. The larger crates were stacked and awaited the truck from camp. With two huge planes to unload, the men would be there for hours. Unfortunately for the four members of the team watching from the woods, they couldn't see anything other than crates of various sizes. They were happy to report back to the fish farm, however, that no tanks or armor drove off the planes.

CHAPTER 28

Cascaes and Mackey sat together and called Langley, where Dex Murphy and Deirdre Gourlie were sitting with Darren Davis watching a bank of televisions showing still photos and live images of the Democratic Republic of Congo.

Mackey spoke first, "Boss, we've got news."

"Good," said Dex. "Because we were getting ready to call you. What the hell just happened over there? You start World War Three already?"

"Sir?" asked Mackey, not sure how Dex could know what had happened before he even told him.

"I am looking at the satellite feed of the camp, and it looks like you crazy fuckers just shot down a plane."

"Negative, sir! We have men observing only. The third plane crashed upon landing. My men report major secondary explosions. We're almost three miles away and could hear and feel the explosion."

"I'm sure. It lit up like a Christmas tree on the sat-pics," said Dex. "What can you tell us about the cargo?"

"Not much, other than lots of crates. Most likely individual heavy weapons, or maybe crew served stuff. No armor or vehicles, and no Chinese troops. But, there were a shitload of boxes, boss. Probably a few million rounds of ammo. Not sure what was in the third transport, but whatever it was, it made a good sized black cloud. If there was armor coming in, it's gone now."

"Okay," said Dex. "Just keep tabs on our friends over there. Any more word on Nigel?"

"Nothing new to report. He's still at the camp with his army and new best friends."

"Okay," said Dex. "I need Cascaes a second."

Mackey passed the phone to Cascaes. "Boss wants to speak to you."

"Cascaes here," he said.

"Bad news, Chris," said Dex, who rarely called him by his first name. "I regret to inform you that Major Adam Stone passed away last night in his sleep. A doctor at the hospital called your number and it was forwarded to your office mailbox."

Chris felt his eyes water, and said, "Thank you. Is that all?"

"That's it. Stay in touch. Sorry to have to tell you. Out."

Cascaes handed the phone back to Mackey and walked outside. Julia had seen his face and followed him out to the quiet African morning.

"Everything okay?" she asked quietly, putting her hand on his arm and not caring who saw.

"Pop's gone," he said quietly. "Won't even be there for his funeral. Not sure who'll be there, really. Most of his friends and family are already gone."

Julia rubbed his back. "At least you got to say goodbye," she said quietly. "Come on, I'll buy you a cup of coffee."

They walked over to the campfire, where Jon Cohen and his crew were just pouring some of the dark coffee and eating breakfast bars.

"Hey, Skipper," said Jon. "Just heading out to dive. Wanna' come do some fishing?" His smile was genuine. He sure did love being underwater.

"I'd love to," said Cascaes, "but I'm afraid we're going to be a bit busy today. The PAC received their shipments last night. Well, two out of the three, anyway. That explosion was the third plane landing poorly."

The men around the fire smiled.

"So what now?" asked Jon.

"You go fishing and act like everything is normal. We're going to stay out of camp today in case the Chinese or PAC comes snooping around. They come by, you just stick with your story. We'll have you covered. Anything goes bad, we've got your back, but remember, we don't want to engage them yet, so stay cool."

Chris and Julia drank some coffee and chatted with the rest of the team as they joined the campfire for coffee and MREs. By oh-eight hundred, Mackey walked over and sat on an ancient log by the campfire that served as a chair.

They finished breakfast and discussed how they would spend the day. Cascaes related to Mackey that hanging around camp wouldn't be smart after the fishing expedition's run-in with the PAC. They also didn't love the idea of having all of them hanging out too close to the PAC camp. They were a large group in broad daylight and it was too easy to be spotted. They decided to gear up and split into two groups. One group would cover the camp and Jon's team, the other would campout closer to the PAC camp and relieve the observation teams in shifts. As they say in the army, "hurry up and wait."

CHAPTER 29

United Nations General Assembly, New York City

The Ambassador from the Democratic Republic of Congo had just finished a passionate speech accusing the Chinese of supporting the People's Army of Congo, the rebel army that threatened his country's stability. He went so far as to cite an explosion near the "rebel base" that witnesses say was the crashing of one of several planes that violated the DRC's airspace without authorization. He had spoken for almost twenty minutes, at one point screaming and pointing at the Chinese delegate, who merely removed his headphones and sat glaring at the African. When he was finished, the Chinese ambassador put his headphones back on and demanded a chance to reply to these outrageous accusations.

For the next thirty minutes, the Chinese ambassador berated the Congolese ambassador for being completely unappreciative of their humanitarian efforts in his country. He insisted that the current regime of the DRC was corrupt and afraid of the fact that the people of his country were demanding changes. He made reference to the accident at the humanitarian aid station that cost the lives of several heroic Chinese relief workers who were bringing in food and medicine. That comment was interrupted by the DRC ambassador who was screaming that "rice doesn't send fireballs a kilometer into the sky."

The Chinese ambassador ignored him and kept on speaking, explaining that thousands of Africans were starving, and that China was sending an example to the world of how a great nation was helping a weaker one recover. He used the spotlight to take a potshot at the United States, saying that while some nations only seek to invade or help those countries that serve their own interests, China was helping one of the poorest nations on Earth, and wanted nothing in return. They were merely trying to help.

That sent the Congolese ambassador over the edge. He threw off his headphones and began screaming. Eventually, the ambassador from South Africa, seated next to him, held him back and calmed him down. The Chinese ambassador smiled and continued.

"The ambassador makes wild allegations. Does he offer any proof? Has there been violence in the Democratic Republic of Congo? No. There is no rebel army. If people protest against the government, it is only because of the government's corruption and inability to govern. China will continue to help the refugees and starving children of the Congo as long as the people continue to ask for our help, which they do daily. Perhaps it is time for President Kuwali to step down. I ask the other nations of the UN, have you heard reports of war and violence in the Democratic Republic of Congo? Have you seen China do anything other than help a weaker nation during its time of crisis? No. You have not."

The American Ambassador to the United Nations, Ted Rogers, was quick to respond when the Chinese ambassador was finished. "The United States recognizes the right of the legitimate government of the Democratic Republic of Congo to defend itself against rebel guerrillas. Should the Congolese government request our help, the president would consider sending American troops to maintain order. We have marines nearby that can be called in should the situation arise."

The Chinese ambassador rose to his feet and pointed at the American. "China has relief workers in the Congo. It would be very dangerous for the United States to send troops to the Congo, as China would be forced to defend its citizens and also send a defense force. If the Congo needs help, it should be from the United Nations, not the United States!" (Knowing full well that the UN would not be prepared to send any forces back to the DRC.)

The posturing continued for another hour, and, at the end of the session, there was no final conclusion. The secretary general warned both the United States and China that their troops' presence in the DRC would only antagonize the tensions between the two superpowers, and the DRC was best left to solve its own internal problems. There had been no confirmed reports of violence in the DRC, and therefore, the United Nations could not afford to send in troops at this time, as their resources were already spread so thin. The Chinese ambassador smiled, then left to call Beijing and report his success.

CHAPTER 30

Shen Xun-jun was furious and screaming at his officers to push the men harder. The Africans were still unloading the two planes, as the third wreck continued to smolder. The fire had been so intense that much of the plane had actually melted. Occasionally, rounds would go off and the Africans would dive for cover, dropping crates and boxes and infuriating Shen Xun-jun even further.

Mackey happened to be watching when one of the crates was dropped and three RPGs fell out of the case.

"RPGs," he said quietly to Cascaes. "Look for similar crate sizes and count. Looks like six to a crate, two layers of three each." They watched for a while until the crates changed shape.

"I counted fifteen," said Cascaes.

"Okay, so that's ninety," said Mackey. "Plus however many they already had brought in. That's enough to make some noise."

"And some big holes," said Cascaes.

Julia was looking at the destroyed plane when she spoke up. "Look into the smoke, inside the plane. Looks like trucks or something were inside," she said quietly.

Mackey and Cascaes readjusted their view. It was hard to see anything inside the billowing black smoke, but there were destroyed vehicles inside.

"Good catch," said Cascaes. "Can't tell what it was, but you can bet it was light armor. They must be pissed. Probably why he had trouble landing—must have been heavy as hell for that dirt runway."

Mackey was smiling. "I bet that puts a crimp in their plans. Looks like three vehicles were in there. There weren't any on the other planes—they didn't spread them out. Knuckleheads." He smiled.

"Okay, so it looks like the PAC is going to have somewhere around ten thousand heavily armed infantry, with light artillery only. They won't have anything heavier than mortars or RPGs most likely. What do you think the president's troops have?" asked Cascaes.

"According to Langley, their air force has a few old helos, nothing armed. No operational combat fixed-wing at all. Maybe a half dozen forty-year-old tanks, and some poorly equipped. Maybe a few APCs. If they're going to prevent a coup, they need to hit this base now while they're all still here. If this army moves out into the countryside, they'll pop each village along the way until we have another Congo war."

"Send in the Marines?" asked Cascaes.

"Above our pay-grade," said Mackey. "When we get back later, we'll check in with the boss. Of course, by the time someone makes a decision, it'll be too late."

"Think we could move in at night with some explosives? Disrupt their camp, break moral a bit, inflict some casualties…" said Cascaes.

"I know we could get it done, but once we go there, the fish farm is closed and we'll be running from an army of pissed off, well-armed guerrillas. Unless we coordinate with the regular army and have them move in after we get things started."

Cascaes spoke quietly, "I know—still above our pay-grade. I just prefer being on offense."

"I hear ya," said Mackey.

The sound of trucks in the distance caught everyone's attention. They all went prone and concealed themselves better as the sound grew louder. It was a small convoy of light trucks flying the government's flag.

"Speak of the devil. This ought to be interesting," said Mackey. "Looks like the president is doing a little recon himself."

Cascaes scanned the camp. They had heard it too—maybe seen the dust. "We have movement in the camp," said Cascaes quietly.

Shen Xun-jun was screaming orders at his officers, who were then screaming at the Africans still unloading the planes to hurry up. Several officers had run inside the fence to organize a few platoons of infantry and had them run out to the airstrip in defensive positions. By the time the trucks were a few hundred yards away, and slowing down, Shen Xun-jun's men had made a decent showing of discipline. There were several thousand armed men now scattered around the camp. The convoy couldn't have numbered more than a hundred soldiers.

The lead vehicle continued towards camp while the other five open transports spread out and stopped, allowing the soldiers inside to unload and take up positions behind the trucks. The Jeep in front, obviously with an officer or government official continued slowly towards camp. One of Shen Xun-jun's men used a bullhorn to scream in French that the camp was a secure area and to turn back. The Jeep ignored them and continued to get closer. Two of Shen Xun-jun's commanding officers walked slowly out towards the airstrip where their men lay spread-out with assault rifles locked and loaded. They repeated the order to turn back, which Julia translated. Again, the Jeep ignored them.

When one of the officers pulled out a sidearm and aimed it at the Jeep, it stopped moving. A single man got out and walked up to the Chinese officer. Cascaes was too far away to hear their conversation.

CHAPTER 31

The colonel from the DRC Army was very nervous as he walked towards the PAC camp. Two Chinese officers were standing before him, aiming a pistol at him. He put on his best game face and tried to sound tough.

"By order of President Kuwali, you are to put down all of your weapons. You are assembled here illegally, and you will be arrested if you do not cooperate."

The Chinese officer smiled and lowered his weapon. "We are operating an aid station for the Congolese people. You are interfering with humanitarian aid to your own people. We have a security force here to protect the food against those who would steal it. I suggest you return to you vehicle and leave at once."

The colonel spoke a tribal language to his driver, who picked up a camera and began filming the "aid station."

"What do you think you are doing?" asked the Chinese officer, who walked quickly to the driver. "Give me that!"

The driver kept filming, his hands shaking.

The colonel stepped in front of the Chinese officer. "We are government officials and have a right to film what you are doing here. You are interfering with a government investigation. Step away!"

The two Chinese officers spoke quickly to each other in Mandarin. They had been told by Shen Xun-jun to avoid gunfire if at all possible. After a few seconds of debate, they stepped back.

"You have been warned. Our security force is here to protect the supplies. If you return, we will have no choice but to protect ourselves and the civilians."

They eyeballed each other for a few more seconds, and the colonel returned to his Jeep, his uniform soaked with sweat. As he hopped into his seat, he barked the order to "drive," and they sped off towards their own convoy. He had survived the ordeal, and had what he needed. The president would show the UN and the world the film of the PAC forces and Chinese officers, assuming he was still in power in the coming days.

The convoy sped off to Kinshasa as fast as it could move.

⊕

"That must have been an interesting discussion," said Cascaes quietly.

"He had a camera," said Julia. "They had serious balls."

"Yeah, I thought for sure they were all dead when he started filming. The Chinese must be getting ready to move quickly, or they never would have let them go."

"Or they need more time," said Julia. "Maybe they're waiting for more supply planes? Stalling? Trying to stick with their story as long as they can until they are totally prepared to take on the army?"

Mackey was watching lots of activity in the camp, as platoons of soldiers began opening crates of weapons.

"Keep four men here to keep tabs, and we'll get back to the farm. We need to update Langley."

Cascaes pulled Moose, Ripper, Hodges and Jones aside and told them to sit tight and keep track of whatever weapons they could see. They would be in contact soon. With that, Cascaes, Mackey, Julia and Theresa quietly snuck out through the small forest back towards the fish farm.

By the time the four of them returned to the fish farm, it was midday and blistering hot. They each drank a few liters of water and collapsed on the straw mat inside the command hut, where they called Dex Murphy again. As they set up their secure phone call, Julia groaned exhaustedly.

"As soon as we're finished, I'm jumping in the lake," said Julia.

"I'll be right behind you," answered Cascaes, hoping for a few minutes alone with her. Mackey pretended not to hear, wishing he was enjoying himself on this mission as much as they were.

Murphy answered the phone while eating a doughnut and drinking coffee—the breakfast of champions.

"Morning boss," said Mackey.

"And how's it going on your side of the world?" asked Murphy. "According to our satellite pictures, nothing has blown up in at least a couple of hours."

"Yeah, well, it's still early. Listen, the plane that went down, it had what looked like three armored vehicles in it. They were the only ones. The PAC will have a hundred RPGs or more, plus plenty of squad sized automatic weapons. They won't run out of lead for another six months, either. The Chinese brought in plenty of ammunition. Also, something interesting happened while we were there."

"I'm all ears," said Dex, munching his doughnut.

"The DRC sent a guy over with a set of brass balls and a camera and filmed their operation. The Chinese exchanged words with them, and the Vegas money was on the DRC officer getting his head blown off, but nothing happened. He left with his camera."

"Interesting. The DRC was just making noise at the UN late yesterday. They were talking about the plane crash right after it had happened, so they must be watching over there, too. You see any DRC forces nearby?"

"Negative contact, and we've been sitting on the airport twenty-four-seven for over two days. The Skipper and me were thinking we should hit them before they get armor support flown back in. It will take another day probably. We could go in tonight and 'disrupt' things a bit. They won't think it's us—they'd blame the DRC."

"I'm not sure. I'll have to ask the director. You were sent there to find out what you can about uranium and to rescue Nigel, not start a war. And just so you know, the Chinese at the UN still deny any involvement with the PAC forces."

"War is coming anyway, boss. We're just trying to even the odds a bit for the DRC army. The PAC looks pretty well trained. And there sure are a *lot* of them. The Chinese can say whatever they want, when that tape gets aired, it will be pretty clear what's going on over there. I think it will push up their timetable."

"Okay, sit tight for now and stay near the phone. I'll get back to you ASAP. And Mac, you're sure about Nigel, right? I mean, the guy's been with us a long time. A-desk is pretty upset. She trusted him."

"Boss, if he hasn't changed sides, then he's the best agent I've ever seen. Academy Award material. Sorry, boss. He's flipped, man."

"Okay. Let me get to the director. He's up to his ass in alligators, as usual."

"Roger that. I'll have a couple of the guys snoop around near the uranium mine and see if they find out anything."

"Okay, just stay low. Out."

Mackey hung up and looked at Cascaes. "Okay—enjoy your swim. Take an hour off, grab some chow and pick three guys to go uranium hunting."

"*Guys*?" asked Julia sarcastically.

"You can take Julia, too, if you want." He looked at her. "If you aren't afraid of your hair falling out." He looked at Cascaes, whose cropped head was getting thin on top. "I wouldn't worry about yours too much."

"Fuck you," said Cascaes with a smile. "I'm gonna' go jump in a lake."

"I'll protect you from alligators," said Julia, getting up off the floor mat.

"Who is going to protect him from you?" asked Mackey, with a knowing smile.

She winked and tussled Mac's longer salt and pepper hair. "Jealous," she whispered.

"You bet your ass," he replied.

CHAPTER 32

Julia and Chris had gone for a long swim, found a secluded spot, and got reacquainted. When they were finished, they swam back to the fish farm and found Jon and his crew sitting down for lunch. They joined them for a meal of MREs, improved with some fresh barbequed fish.

"Bony little fuckers," complained Jon, spitting tiny fish bones out of his mouth.

"Yeah, but tastier than the plastic hotdog looking thing I just ate. What the hell *was* that, man?" asked Ryan O' Conner.

"I think the package said 'beef' on it—it just didn't say from what animal. Stick with the fish, man," said Ray Jensen with a laugh.

"You guys seen Ernie P. or Smitty?" asked Cascaes.

"Down in Fish Central, playing with claymores. I think those two guys are fucking crazy man. They are getting this place rigged to repel a major assault."

"That's what they get paid to do," said Cascaes.

"Yeah, Skipper, but these guys are *nuts*. They were taking stuff apart and making their own explosives and shit. They've got wires and sensors running all over camp. While you guys were out at the airstrip, Smitty and Ernie were *busy*. I mean, don't get me wrong—I appreciate the help, since it's our asses on the line if the PAC comes cruising in. But damn—I've never seen anybody do *this* kind of shit. Those guys engineers?"

Cascaes laughed. "I told you—Department of Defense."

"Oh, yeah—spooks like Mackey," laughed Jon. "That explains it."

Cascaes laughed. "They were imbedded with Rangers in Afghanistan for two years. Making 'things that go boom' is a specialty. You think only the Iranians know how to make IEDs?"

"Yeah—that's a good word for it. Improvised Explosive Devices. That is definitely what this shit is—*improvised*. I just hope I'm not in camp if those two fuckers start setting shit off. This whole place is going to be one big black hole."

"Okay, you have my curiosity piqued," said Cascaes getting up, tossing his unfinished fish into the fire. "Come on Julia, let's go get our other two volunteers."

Julia and Cascaes walked down to Fish Central, the large fish packing building on the lake that would serve as a final defensive position if the shit hit the fan. When they walked in, sure enough, Smitty and Ernie had taken apart a dozen Claymore mines and had parts everywhere. They were laughing and joking as they worked.

"You two guys enjoy your work *way* too much," said Julia.

"If you can't have fun at work, why work?" asked Ernie, with a fuse and wires between his teeth. Ernie P. was a short Hispanic man with a bright smile and brown eyes that smiled when he did. For a good-natured guy, he was as deadly as they came.

"What the fuck are you doing with my explosives, sir?" asked Cascaes with a smile.

"Improving on them, Skipper," said Smitty, holding up a large bucket of chain links.

"Ah, I see," said Cascaes.

"You see what?" asked Julia, confused.

"Watch and learn," he answered. "What's the container?" he asked Smitty.

Joe Smith held up a large metal box that had once housed something mechanical in the fish farm.

"Gotcha. How many?" asked Cascaes.

"A dozen," said Smitty, then he flashed a smile. He really *did* love blowing things up.

"Damn. They really did pack a lot of shit into our SCUBA crates," answered Cascaes.

"Chris, you want to fill me in?" asked Julia.

"You see, my dear," he said dramatically, "our ingenious friends over here take a Claymore mine, which is a shaped anti-personnel charge designed to throw hundreds of small ball-bearings…"

Smitty cut him off and walked over with steel balls in his hand. "Allow me, Skipper," he said with a bow. "The M18A1 fires seven hundred spherical steel balls over a sixty degree fan-shaped pattern approximately two meters high and fifty meters wide at a range of fifty meters. It is effective up to a hundred meters, although the optimum range is about fifty meters."

Ernie P. walked over with chain links in his hand. "Your very devious team mates have combined several claymores with chain links and assorted metal odds and ends with increased shaped charges to double the field of fire and effective kill zone. By the time we are finished with camp, we will *want* the PAC to attack us."

"You may want to be in Tanzania when we set this puppy off though," said Smitty.

"Wow," was all Julia could muster.

"Yet again, I leave a beautiful woman speechless," said Smitty with another dramatic bow. "Now if you will allow me to continue my work, I have lots to do."

"Okay," said Cascaes. "You have just gotten yourself out of a scavenger hunt for uranium. Keep up the good work and I'll find another victim."

Chris and Julia walked back out, up the small slope towards the campfire. "Holy crap, Chris. Those guys know their shit, huh?"

Cascaes smiled. "This team was picked from the best of the best Julia, including you. If they tell me this place will be covered, I will take that to the bank. They were pretty famous in Kost, back in Afghanistan. Set up an ambush and took out a few hundred Taliban soldiers in a series of controlled blasts. The Rangers they were with were damn good, and they all said that they'd never seen anything like those two. I'm glad they're with us."

She smiled and whispered, "I'm glad I'm with *you*."

He winked and fought the urge to kiss her since they were near the campfire.

"Okay boys, I hate to break up the diving for the day, but I need two of you to come with us. Smitty and Ernie are busy, and Moose, Theresa, Hodges and Jones are at the airfield. Who wants to dry out for a bit?"

Jon nudged Pete McCoy. "C'mon Petey, we'll give R and R some R & R."

"R and R?" Pete asked.

"Ray and Ryan."

Pete didn't complain. "Aye, aye. I always wanted to go on safari anyway."

Cascaes smiled. "Hopefully we won't see lions—just uranium mining activities. Bring the cameras; we'll be linking directly to Langley."

"How far a hump?" asked Pete, planning gear in his head.

"Probably five to eight klicks. The mine is north of Lubumbashi, and a bit west. When we came up from the airport, it was on our left about two klicks. We'll be humping in the hottest part of the day, so bring plenty of water. The walk back should be cooler."

"We're carrying, right Skipper?" asked Jon.

"I won't walk out of my hut to take a piss without a sidearm around here," said Cascaes. Then he looked at Julia. "Excuse the expression," he added.

"No problem. When I take a crap in the woods, I bring a grenade," said Julia. Jon and Pete cracked up.

"I'll hang with you anytime, lady," said McCoy.

She blew him a dramatic kiss. Cascaes smiled and switched back to serious mode. "We'll carry assault rifles and silencers, night viz in case we run late, commo equipment, local currency, water and food for two days."

Pete and Jon were making the mental list, and then hustled off to load packs for the four of them. They had served as SEALs with Cascaes as their commander for almost eight years, and would follow his orders to their deaths. They had extreme confidence not only in their own abilities, but in his command experience and expertise. As they hustled off, Julia spoke quietly to Chris.

"It's going to start getting busy around here, huh? Between babysitting the PAC, defending this little fish farm, keeping track of Nigel and finding the story on the uranium mining, it's really going to cut into our dating."

"Yeah, and you left out the part where we take on the PAC army of ten thousand infantry with heavy weapons."

"Right. And there's that," she said. She looked around and no one was nearby. She leaned over and kissed him. "I love you, by the way."

Cascaes smiled and felt startled. While he had made the comment before their trip about marrying her one day, neither of them had ever actually used the "L word" before. She laughed at his startled face.

"I only said that because we'll both probably be dead in a couple of days."

"Whew, for a minute there I thought this was getting serious," said Chris.

"Pretty serious," she said, this time seriously. He leaned over and kissed her back. "I love you, too," he said, "but that is classified."

They walked back to their command hut where Mackey was on the horn with Moose over at the airfield. They packed gear quietly as Mackey spoke with the team at the PAC camp. They finished packing and were starting to head out when Mackey ended his conversation and turned to Cascaes and Julia.

"Moose said the camp is getting busier. Lots of shooting—live fire exercises with their new weapons. Maybe they are getting ready to go operational sooner than we think. They'll stay out their watching all night. You guys be careful and get back tonight. Stay in radio contact every hour and make sure your GPS locators are working. I hate having my people scattered all over when there is a chance that World War Three is gonna start. Who are you taking?"

"Julia, Cohen, and McCoy are with me. Smitty and Ernie P. are finishing the defensive preparations for the farm. They've got daisy-chains a mile long. Moose, Ripper, Jones, Hodges, Koches, Woods, and Theresa are still up at the PAC camp?" asked Cascaes, counting on his fingers.

"Check," said Mackey.

Cascaes was doing roll call in his head. "Where's Cory?" he asked. Cory Stewart was CIA, and was an old contact of Mackey's. Cory was older than most of the others, and a quiet, loner type who was all business, all the time. While he enjoyed listening to the joking and funning amongst his team, he was usually just the observer. Like many CIA field agents, Cory tended to be "in the background" and easy to miss in a crowd. Prior to his recruitment to "the team," Cory had always worked alone in the field.

"He should be halfway to Kinshasa by now," said Mackey.

"What the fuck?" asked Cascaes, obviously pissed that he wasn't informed ahead of time.

"Sorry, Skipper," said Mackey. "Langley's orders. He's supposed to make contact with the DRC government contacts we have and update them on their options. The director sent the order a couple of hours ago."

"You might have mentioned it," said Cascaes. "Anybody else?"

"Nope. Just Cory. He hopped the train a few hours ago. It's almost 800 miles—gonna take a while on that piece of junk. I'll brief you later. For now, get what you can at the mine, and hustle back. By tomorrow, we should all be reassembled and prepared to take offensive action against PAC forces, if we get the order. The situation changes every time I call. Just go take some pictures, and get your ass back here in one piece."

Cascaes wasn't particularly happy being left out of the loop, but was somewhat used to it. Rarely did anyone ever have "all the pieces" of the puzzle. He grunted a "yes, sir" to Mackey and grabbed his combat pack. "Let's go," he said to Julia, and headed out to find Jon and Pete and start the journey to the uranium mine.

CHAPTER 33

Chris, Julia, Pete, and Jon met up at the campfire and hopped in the old pickup truck. They headed off towards the reported location of the illegal mining operations north of Lubumbashi. It would be three hours or so each way, bouncing along the dirt roads. At a little after two o'clock, and eighty-five degrees with relatively high humidity, it was not a great day for a drive in the country.

They drove through tall grasslands, remaining relatively quiet as they observed the raw beauty that was Africa. The countryside was wide open and there were no signs of human activity for the first two hours. As they grew closer to the mine, a makeshift village appeared. Thousands of Africans, mostly very young men or boys, had come to the area to work the mines. One of the biggest problems in fighting illiteracy was combating the dropout rate of boys who could easily be talked into working for low wages at the mines. The village was merely a shantytown of sorts, with garbage strewn everywhere. When they got closer, they stopped the truck and got out to walk. They spread out and approached the edge of the village cautiously.

Cascaes called in their location and the fact that they had made contact. Pete snapped a few pictures that were uplinked to Langley, and they walked closer. The first thing that got their attention was a small graveyard outside the village. There were easily a hundred recently dug graves with small stones as markers. Pete snapped a few pictures of that as well.

"Radiation sickness?" asked Julia to Cascaes. He shrugged.

They walked closer until they were at the edge of the village. The place reeked of latrines and garbage. "That's what happens when a village has no women to oversee the men," thought Julia. Chris motioned for Jon and Pete to stay put and cover them, while he and Julia dropped their packs and weapons. They walked slowly into the hellhole that was the village until they saw their first person, a young boy of maybe ten or so. Julia approached him with her warm smile and said "hello" in French.

"Hello," he replied, but didn't smile.

"What's wrong?" she asked.

"I can't work today," he said. "My little brother is sick."

"Where is he?" she asked.

He pointed to the small hut behind them. "Sleeping inside."

Julia asked if she could see him, and maybe help. That got a smile. "Are you a doctor?" he asked.

"No," she said, "but I have some medical experience."

They followed the boy inside the hut. It was even hotter inside. A boy of maybe seven or eight was lying on his side on the dirt floor. He looked seriously ill. His skin color was pale for a dark-skinned boy, and his eyes were glazed-looking in hollowed out cheeks. He looked like he was freezing. He didn't stir when they walked in.

The older brother sat next to him and whispered to him in Swahili, "The white lady is going to make you better." Still no response.

"How long has he been sick?" she asked.

The older boy, who told them his was named Soffee, said that his little brother, Imika, started with diarrhea last week, and wouldn't eat. Then he started getting cold, then hot and weak. He had drunk water from the creek by the mine, even though they had been told not to. Imika had boiled it first, which they had been taught would kill bad things in the water by the Peace Corps some years back, but they didn't understand that uranium and heavy metals couldn't be boiled out.

Cascaes asked Julia to translate his questions. "How many times did he drink that water?" Soffee shrugged. Most of the villagers had been drinking it for weeks. Cascaes asked where the water was, and Soffee said he threw it away. Cascaes asked where the creek was, and Soffee said he would show him if Julia would help his little brother. Cascaes quietly told Julia not to even think about bringing the boy back to camp. Julia narrowed her eyes with anger.

She stayed with Imika, holding his cold hand, watching his labored breathing, trying not to cry. He was too weak to even lift his head. Chris followed Soffee through the center of "town" towards the site of much activity. They walked on baked mud and dead, brown grass, past the huts that housed the laborers. Beyond the corrugated steel huts and makeshift cabins, thousands of Africans were digging by hand in an open pit with the aid of water cannons that ran off large generators near the town's water source.

The open pit mine was the size of ten football fields, but there was very little in the way of heavy machinery. The land was simply being "overpowered" by sheer will. Water cannons tore open huge holes in the mud, and then workers with pick axes and shovels would dig through the dirt looking for the Uraninite ore, or "pitchblende," that they had been trained to identify. They stood in ankle-deep, orange-tinted, foamy water and oozy mud that would kill a fish or frog in a matter of seconds. The ore in this location held the highest concentration of uranium yet discovered on the planet. "Oh great," thought Cascaes, "Use the water to mine the ore, then drink the water."

Cascaes stopped when they got close enough to see several Chinese men overseeing the workers. The Chinese wore lead lined waterproof boots and took iodine tablets daily. The Africans were barefoot in the poisoned mud.

He stepped behind a hut and called back to Jon on his throat mic. "Fishboy—you read me?" he asked.

"Loud and clear, boss," said Jon.

"Come up the center road, quick and quiet with your camera and concealed side arms only. Chinese are on site. Jackpot. Out."

He waited for almost five minutes, and sure enough, Jon and Pete came hustling up the same dirt road through the shantytown. Cascaes called to them when he saw them, and they ducked back behind a shed with him and the small boy.

"Smells *great* around here," said Jon quietly with a grimace on his face.

"Like a shit sandwich without the bread," said Cascaes. "The mine is up ahead. This little kid is Soffee. His brother is dying up the hill over there. They've been drinking the water. Same water the Chinese are using in the water cannons to strip mine."

"Brilliant," said Jon. Pete pulled his lens cap off and hustled up ahead to get a look. He started filming, taking particular care to show the Chinese men directing the workers. He also filmed the African workers carrying out another small body and laying it to the side for burial later. They couldn't stop working yet.

"Unfuckingbelievable," said Pete to himself as he filmed. When he had ten minutes of footage, panning over the huge area of ravaged earth where thousands of boys and men dug through poisoned mud, he hustled back to Cascaes. "Got it all, Skipper."

"Okay, let's get Julia and get the fuck out of here," said Cascaes. He held up several small vials filled with water samples and showed them to Pete.

They ran back to the hut where Julia sat crying with the young boy. His eyes were rolled back, showing only the whites, and he was convulsing quietly.

"Oh shit," said Pete when he saw the kid.

Julia shook her head at Chris. "He's so sick, Chris. He'd never make the trip anyway." She held up her hand to Soffee, who took it, looking scared. She explained in French that his little brother was dying, and that Soffee should go home as soon as Imika had passed on. He should go home and never come back to this place that was poisoned.

Soffee sat next to his brother and cried, and Cascaes gave him his thermos of fresh water and some MREs. "Tell him to eat and drink only this until he gets home."

Jon looked at Cascaes. He pulled a few morphine syringes out of his fatigues. "Skipper, we can make it easier for him."

Cascaes squatted next to the two young boys and asked Julia to translate. "Tell Soffee that this will help his brother sleep comfortably until he goes to the next world. He'll have happy dreams."

Julia translated and Soffee hugged his brother and cried and nodded his head.

"Who's gonna do it?" asked Jon, his mouth suddenly so dry he could barely get the words out. They exchanged glances in complete silence.

Cascaes took the syringe from Jon, swallowed hard, and popped it into Imika's skinny thigh. They watched the boy drift away. At least he wouldn't be suffering. They sat with Imika while he sang a song they didn't understand, but cried just the same. They shared a quick prayer, and left the boys, all four of them wiping tears, and jogged out of the village back into the grass, where Pete set up his satellite computer and sent the film to Langley.

Julia wiped her eyes with the back of her hand. "Different country, same shit. Sweatshops in China, slave-wage farmers in Mexico, baby miners in Africa—no one gives a shit as long as what they want to buy is cheap."

"That about sums it up," said Cascaes.

Jon kept seeing Imika's face and skinny body. "I've never been able to understand how it is that Africa and South America, two continents so rich in natural resources, are so fucked up."

"Don't get her started," said Cascaes, stiffening. "You two can figure out the world's political and economic picture when we get back to the Land of Wasteful Spending. For right now, keep your shit together and stay focused. We've got 10,000 armed thugs itching to start a revolution so they can make this little mine scene a national pastime. If you really want to help these people, stay alert."

Pete whispered over to the three of them. "Uplink is finished, Skipper."

"Okay, let's boogie on back to the fish farm and see what's going on. World War Three could have started already for all we know."

They stood up and started walking. Julia looked at Cascaes. "You know, she was right."

"Who was right?" he asked.

"Deirdre. Back in Langley. That slide show didn't really paint the picture."

CHAPTER 34

Kinshasa

Cory Stewart walked through the streets of Kinshasa in jeans and a polo shirt, looking like the other white men trying to find business opportunities in the third world. Kinshasa was a strange city. Some avenues were the same wide streets you would see in any major city, except that some of the side streets were literally dirt roads. Old primitive houses were down the block from large apartment buildings. An occasional new Mercedes would zip past an ox drawn cart. Worlds had definitely collided here.

Most of the people on the streets were Africans, but the whites and Asians seemed to be from every corner of the globe. As Cory walked, he could hear the lilt of Irish accents, Indians speaking in Hindi and accented English, Russian, American English, and various Middle Eastern dialects. Occasional Chinese banter would catch his attention, but there was nothing to be learned by walking the busy business district. He was on his way to a secret meeting with one of Prime Minister Gugunga's most trusted people, his chief of staff, a man named Lucien Zabanga.

The meeting between Zabanga and Cory Stewart had been set up by a Congolese businessman named Michael Motumba that Langley had recruited the year prior. He was in the computer business and anxious to see his country enter the twenty-first century. CIA had convinced him that his cooperation would ensure the future of his nation, and more importantly, his failing company. Langley had "signed a contract" for his computer services for 50,000 dollars, US. They had received nothing for this contract other than the ability to call Michael whenever they needed him. He was a low-level asset, but in this case, he had ties to the prime minister that made him extremely valuable.

Michael Motumba had contacted the prime minister's office to arrange the meeting, but never actually spoke to him personally. He had been given to Lucien Zabanga, his chief of staff, and Zabanga had agreed to meet with Cory Stewart. Motumba had told Zabanga that Stewart was an important American with government ties, and came to offer the prime minister and the president support 'in this most perilous time for their government.'

Michael led Cory down the busy streets of Kinshasa until they reached an office building that appeared fairly new. It was ten stories high, and was impressive looking in a skyline that lacked many skyscrapers. When they arrived, Michael told Cory to go to room 515 on the fifth floor. He would meet him down the block at the outdoor cafe on the corner when he was finished.

Cory entered the building and waited for almost five minutes for an elevator that never came. He ended up taking the stairs with the rest of the sweaty, grumpy businessmen traveling up and down the staircase in the building whose elevator hadn't worked in five months. "Waiting for parts from Belgium," was the standard line from the building's superintendent. He walked down the hall and stopped at 515 where he wiped the sweat off his face and onto his jeans. He took a deep breath and walked in, and as he closed the door behind him he knew he was a dead man.

Seated in front of him was indeed, Lucien Zabanga. But, seated next to him were two Chinese men and three large Africans with their automatic weapons across their laps. As

Cory reached for the doorknob behind him, to try and make a break for it, a large man stepped up from behind him and pressed a Glock 17 into his ribs.

"Have a seat, Mr. Stewart," said Zabanga. "Or shall I call you something else? How many names do you have?"

Cory felt the sick feeling of defeat creep into his stomach. The air seemed to leave his lungs instantly. He had been a field agent for fifteen years and been in and out of some hairy places. To be taken down so casually was as embarrassing as it was final. He felt a sudden calm as he realized his fate. With such a large team in the field, he made his decision instantly. He was dead anyway. He wasn't going to say anything that would get the entire team killed with him.

Cory threw his elbow as hard as he could into the man's throat behind him, and with his other hand, grabbed the pistol. The gun went off as he grabbed it, but missed Cory. He popped his knee twice into the man's face as he went down, the three large men behind the desk diving across the office at him, furniture flying everywhere. Cory yanked the weapon free from the man's limp hand and rolled across the office floor getting his finger into the trigger guard. The three men dove at him, wanting him alive, and Cory managed to fire three rounds quickly into the first man now grabbing his ankles. The other two were on him quickly, tackling his legs. Cory knew he'd never take them all. He couldn't risk it. He shoved the Glock into his mouth and pulled the trigger before the men could get it out of his hand. He never heard the gun go off or the screaming of Lucien Zabanga and the Chinese, desperate to take him alive.

⊕

Michael Motumba sat at the coffee shop watching the front of the building for Stewart. He figured it would be at least a half hour, so he ordered a small meal and got comfortable. The sight of a black SUV roaring up the street took him by surprise. More surprising was watching Lucien Zabanga hustle out of the building with two Chinese men and two large bodyguards. They piled into the large truck and took off in a cloud of dust. Motumba dropped his coffee mug, quite literally, on the floor.

He was up and running as the truck sped away, a waiter chasing and screaming at his for leaving without paying his bill. He raced up the stairs to the fifth floor, drawing comments from the people he pushed past on the staircase. When he got to the fifth floor, he ran down the hallway to the office reading 515 and threw the door open. It bounced off the body behind it. Michael pushed the door until it was open enough to slide inside the office. He had never seen anything like the scene inside. Cory Stewart was on the floor, most of the back of his head splattered across the wall next to the door. A large black man lay at his feet covered in blood, his eyes half open, but not seeing. Another was leaning up against the wall behind him, his mouth open and tongue already swollen.

"Oh God," he said quietly. He stood staring for a moment, not knowing what to do. Then fear overtook him. Zabanga knew his name—knew the name of his company—knew where he lived and worked. Michael stepped back over Cory, saying a prayer as he closed the door behind him and ran back down to the staircase. When he hit the street, he kept running, not even knowing where he would go.

CHAPTER 35

Cascaes, Julia, Jon, and Pete stopped the truck outside camp and walked in cautiously, after observing it from a distance to make sure all was as it should be. When they saw Smitty and Ernie P. walk casually to the campfire to start cooking dinner, they figured it was safe. They headed right for Mackey's cabin where they would debrief him on what they had seen. They were surprised when they entered and found Mackey throwing things all over the cabin like a drunken lunatic. Mackey stopped, embarrassed, when they entered and caught him wild-eyed in mid-throw of a box of MREs.

"What's wrong?" asked Cascaes, shocked to see the boss so out of control.

"God damn it!" he screamed. "They got Cory. Those fuckers killed him."

"*What*?" Cascaes exclaimed, equally shocked. "What happened? How did you find out?"

Julia's hands covered her open mouth without her even realizing it.

"Dex just called me. He got a frantic call from their asset in Kinshasa—some low-level informant that set up the meeting." Mackey sat down on an ammo crate and took a deep breath to regain his composure. "According to this guy in Kinshasa, Cory went up to meet with Lucien Zabanga, the prime minister's chief of staff. He was there to get permission for us to go on offense and disrupt the PAC camp. Washington wasn't going to do anything without direct approval from the government. So Cory goes up to some office and they bushwhacked him. This guy that set it up

157

said he saw Zabanga with his own eyes, with two Chinese and some bodyguards. Cory apparently took two of them out before they shot him in the head. At least it was quick."

"Think they got anything out of him?" asked Cascaes, wondering how long before an armed column moved into the fish farm.

"No. Dex said that the guy saw Cory's body. He had been shot in the head right by the door of the office relatively quickly after he went up. He must have realized it was wrong right away and put up a fight. Dex said there were no signs of torture. Cory would've died before he gave us up anyway."

"He did, boss," said Cascaes quietly.

"Fuckers. And Washington still won't give us a green light. And that's *after* we know that Zabanga is with the Chinese."

The satellite phone rang right on cue. They all looked at each other.

"Until right now, you mean?" asked Cascaes, hoping it was the order to blow the shit out of the PAC camp.

Mackey picked it up right away. "Fish central," he said.

"Mac, be advised, you are 'green light' to take out Zabanga. Move quickly before he takes out Prime Minister Gugunga. They must all be getting nervous by now. They know we have assets on the ground and the Marines offshore. You need to move immediately. We will be sending you coordinates, addresses and photos of all of the known regular locations."

"Zabanga? Why doesn't the PM go after Zabanga himself and let us take a whack at the PAC camp? Zabanga is all the way in Kinshasa—the PAC camp is walking distance. We could be in and out before they knew what hit them."

"The prime minister never knew about the meeting, Mac," said Dex. "Our man arranged it through Zabanga's office. By the time Washington is able to speak to him directly and convince him that Zabanga is with the PAC, he'll be dead. And Gugunga won't know whom to trust, anyway. Hell, we don't know whom to trust over there, either. The sitting government is going to come apart at the seams if the PM or the president is assassinated. The PAC will move in and whole civil war will last about ten minutes. You need to take out Zabanga and anyone that gets in your way, and we'll try and reach the PM and the president through Washington. Tonight, Mac. You need to move out right away."

Mackey exhaled slowly, trying to keep from getting angry again. The mission seemed to be spinning out of control. Mackey tried to catch up in his head—he had half of his team watching the PAC camp, dozens of villagers wandering in and out of his base every day to sell and transport fish, a casualty from a mission that he hadn't designed, and now an assassination mission in Kinshasa all the way on the other side of a very large country, the same place his man was killed, that would require his best sharpshooter and spotter, *plus* a team for close quarter contact if necessary. He was getting stressed.

"All right, Dex. I'll put together a team for Zabanga, but what about the PAC? They're training every day that we sit here with our thumb up our ass. We can still disrupt their camp. They'll never know what hit them."

"Look Mac," Dex said. "I'm feeling the pressure at my end as well. I know you'd love to blast that base, but we don't get to make that call. So far, the Marines are just there to rattle the saber back at the Chinese, but I don't think the president wants to go toe to toe with a billion Chinese. If you go starting up a firefight over there, you'd be on your own against ten thousand guerrillas. President Kuwali doesn't even know you exist, so you wouldn't be getting any help from them. If the PAC moves against Kinshasa, it will take a couple of days. Just keep watching the base for now."

"All right, all right," said Mac, frustrated.

"And listen, we got the photos and video from your boys over at the mining operation. The little kids they have working are their 'canaries in the coal mine.' The director is meeting now to try and decide what to do with the evidence of the mining operation that is supposedly shut down."

"Yeah, well maybe the World Health Organization will invade and take out the PAC," said Mackey sarcastically.

"Yeah, right after the UN," said Dex. "Keep me in the loop, Mac. Good luck, out."

Mackey leaned back against the wall of the cabin. "This mission has been fucked from day one," he grumbled to no one in particular.

"So what now?" asked Cascaes.

"I'll call Hodges and Jones back from the PAC camp. They've been sitting up there with Moose, Ripper, Woods, Koches, and Theresa watching the base. Hodges and Jones can try and snipe Zabanga, but I need a team of four to get in closer in case they can't get a shot."

"There's four of *us*," said Cascaes.

"You haven't even sat down from your trip to the mine yet," said Mackey.

"No biggie. We'd need a truck for Kinshasa anyway. We can grab a nap on the way."

Mackey's eyes went to Julia then back to Cascaes. "Who are you gonna bring?" asked Mackey.

Julia had seen it. "Mac, don't give me the macho bullshit. I've done my share of wet work before. Chris and I can walk on the street without anyone looking at us twice."

Mackey rubbed his eyes, feeling very tired all of a sudden.

"And we've got their back," added Jon.

Mackey threw his arms up in surrender. "Fine. Go get something to eat, get cleaned up because you smell like shit, and meet me back here in two hours ready to move out. Hodges and Jones will be here waiting for you. You can take the truck."

Julia thought about the old piece of junk truck. "We might be faster walking," she said with a smile. Her smile broke the tension, and she patted Mackey's shoulder. "And I'm sorry about Cory," she said quietly. The four of them walked out to change and grab some food before gearing up for a long trip to Kinshasa.

CHAPTER 36

Moose was watching the PAC camp through high-powered binoculars when his earpiece crackled. It was Mackey from the fish farm telling him to send back Hodges and Jones immediately for a different mission. The choice of personnel wasn't lost on Moose.

"They get to pop somebody?" he said quietly. "Because they can pop the head dink right now if you want." Moose was watching Shen Xun-jun at the head of the parade ground observing his troops on an obstacle course. Hodges did, indeed, have Xun-jun's head in his crosshairs at that precise moment. He would have been very happy to separate the man's head from his body.

"Just get them back here and stay out of sight. We still aren't cleared to engage the PAC yet. Observation only."

"Yeah, well I am observing a shitload of them practicing to kill us," said Moose.

"Just be sure they don't. Out," said Mackey as he hung up.

Moose relayed the order to Hodges and Jones, who packed up and double timed it all the way back to the fish farm. They arrived, somewhat winded, at Mackey's cabin just as Chris, Julia, Jon, and Pete arrived in civilian clothing.

"Y'all got a date?" said Hodges in his southern drawl.

"Yeah, with you, hotshot," said Cascaes. Trade the ghillie suits for civvies. We are heading to Kinshasa. We have a target for you."

"No shit?" said Hodges. "Who's the sad sumbitch that's gonna meet the Reaper?"

"The same guy who had Cory killed," said Cascaes.

"Oh shit," said Hodges and Jones simultaneously.

"What happened to Cory?" asked Hodges.

"He went to meet with Lucien Zabanga, the chief of staff for the prime minister, and Zabanga set him up. Now you get to even things up." Cascaes handed Hodges a headshot of Zabanga that Mackey had printed for him off of his computer, downloaded from Langley only an hour before. "This is your target. If you can't get a shot from a safe distance, then we'll have to take him out the old fashioned way. But that may get complicated in downtown Kinshasa—the PM doesn't even know that Zabanga betrayed him yet."

"When are we heading out?" asked Hodges.

"As soon as you can change and grab an MRE for the road."

Hodges and Jones both hustled off to get changed and gear up for the next mission, while the four of them entered Mackey's cabin.

"The boys are back," said Cascaes. "We should be ready to roll in a few minutes."

"Okay. Here are the GPS coordinates and addresses of his most likely locations," said Mackey as he handed him photos and a small hand held computer. He has a large house just outside the city that is actually on the way to Kinshasa. I would make that your first stop. He will most likely have plenty of bodyguards there with him. If you can take him out there, you can get out fairly easily and get right back here. If you have to go to one of his other known addresses, it will be trickier. They are in the city and a sniper shot is unlikely. Just get in, and get the hell out in one piece. I don't have any safe locations in Kinshasa for you."

They were interrupted by Mackey's secure phone buzzing. It was Moose.

"Hey boss, we got lots of activity over here. Looks like maybe two company sized units gearing up and getting ready to move out. You boys better get out of Dodge. If they're heading your way, they'll outnumber you a hundred to one—

which would be okay if I was there with you, but you're on your own, you better beat feet."

"Have they left yet?" asked Mackey.

"Negative, but the gates are open and they are forming up columns of vehicles. They look pretty damn organized, Skipper. They must have had trucks under cover, 'cause I am looking at dozens of pickup trucks. Some of them have machine guns mounted in the back; most of them are just transport."

Mackey cursed under his breath. "Okay, sit tight and keep watching. You call me back as soon as you have anything else. Out."

Mackey reiterated the information to the others.

"So now what? You want us to stay here?" asked Cascaes.

"Now you sound like Moose. Two thousand against nine— you being here is going to even the odds? No—you go find Zabanga. I'll monitor things from here, and if they head this way, we'll take off and contact you when we can. Smitty and Ernie P. have this place so full of C4 that if they show up we'll blow them all to Hell anyway."

"Yeah, we saw," said Julia.

"Okay, get on the road. Stay in touch. Take the truck west along the Lukuga River until you get to the railroad station. You can't miss it, it's the only thing out there. Get on the train at Kabalo. You can pick up the Kinshasa Express there. You might make it by tomorrow night."

"Mac, by tomorrow night, you may have a full scale war on your hands. Are you sure about this?" asked Cascaes.

"Nope. I'm not sure about a damn thing. Like I said, this mission is one giant clusterfuck. I am going to have my team spread out all over the damn country when the shit hits the fan, and I don't like it one bit. But I'm not calling the shots, Chris."

Cascaes looked at Julia. "Mac—I'll leave Jon and Pete with you. Four of us can handle Zabanga. You may need the extra firepower here."

Mackey bit his lip and thought it over. "You sure, Chris? Zabanga may have a small army himself over there."

"One hundred percent, boss. We'll take him out and be gone before his men even know what happened."

"Okay. Jon, Pete—you two are spared the train ride. Instead, you can circle the wagons with us and wait for the PAC forces to assault this little fish farm."

Jon and Pete looked at each other and shrugged. "Whatever you say, boss. And the boat is still good to go if it gets too hairy. We can be in Tanzania in forty minutes."

"Okay, that's it then. We're out," said Cascaes. "Good luck, boss. We'll check in when we arrive."

CHAPTER 37

Mining Camp

Soffee had walked down the muddy slope towards the open pit mine to find help burying his brother. He had the new canteen over his shoulder, and foil packs of MREs shoved in the waistband of his tattered shorts, his only clothing. A Chinese supervisor stopped him and spoke to him harshly in French.

"Where are you going? Who are you?"

Soffee, his big brown eyes still full of tears looked up at the man in the gray jumpsuit, whose pants were tucked into tall rubber boots. His white hardhat had Chinese characters on it. "My little brother is dead. I need help burying him."

The Chinese man grabbed the canteen and pulled. "Where did you get this?" He grabbed the silver MRE packets from his waistband. "Where did you get this?" he repeated louder and faster.

Soffee was scared. "The white doctor gave it to me. He said not to drink or eat anything here—it's all poison. It killed Imika."

"What white doctor? Where is he?" he snapped. His Chinese accent made his French difficult for Soffee to understand.

"They left this morning," he said, terrified of the man gripping his little arm.

"They? There was more than one?" he was screaming at him now.

"There were four of them," he said quietly.

165

The Chinaman grabbed the boy hard by his wrist and walked quickly towards their prefabricated office building near the pit, practically dragging the small boy. Soffee had to run to keep up. One of the foil meals dropped on the ground, and Soffee couldn't stop to pick it up. He started to cry and scream that he wanted to go home. His cries were ignored all the way back to the small white building—the only building in the entire camp that didn't look like a mound of garbage.

The man threw the door open and pulled Soffee inside, practically throwing him at two Chinese men seated at a large table covered with computers and phones. He began screaming in Chinese, and grabbed the MREs and canteen from Soffee, waving them at the other men. The older man stood up and walked around the desk, then sat on it facing the skinny little boy. He said something quietly in Chinese and the man that brought Soffee in walked out in a huff.

In French, the older Chinaman asked Soffee who gave him the canteen and food, and Soffee repeated the story. Then the man started asking detailed questions—did they have computers? Cameras? Guns? Soffee answered everything honestly, as best as he could remember, and asked about burying his brother. The Chinaman promised he would get Soffee help burying his brother, and asked him who else knew about the white visitors. Soffee shrugged, and the man patted his head and told him he was a good boy and could show the other man where his brother's body was. Soffee reached for the MREs and canteen, and the man grabbed his hand. They no longer belonged to him.

Although upset that he couldn't have the good water and food, he was more scared than anything else, and was relieved just to get out of the small office. As he led the other Chinese man back to his small shelter, the older man picked up the phone and dialed. It rang a phone on Shen Xun-jun's desk at the PAC camp.

Although the mining operation didn't answer directly to the army general, the mining company was under the jurisdiction of the Chinese government and answered to the highest-ranking Chinese government official in the country—currently Shen Xun-jun. The Engineer, Dr. Fong, was surprised when the general answered his own phone. He explained to the general that his mining camp had apparently been visited by a team of Americans. The MREs and canteen were American issue, and the boy had said they were four white people—three men and a woman. The conversation was brief, and Shen Xun-jun was not happy when he slammed the phone down.

Shen Xun-jun stormed out of his cabin to where his army was preparing to load up for the trip to Kinshasa to take the capital. The plan called for his army to link up with another smaller PAC force from the south, just outside of Kinshasa, by tomorrow night. They would camp secretly in the woodlands to the south of Kinshasa and wait for Shen Xun-jun's army to take out the president and prime minister. Once the heads of state were assassinated, his army would sweep into the city, and Nigel Ufume would lead the coupe, which hopefully wouldn't last more than a few hours. Having Americans on the scene operating nearby was unacceptable, particularly with the ship full of United States Marines off-shore that Shen Xun-jun was very much aware of.

Shen Xun-jun screamed for Sergeant Major Han, who was directing troops into vehicles in the total chaos that was the camp. Sergeant Major Han grabbed a Congolese sergeant to keep everyone moving as he ran off to the general. He snapped a salute.

"Yes, sir!"

"There is a slight problem. Americans have been spying on us. I want patrols sent around the perimeter of this camp, and two platoons sent to find those Canadian fishermen. They may be our American spies. I want them now!"

Sergeant Major Han snapped a salute. "Shall the rest of the men proceed according to plan?"

"Yes. You lead the patrol *personally* to find the Americans—you can catch up to us tomorrow. I want you to round up everyone you find and bring them along to the rendezvous point south of the city. I will be with my men and will deal with the Americans there. There are three men and a woman that we know of."

The sergeant major snapped a salute and ran off to pull two platoons for a trip southeast to find the fish farm. He also began shouting orders for guards to begin moving out into the grass surrounding the camp to make sure there were no spies watching their camp.

Out in the grass, Moose radioed back to Mackey again. "Hey Skipper, you read me?"

Mackey was seeing Cascaes and his crew off to Kinshasa when his radio buzzed.

"What have you got Moose?"

"Skipper, I'm not sure, but I think we've been made. We're in the wind, boss. They've got patrols moving out all over the place, and about twenty vehicles just took off in your direction. We are going to head south, parallel to your location, due west one klick, you copy?"

"I copy," said Mackey, now getting anxious.

"And, Skipper, it looks like the rest of them are all mounting up and breaking camp. Might be the big move to the capital. I think they're taking every weapon they got off those planes. I need to sign off and beat feet, Skipper. Out."

Mackey listened to the radio go dead and exhaled slowly. He was used to running a tight operation where every detail was well planned ahead of time. They were now reacting and trying to keep up to events as they occurred, and he hated being on his heels. He hustled out of his cabin and yelled to Smitty and Ernie P.

⊕

Ernie P. and Smitty were digging in the dirt outside "Fish Central" when Mackey found them. They had been planting their explosives and coordinating the firing sequence in the event of an assault. The one that they were about to find out about.

"Hey!" yelled Mackey as he approached. "I hope you boys are almost finished."

Smitty stood up from the hole and smiled. "As a matter of fact, we are just finishing up now. What's up?"

"Looks like you are going to get a chance to play with your firecrackers. What's the maximum range from which you can detonate?"

"Shit, boss, we can set these puppies off from a few miles out. We gonna have company?"

"Yeah, and maybe a *lot* of it. I'm thinking we observe from the lake, draw them into camp with some bait, and then bring the whole thing down on their heads as we take off. There will be too many of them to take on in a firefight, but at least we can beat them up a little and take out some personnel."

"Roger that, boss. Give us another ten minutes and we're finished here. Look around you—you see anything suspicious?"

Mackey glanced around quickly. Everything looked normal. "No," he said suspiciously.

"Exactly. And neither will they." He smiled and knelt down to finish covering the box in the hole.

CHAPTER 38

Cascaes drove the truck as fast as he could and still maintain some control on the bumpy dirt roads. Getting to Kinshasa before the PAC was vital. By the time the United States was able to speak directly to the president and prime minister and convince them that the PM's chief of staff was a traitor, the PAC forces would be driving through the gates of the Presidential Residence. They hung on as tight as they could and bounced and swerved all over the dirt road—more like a path, really, until they made their way to the train station.

Once at the station, they grabbed their duffle bags full of weapons, night vision equipment, gear, and camos out of the back of the truck and walked to the platform. They were the only ones there, except for the two old men who ran the station. "Station" was being kind. It was really more of a simple platform with a tiny house next to it. The house served as the area train station, post office, local news stand, and gossip column.

Julia approached one of the old man. He was dark, with a grey beard and hair, and only a few remaining teeth. He smiled broadly when she approached and said hello in French. She asked when the Kinshasa Express would be here, and he laughed and shrugged.

"Should have been here an hour ago, but she comes when she wants," he said with a smile. "Where are you coming from?"

She told him about the fish farm, and explained they had business to conduct in Kinshasa. Time was of the essence, of course. This led to the two old men chattering for a few minutes in Swahili, then the man switched back to French. "If you have enough money, I could get you a plane," he said. He saw her surprised expression. "It's a good plane—a new one. And it could fit all of you in one trip."

"Who is the pilot?" she asked.

"My nephew," he said with great pride. "He has the plane down in Lubumbashi—a private charter company. I can call him and you could speak to him."

"You have a phone here?" she asked, not seeing any signs of electricity.

To her amazement, he pulled a cell phone from his pocket— life in the twenty-first century—no lights or toilet, but a cell phone. She smiled and giggled quietly, which got Cascaes's attention. He asked what was up and she told him. "Hell, yeah!" he said. "Get us a damn plane!"

The old man called his nephew the pilot, who answered right away and was happy to find new customers. He would arrive within the hour, instead of the half day truck journey it had taken the team when they first arrived from Lubumbashi. Things were looking up. Cascaes radioed Mackey, who sounded out of breath when he picked up at his end.

"You okay, boss? You on the run?" asked Cascaes.

"No—not yet, anyway. Just getting our 'welcome' prepared. You at the train station?"

"Yes, and good news, we have a plane for transport."

"A plane? No shit? You trust the pilot?"

"Well, we haven't seen him or the plane yet, but it's the railroad guy's nephew from Lubumbashi. He runs charters. It will save us an entire day."

Mackey chewed his bottom lip. "All right, Chris. If you think the guy is on the level and the plane is safe, go for it. You'll get way ahead of the PAC. And we plan on decreasing the number heading your way," he said as he watched Ernie

P. and Smitty run down to the boat with boxes of ammunition and weapons.

"Hey, boss—does the name Custer ring a bell? You don't want a firefight with the whole PAC army—what are you doing?"

"I have no intention of a standup fight, just some good old fashioned booby-traps and daisy chains. Then we'll be across the lake and show up somewhere nice and quiet when the dust settles."

They said their good lucks and Cascaes briefed Hodges and Jones about the plane. They sat on old benches at the platform and waited for the plane. Julia tried to get the latest gossip from the old men, who were free enough with sharing whatever they knew, until she mentioned the PAC. Their smiles disappeared instantly, and it wasn't lost on Cascaes, even though he didn't speak much French.

She pressed them further, in her diplomatic and disarming way. Stories of the last Hutu-Tutsi War came out of the old men. They had seen the killing and behavior that made them ashamed to belong to the human race. By the time they finished chatting, Julia and the old men were both in tears, holding each other's hands. As far as the PAC was concerned, he had only heard rumors about the aid station to the east, but he was old enough to know the ancient wisdom of "no such thing as a free lunch." They were still speaking and sobbing when they heard the noise of the plane.

The plane circled twice, waving its wings as the old man walked out to the grassy plain and waved back. The plane landed on the grass, and slowly drove up towards the station. It was a Beechcraft twin prop eight seater, maybe twenty years old—new to the old man at the station. The engines cut off, the door opened, and a tall skinny African in a white captain's shirt complete with epaulettes stepped out. Somehow, the blue shorts made him look even taller and the shiny black shoes with no socks made him look goofier. He smiled and gave a huge greeting to his uncle, and they hugged and chattered a hundred miles an hour for a few minutes, until the old man introduced him to the 'Canadians.'

It would be 36,000 Congolese francs per person, roughly a hundred bucks each, to go to Kinshasa. Cascaes asked Julia to ask the pilot if the price was firm. He explained it was a fair price, and Cascaes agreed, but said he would have to pay in Canadian dollars. They ended up settling on 400 Canadian, and quickly loaded the plane. Chris and Julia intentionally took the two rear seats so they could at least occasionally hold hands, or touch a leg, or *something* without Jones and Hodges seeing them.

CHAPTER 39

Sergeant Major Han was not happy about being pulled from his original assignment leading the assault against the prime minister's house. While he still might be given that honor if he made it back in time, being sent to go round up these Canadians or Americans seemed beneath him. The odds of these four people just sitting around the fish farm waiting to be arrested seemed unlikely. He was merely wasting his time and being distracted from his more important mission. As he sat in the cab of the truck rumbling towards the village of Buwali, he remembered the chief there telling him the Canadians had been there for years. Perhaps the old chief was a liar. Buwali was on the way to the fish farm, and the villagers would know the exact location. They would stop on the way for a 'heart to heart' with the old man.

As they approached the village, the sun was setting behind them in a brilliant red fireball, just like the painting that Sergeant Major Han had in his small apartment outside Beijing. He didn't like Africa, and would be happy when this business was finished and he could return home where he could get a good cup of tea and bowl of properly cooked rice. The longer they drove, the angrier he became. By the time the trucks rumbled into the quiet village, Sergeant Major Han was at a rolling boil.

The villagers saw the trucks and ran out to greet their best customers, the Chinese from the aid station. They were singing and waving as the trucks started to unload with angry looking soldiers wielding Chinese assault rifles. Most of the singing stopped as the PAC soldiers began pushing the villagers away with the butts of their rifles as Sergeant Major Han began screaming orders in his *"rousy"* French. He walked through the crowd, which backed away from him in fear as they read his angry face. His hands were on his hip and holster as he walked bow-legged to the center of the village.

Chief Ma-Fafe read his face and was confused. Had they not been happy with the fish? They were all freshly caught—what could be the problem? He approached the sergeant major and respectfully clasped his hands together and bowed, giving blessings and greetings in traditional fashion. This was met with an overhand right to his ear, which knocked him to the dirt. Sergeant Major Han began screaming in French that the chief was a liar and was hiding American spies. Ma-Fafe looked up at the bulldog of a man standing above him. He was completely shocked. One of his sons ran to his aid, and Sergeant Major Han pulled the pistol from his holster and aimed it at the man's face, cocking the hammer. The chief screamed from the ground for everyone to stop. His son froze, Sergeant Major Han's gun only a foot from his nose.

The chief placed his face and palms against the ground and began begging the sergeant major not to kill his son. Sergeant Major Han slowly holstered his weapon, now that several PAC troops had come up behind him.

"Where are the Americans? The woman and three men?" Sergeant Major Han demanded.

The chief looked up bewildered. "I have seen no woman," he said. "I only have seen the Canadians from the fish farm…"

This brought a kick from Sergeant Major Han's boot to the old man's face, sending him rolling across the dirt road into some grass, where he howled in pain. Sergeant Major Han pulled his gun again and once more pointed it at his son's head.

"Tell me now or I will shoot," he said slowly.

Ma-Fafe knelt, holding his bleeding left eye. "The fish farm is not far—just down along the lake. I don't know if there are Americans there."

The villagers crowded in the center of the village, frightened to see their chief cowering before armed men. Many of them remembered similar scenes during the last Congo War, when entire villages disappeared overnight.

Sergeant Major Han tried to get a more exact location, but clearly, kilometers meant nothing to the old man. His son was the one who finally said it wasn't more than fifteen minutes by truck. Sergeant Major Han squatted down by the chief's face.

"If I find out you have been lying to me, I will come back here and kill everything that lives in this village including you."

Sergeant Major Han barked the order for his men to reload into the trucks, and they left in a roar of diesel engines and cloud of dust. Ma-Fafe's son ran to his father as soon as Sergeant Major Han left, helping the old man up and asking him what was happening. The chief answered that he didn't know, but he could smell blood coming.

CHAPTER 40

Near Kinshasa

In two hours, Cascaes and his crew travelled the distance it would have taken the train an entire day to cover. Assuming the train ever arrived at the station to pick them up, which still hadn't happened. The pilot yelled back to Hodges, sitting behind him, that they would be at Kinshasa airport in twenty minutes.

Cascaes handed up a piece of paper with map coordinates and two hundred dollars Canadian. "Ask him if he can drop us off here instead. It's closer to where our meeting is."

The pilot looked at the coordinates and adjusted the GPS computer on his dashboard. "There isn't much out there. Are you sure?" he asked. No one responded so he just shrugged and banked hard to the right as he adjusted for their new heading. They touched down on a grassy savannah in the middle of nowhere. The pilot again asked if Cascaes was sure about the location—they were several miles from the outskirts of Kinshasa, and it would be dark soon. They assured him they would be fine, thanked him for the ride, and told him they would call him again one day soon.

As soon as the plane took off, the four of them stripped from their civilian clothes into camos. Hodges and Jones tried their best to be inconspicuous as they watched Julia get changed, her beauty much more evident in a bra and panties.

Cascaes cleared his throat when he saw them gawking, and they quickly pulled on their clothes.

"Looks like about an hour walk due west to get to Zabanga's house. If we get lucky and he's there, we'll try and take him out from a distance and just disappear. If you can't get a shot at him, then we'll figure out a way into his place, but I have no idea what kind of security or surveillance he has. We'll just take this nice and slow and sort it out when we get there." With that, they began the long walk to find the traitor's hideout.

Seven hundred miles to the east, Shin Xun-jun's column of troops rumbled through the Congolese highlands, like an African serpent winding its way to its prey. Major Wu had the plans of the prime minister's residence, and would be leading that assault, although now perhaps without Sergeant Major Han. He hated relying on the poorly trained PAC guerrillas, but the decision wasn't his. In another truck, Nigel Ufume reviewed the maps of the city and planned on how they would use a small team to infiltrate the president's compound while the remainder of the troops waited for the signal to begin the major assault that would bring the ruling government to its knees.

They would drive all night, stopping only to refuel, and rendezvous with the 2,500 other PAC guerrillas that had been formed further west. Many of these men were mercenaries, trained during the last Congo War, and very content to kill anyone so long as they were paid and fed. The relative peace of the past few years had many of them desperate to keep food on their tables. The Chinese paid well, kept them fed, and offered shelter in the camp they had built. Although a much smaller camp than the one Shen Xun-jun ran to the east, these men made up in skill what they lacked in numbers. The general who ran that "aid station," a man named Wong Fu-jia, was almost as fanatical as the guerrillas in that camp. While Shen Xun-jun didn't know him personally, he had seen his file, and was pleased to have him and his men joining them outside Kinshasa.

CHAPTER 41

The Fish Farm

It was almost eighteen hundred hours when Mackey's handheld computer blinked to alert him that one of the sensors on the perimeter had been tripped. He and his men had scattered around the farm's perimeter to watch for any movement. When his computer flashed, his adrenaline immediately started pumping. He whispered into his throat mic to his men.

"Be advised, sensors indicate movement to the north, eight hundred yards. I want everyone to get to Fish Central and prepare the boat. Prepare to be assaulted."

Mackey and the rest of his crew sprinted through the jungle back into the camp and ran down to the dock. It was getting dark, particularly out on the lake. Everyone piled into the boat, which had been stockpiled with most of their gear, and Mackey took the helm and started the engine. Smitty and Ernie P. had opted to stay behind with SCUBA equipment. They would control the detonations from the water's edge where they could see better, and then slip into the water and get out to the boat.

Mackey, Jon, and Pete headed out into the lake as fast as they could, knowing they would only have a limited amount of time before they had to kill the engines and hope they wouldn't be seen out on the water. Smitty and Ernie P. hid beneath the old wooden pier and watched the village, waiting for the approaching vehicles to enter their extremely large kill zone. They had been methodical in their planning, and true to their nature, anxiously awaited the fruits of their labor.

Mackey called to Ernie and Smitty, speaking quietly into their ear pieces. "Multiple sensors lighting up at 300 yards, they must have dismounted. Out."

Smitty smiled and picked up his night vision binoculars, scanning the woods outside their small compound. He could see headlights in the distance.

"Got 'em. Looks like they are fanning out in the woods. We'll be ready."

Ernie opened a small computer screen and entered some codes to arm their explosives. His touchscreen monitor showed all of the sensors, lighting up one and two at a time as the enemy approached through the woods.

"Ooh, they're so sneaky," said Ernie sarcastically as he watched them getting closer on his monitor.

Ernie and Smitty allowed the guerrillas to get to edge of the camp unchallenged. Once there, he could see a Chinese officer directing squads into different parts of the village. Evidently, they planned on assaulting all of the buildings simultaneously, which would be perfect for their daisy chain. It seemed to take forever for the guerrillas to get into position. As they squatted outside the buildings preparing to enter, Smitty quietly said, "*Now.*"

Ernie touched his screen and set off multiple claymores that had been set in the woods facing both in and out. With a deafening roar, tens of thousands of ball bearings were sent through the woods and open center of the camp. The majority of the guerrillas disappeared in a cloud of human flesh. The screaming was as loud as the explosions, which were pretty damn loud. Those soldiers furthest from the forest edge assaulted the buildings to get out of the ambush, not realizing they were entering kill zone number two. The doors had been rigged, and as each cabin was entered, explosions rippled through the camp. With the woods exploding and the buildings blowing up, the only safe place to run was towards the river—towards fish central where Smitty and Ernie sat saving the best for last.

Ernie turned to Smitty and said, "This is it!" as he touched the final trigger and covered his ears, opened his mouth, and crossed his ankles. Smitty did the same thing, trying to protect his eardrums and family jewels from the huge concussion as their homemade explosions took apart the entire camp. Shrapnel, chains, ball bearings, nails, and whatever other scraps they had packed into the huge tubs of C4 screamed through the camp, slaughtering whoever was left, including Sergeant Major Han. It took a full minute for all of the pieces to float back down to earth. Smitty and Ernie slipped into the water and put on their BCDs and SCUBA masks, disappearing into the dark water of the lake before the last remnants of the invading army had even settled back down to earth.

In less than a minute, Sergeant Major Han's entire patrol and the fish farm had simply ceased to exist.

CHAPTER 42

Residential compound of Lucian Zabanga

Hodges and Jones had set up their sniper position on a small hill a few hundred yards from the electrified fence around Zabanga's large villa. Large bull mastiffs trotted along the inside of the fence looking as menacing as anything that might come out of the jungle. Chris and Julia had taken a position on the other side of the compound in the woods. With their high-powered binoculars and spotter-scopes, the two groups hunkered down and watched, waiting for a sign that Lucien Zabanga was actually there.

Inside his study, Zabanga sat at his desk smoking a very expensive cigar, trying to reach Shen Xun-jun. The phone at the aid station went unanswered, and now he was calling a cell phone number that was for "emergencies only." Zabanga's nerves constituted an emergency—he was getting panicky. He was relieved when General Shen answered the phone gruffly in French.

"It's the tiger. Is this the Lion Hunter?" asked Zabanga.

"This is the Lion Hunter," said Shin Xun-jun. "The hunt has begun. The lion and leopard will be skinned by tomorrow night."

"The sooner the better. We had a visitor near the Lion's Den. We had hoped to question him, but he's dead. He must have friends nearby. I'm worried they know about the hunt."

Shin smiled as they bounced along the dirt road in the dark. "There is nothing to fear. Another smaller hunting party is taking care of that problem as we speak. I expect to hear from them almost any time now. You're in a safe location?"

"Yes. I'm out of the city. Call me when you're close."

Zabanga hung up the cell phone and poured a glass of twenty-year-old rum. As he puffed on his cigar, he wondered if he should have been more insistent on being named president instead of prime minister. Why should this man Mboto Kangani be allowed to run the country? While there would be plenty of money and power as the number two man, why settle for being number two? He decided the new president's career wouldn't be a long one. As soon as things calmed down, the new president would have an accident, and the prime minister would take control of the entire government. He smiled as he contemplated living in the presidential residence.

Lucian stood up and stretched, then walked out to the large open den outside his office. Three of his bodyguards sat by the fireplace drinking beer. They stood up when he entered.

"Tell Duma I'm hungry. Have him bring my supper to the back porch. There's a nice breeze this evening."

One of his men walked off to find Duma, the chef, while the other two men walked with Lucien to the rear porch. They lit the torches outside and walked the large rear yard of the compound, where the giant dogs trotted loyally alongside them. Lucien sat at the large table by himself, smoking his cigar and sipping his rum. It was a beautiful night, indeed. By tomorrow at this time, he would be on his way to becoming one of the richest men in Africa.

"Skipper," whispered Hodges. "You seeing this?"

Cascaes was smiling from the other side of the compound. "Affirmative. Was just getting ready to call you. That's the target. Confirmed. You're cleared to fire as soon as you have the shot. Move to rendezvous point as soon as the target is eliminated."

"What about his guards?" asked Hodges.

"You're cleared to take out any hostiles. And do *not* allow them to release those dogs," said Cascaes.

Jones began quietly giving Hodges the range, wind direction and speed, and Jones adjusted his scope. Lucien's head was as clear as a close-up photo in the night vision scope. The man was actually smiling.

"This is for Cory, motherfucker," Hodges whispered as he slowly squeezed the trigger. His silenced sniper rifle made a quiet crack, and a little less than a second later, Lucien Zabanga's head exploded all over his table. He sat there, face down in his own blood and brains for almost ten minutes. Duma, the chef, walked out with a tray of food, at first thinking Zabanga was sleeping at the table after drinking his share of rum—it wouldn't be the first time. When he saw the blood and brains all over the wall and table, he dropped the tray and began screaming.

The screaming brought barking dogs and running guards. As the guards ran to keep up with the dogs, Hodges tried his best to lead the fast animals correctly. He squeezed off a round, and although he missed the dog at which he was aiming, he hit the one behind it.

"God damn, those things are fast," he whispered to Jones.

"Two more dogs in the yard, four guards I can see," said Jones quietly. "500 yards, wind speed is steady at is one knot, southeast."

Hodges adjusted and fired, dropping another dog. He chambered another round as Zabanga's guards hit the deck and began spraying random fire at the perimeter fence. They had no idea where the shots were coming from, and were panicking as they watched the last dog drop before it could be released at their attackers, dead before it hit the ground. Cascaes and Julia began firing short bursts from behind them, moving every few seconds. To the guards inside the compound, they appeared to be surrounded and under attack from a large force. The guards tried to get back inside the house but were hit with deadly accurate sniper fire. As soon as everything went quiet, Cascaes, Julia, Hodges and Jones packed up and began sprinting to their rendezvous point west of Zabanga's villa.

Shen Xun-jun was getting anxious. There was still no word from Sergeant Major Han, and they should have made contact hours ago. He tried calling him on his radio and got no answer. He cursed under his breath as they plodded west. Where the hell was Sergeant Major Han?

He had no way to know a wild dog was trotting around with a piece of Sergeant Major Han in his mouth.

CHAPTER 43

Moose, Ripper, Theresa, Lance, and Jake hustled through the tall grasslands and woods to get away from the PAC camp as quickly as possible. They had been extremely careful about covering their tracks and left no evidence of their visit. The patrols had driven past their stakeout location without even slowing down—they were safe for the moment. They headed back towards the fish farm on a course parallel to the path they normally used, but which was now being used by that convoy of six trucks loaded with fifty PAC guerrillas and two Chinese officers, including Sergeant Major Han.

The five of them moved single file quickly along the narrow path, they were at a brisk jog, but they had a long distance to cover by foot, so they paced themselves. After an hour of double-timing it, they took a break for water and rest. Moose called back to Mackey on his radio—the Chinese patrol could have arrived by now.

"Skipper, it's Moose, you copy? You guys okay over there?"

"Moose, its Mac. Take a deep breath and relax. The enemy has been destroyed, over."

"*Destroyed*? It's all over?" Moose was stunned. The enemy patrol had outnumbered Mackey and his men by ten to one.

"Roger that. Thanks to our sneaky little bastards here in camp, it was all over before it started. They never got a shot off. We're reassembling and awaiting your return. We'll regroup and move out as fast as possible. Just return to base, ASAP! Out!"

Moose updated the group, who were as shocked as he was to learn that the firefight they were so worried about was already over. Smitty and Ernie P. had evidently been very successful with their daisy chains and ambush. Even with the threat gone, there was no slowing down. Kinshasa was almost eight hundred miles to the west, and the PAC army had a large head start. They would need some serious luck to beat them to the capital.

CHAPTER 44

The Bush near Zabanga's Residence

Cascaes, Julia, Hodges, and Jones headed to the rendezvous point quickly, winded and adrenaline pumping, but clear headed.

"We need their vehicle. We'll head back to the house. I think we got them all, but move slowly. Find the keys, grab the truck, and get our asses to Lubumbashi to find that plane," said Cascaes.

"There's an easier way, Chris," said Julia. She pulled out a card for the pilot's charter service. Why not just have him pick us up and fly us back from *here*?"

Chris looked at her, feeling somewhat dumbfounded. "You think we could just call his cellphone?"

Hodges laughed. "Yo, Skipper—we have the satellite phone. We can call control in Langley; they call the pilot and say they're us, and tell the guy to return to where they dropped us."

Cascaes smiled, then to everyone's shock, kissed Julia on the lips. "Brilliant!" he said with a laugh. "Hodges, do it now!"

It took almost ten minutes to set up the phone and track down Dex Murphy to explain what they needed. He was quick to follow along, didn't ask questions, and placed the call to a cell phone in Lubumbashi himself. He told the pilot that he needed to be picked up at the same location, saying he was

Chris Cascaes, and the pilot happily obliged, reminding him that, "I told you there was nothing out there."

Dex called Chris back via satellite phone and confirmed their exit. The foursome moved back carefully to where they had been dropped off and set up a quick perimeter, watching all sides with night vision for movement. Zabanga's guards were all dead. Only his chef remained, hiding under a table in the kitchen with no intention of doing anything until the sun came up.

Chris and Julia ended up moving closer in the dark. She leaned closer and whispered to Chris, "You blew our cover!"

He didn't get it at first, then realized he had kissed her in front of Hodges and Jones. "Well, then screw it, if it's already blown," he whispered back and kissed her for a long minute. They both smiled in the dark.

"You're *bad news*, mister," she whispered.

"I love you," he whispered back. "Want to marry me?"

He could see she was wondering if he was serious. "I'm totally serious," he whispered. She smiled in the dark and moved closer until her shoulder was pressing against his. "Did you get the ring?" she said with a giggle.

"Well, we *are* in Africa. Maybe I can go dig for a diamond," he whispered back.

"You can dig up anything you want, the answer is yes. But can we get home alive first?"

He kissed her quickly and said, "Yes. They continued to lay on their stomachs in the dark, scanning with night vision goggles as they waited for the plane.

"You're so romantic," said Julia quietly. "Maybe for our honeymoon, you can take us to Iraq or Somalia." They both chuckled in the dark. Their relationship was anything but normal.

The hour passed quickly, with occasional kisses being sneaked, and Hodges and Jones checking in from time to time. When the plane could be heard, Jones and Hodges threw flares along a straight line in the level grass so the pilot knew where to land in the dark. It was a hairy landing for any pilot. This guy was pretty good after all. His plane came to a stop and the foursome ran to it. The pilot was shocked when his casually dressed passengers reappeared looking like the combat warriors they were, with weapons still out. He was alarmed, to say the least. He began waving them off.

"No, no! I don't need any trouble!" he screamed over the drone of his prop.

Julia ran to him and smiled. "It's okay!" she yelled. "No problem here, we just had to make sure everything here was okay. We'll explain on the way back…"

As she spoke, the men piled in before the pilot could protest. The fact that their weapons were still out didn't give the pilot much choice. He protested and tried his best to get them out of his plane, but he relented, turned the plane around and took off into the light breeze.

"We aren't going to Lubumbashi," said Cascaes. "Plug in coordinates for Kinshasa."

"Kinshasa?" exclaimed the pilot. "I don't have enough fuel to get to Kinshasa! It's 800 miles!"

"You can stop in Kananga," said Cascaes quietly. "We're going to Kinshasa. Just outside the city actually. I'll pick a place when we get close. No screwing around, buddy. And just so you know, the fate of your whole country rests on you getting us there. We are trying to prevent a coup, you understand? A war. Consider yourself the official Air Force of the Democratic Republic of Congo."

"*What* war?" asked the pilot, very unsure of what he had gotten himself into.

"You ever hear of the PAC? The People's Army of Congo?"

"No," he said warily.

"Well, the Chinese government has built an army to take down your president and prime minister. The PAC will be

attacking the capital within a few days. We need to get there
before they do, you understand? "

"President Kuwali and Prime Minister Gugunga are good
men. Why would anyone want another war here? We're still
recovering from the last Congo War."

"Money, power, raw materials—the usual story. Just get us
there. You'll be well paid. And then I have another job for
you."

Cascaes sat back and called Mackey from the satellite phone
he assembled in the rear seat on Julia's lap. They exchanged
glances as he touched her legs. Mackey picked up the phone
after a few rings.

"Mac, you okay out there?"

"Roger that. We're fine. Took out an enemy patrol, and
Moose and crew just got back intact. We're going to truck it
over to the train station and try and beat the PAC to Kinshasa.
Where are you? What's the story with Zabanga?"

"We're in a plane heading to Kinshasa. The target was
eliminated," he said, not wanting to use Zabanga's name in
front of the pilot.

"A plane?"

"Yeah, I just created the first Congolese Air Force. Made
this pilot a general," he said loudly. The pilot heard him and
smiled for the first time this trip.

"We will refuel in Kananga and be in Kinshasa by sun-
up. The PAC will be at least two days out. I'm going to try
and arrange for an airlift for you guys after we arrive. Keep
moving west and keep track of where you are. I will hopefully
be sending you a lift." He eyed the pilot, who heard him and
looked worried.

"Okay, stay in touch. And stay out of sight in Kinshasa."

"Yeah, we'll stay outside the city until we have a plan put
together. 10,000 against a dozen…we need a *really* good plan.
Out."

CHAPTER 45

Shen Xun-jun called Wong Fu-jia from his command vehicle as they moved westward in a seemingly endless convoy to Kinshasa. The vehicles were a mixture of Chinese "deuce and a half" cargo trucks and old pickup trucks, many with machine guns mounted in the bed. All of the trucks were overfilled with PAC soldiers. Before leaving the camp, the trucks had been covered with tarps with large Red Cross symbols on them. "China Relief Mission" was written underneath in five languages. Shen Xun-jun led the procession in his Jeep, the only vehicle that looked military, but armed escorts in this poor country were a common sight.

Shen Xun-jun held the same rank as Wong Fu-jia, but had seniority, and was therefore running the operation as commander of all forces. Wong Fu-jia's PAC forces were smaller than Shen Xun-jun's, but he had been fortunate enough to organize mercenaries and professional soldiers, compared with Shen Xun-jun's large army that couldn't shoot straight. Wong Fu-jia's aid answered the radio and handed it to his general.

Shen Xun-jun updated Wong Fu-jia that they were assembled and heading west. He also informed him that Americans were snooping about and had visited the mining operation. He had sent Sergeant Major Han with a small patrol to find the Americans and bring them to him, but so far, had been unable to make radio contact. He was getting nervous about that.

Wong Fu-jia and his rebel force were currently camped twenty miles south of Kinshasa in a heavily wooded area to avoid being spotted. His troops were ready; they just needed the RPGS, mortars and heavy machine guns that Shen Xun-jun would be bringing.

Shen Xun-jun advised Wong Fu-jia that once they made it to Kinshasa, Nigel Ufume would be leading a small group into the city at night to move on the president while he was at his residence. With a well-coordinated attack using heavy weapons, they could destroy the entire compound before the presidents guards had time to launch a counter-attack. This would happen at oh-four-hundred when almost everyone would be sound asleep. By the time the sun came up, the larger force under Major Wu would be seizing the "Palais du Peuple," Congo's version of The Capital. Li's troops would execute everyone they saw, inflicting heavy enough casualties in the government to cause chaos and lack of leadership.

Wong Fu-jia would then move in at daybreak with his force, at the fastest speed possible, killing everything that moved as they made their way towards the presidential palace. By inflicting huge casualties on the civilian population, the PAC could cause enough panic to demoralize whatever government forces might still be forming up under whatever leadership was left. With the president and prime minister both dead, the Palais du Peuple under PAC control, and the city burning, Shen Xun-jun anticipated the overthrow would be over by sunset. The civilians would flee the city, and the official army would be right behind them in tatters. The PAC would then declare themselves as the new interim government, and call for an immediate election. The election would be rigged so that Mboto Kangani would be the new president, and Lucien Zabanga prime minister. And they would answer to China.

⊕

Up on the side of the small mountain overlooking the lights of Kinshasa, Wong Fu-jia strolled through his small army. He watched the mercenaries sharpening their knives and machetes and cleaning their weapons, and felt extremely confident that his men would roll through the city. The hardest part would be maintaining their discipline to avoid the raping and pillaging that was so common in the African wars. Once these men smelled blood, they would be difficult to control. He smiled. In the worst case scenario, he would simply allow them to do whatever they wanted. They would remain loyal and happy, and Wong Fu-jia would be a hero of the Chinese people.

CHAPTER 46

Sunrise, Near Kinshasa

The pilot was exhausted and worried, but kept it to himself. Julia had fallen asleep against Chris's shoulder, and he was happy to have her next to him so cozily. Hodges was out cold across the center two seats, and Jones was sitting up in the co-pilot's seat. The pilot had stopped once in Kananga to refuel, which had been a little hairy since the team was in uniform, but it was dark and they were in and out quickly. It was almost 5:30 in the morning, and the pink sunrise was spreading across the purple African sky.

The pilot spoke out loud to anyone who was listening. "We're getting close to Kinshasa. I'll have to radio in to the airport soon. I never filed a flight plan for this airport and they aren't expecting us. What do you want me to do?"

Cascaes was in the rear row of the six-seater. "Head northwest and look for a place to set down. I'd like to be within five miles of the city limits, to the south, but not too close to any population."

The pilot banked right and headed northwest, dropping his altitude to only a thousand feet. He scanned beneath him, trying to find a smooth place to set down that seemed isolated. There were small mountains just west of their location, with many small areas of broken forest south and west of the city between the mountains and the city limits of Kinshasa. It would be remote enough for his passengers, but finding a flat level field would take some time. The landing at night had been terrifying the night before, and he never told the team just how close he came to crashing. It had been the bounciest, hardest landing of his twelve-year flying career, and certainly couldn't have been very good for his plane. The pilot flew low and slow, studying his instruments and the ground below him.

Julia woke up and remembered where she was, then gave Chris a little squeeze. Hodges happened to turn around at that precise moment and "busted" her. She blushed.

"Just stretching," she said.

"I had night vision, remember?" he said with a laugh. She didn't get it at first, then realized that Hodges and Jones probably saw everything that was going on "under the cover of darkness" last night while they waited for the plane.

Chris couldn't help but laugh. "What happens in the field stay in the field," he said. "Classified."

"Roger that, Skipper," he said, and turned back around. They all began looking out the windows, scanning the land below them for a suitable place to land and wait for Mackey and his team. Hodges mumbled a quiet, "holy shit," and ripped into his backpack, pulling out his sniper scope and removing the lens caps quickly. He looked back down through the scope and scanned the forest below them.

Cascaes announced to the pilot and his crew, "Come on, general. Land this plane. Once we hit the ground, we hunker down and stay out of sight all day until the rest of the team gets up here and links up. Hodges, get Dex back on the phone. The PAC could be here by tomorrow if they travel all night."

Less than a mile to their west, the PAC force under Wong Fu-jia force hid in the woods, looking out to the city of Kinshasa.

CHAPTER 47

Midnight, White House Situation Room

The joint chiefs stood up when the president hustled in with the secretary of state and his chief of staff. Dexter Murphy stood next to an air force general, with whom he had been discussing air assets. Additional staffers had not been invited, and the meeting was considered top secret.

The president asked everyone to be seated and opened the briefing. Dex Murphy stood and approached a map of the Republic of Congo that was displayed on a very large screen. The image was a live satellite picture, superimposed with city names, major roads, international boundaries and major geographical features. As intelligent as the President of the United States was, his dealings and knowledge of the PRC was limited.

"Mr. President, the Chinese have mobilized the PAC forces and are heading west towards Kinshasa at this moment. Our satellite teams have them here…"

He dialed in a computer and the screen zoomed in on a road near the town of Kananga.

"We've confirmed with our limited assets in-country that a very large convoy of trucks is headed west. They're using Red Cross relief as cover, but it's them, one-hundred percent."

The room watched as Dex zoomed in and showed a live view of a convoy, several miles long. "We estimate their force, based on observations on the ground by our own team, to be somewhere between 8 and 10,000 troops. These aren't highly trained soldiers, but they're heavily armed with new Chinese weapons and ammunition. Most likely have a large supply of mortars, RPGs, heavy machine guns, et cetera. The only good news is one of the Chinese transports crashed while landing, and apparently had light armor vehicles, which they haven't been able to replace."

Dex turned around and faced the room, placed the laser pointer on the table, and took a breath. "The bottom line is this, Mr. President. You have to make a decision *now* about whether or not you want to prevent the current government from being overthrown. The Chinese will have their own people running things within a week, unless we prevent it now. Once the Chinese are entrenched with the PAC government, they have access to the world's largest supplies of uranium, plutonium, and many other rare earth elements that are strategically important. The gold, platinum, and diamonds are just a bonus."

The president nodded thoughtfully and sat in silence a moment. He then addressed the Chairman of the Joint Chiefs. "General Rogers, if we were to take action to intercept the convoy, what are our options?"

The general cleared his throat. "We can certainly destroy the column before it gets to the city—there are plenty of open areas where we can minimize any chance of civilian casualties. But we can't shoot up a bunch of Chinese officers and think there won't be major consequences."

The president smiled. "General, I spoke with the general secretary yesterday and voiced my concerns over Chinese military actions in the DRC. President Jin was very clear that there are *no* Chinese military advisors there. They have an aid station, only. That being the case, if we were to destroy the PAC forces en route to the capital, we know we won't be hitting any Chinese officers." He folded his hands and looked seriously at the general. "Options?"

General Rogers nodded. "PHIBRON Five, our amphibious assault squadron is four hundred miles off the coast with the 11th Marine Expeditionary Force. That's over 1,500 combat-experienced marines, with enough Sea Knight helos on board to get them deployed immediately. The *USS Makin Island* has five AV8-B Harriers with air to ground capabilities. In short, we can destroy the convoy with the Harriers, and reinforce Kinshasa with ground troops if necessary. From 'Go' to target should be less than thirty minutes for the jets."

The president stood. "Gentlemen, please remain here for a bit. I've got a couple of phone calls to make." He looked at his chief of staff. "Susan, get President Kuwali on the horn."

Ten minutes later, the president sat in the Oval Office speaking to President Kuwali. It was six in the morning in Kinshasa. While President Kuwali spoke excellent English, he used a translator anyway, to be sure everything was perfectly understood. Kuwali listened to the entire briefing without saying a word, paying close attention to the location and size of the PAC forces that were heading his way. He was more than happy to accept the United States' offer of military support.

CHAPTER 48

09:00, Southwest of Kinshasa

Cascaes sat with Julia, Hodges, and Jones in a remote, forest outside of Kinshasa. The sun was low in the morning sky, and the four of them cleaned weapons, ate MRE's and monitored the radio. They had paid their pilot 2,000 dollars US, which was several month's salary. Cascaes promised the pilot another five thousand on top of that if he would fly to Niemba, due west of the fish farm, and pick up the rest of the team and return them to this location. While the pilot understood what he was doing was obviously dangerous and suspicious, seven thousand dollars was impossible to turn down. He shook on the deal, and headed back on the long journey back towards Lake Tanganyika to get the others. His return would get the rest of the team back in time for dinner.

Hodges handed the satellite phone to Cascaes, who was sipping coffee on a large boulder, admiring the mountains to their west. It was Dex Murphy back in DC.

"Just finished with the Big Boss. Operation Dragon Catcher is a go," said Dex. "Air assets will be en route to meet the PAC out in the open when the convoy reaches the chosen location. In another few hours, this whole thing will be over before it starts. When the target destruction is reported back to us, we'll let you know. You'll either be tasked with visual confirmation, or more likely, given a rendezvous point where Sea Nights will pick you up and bring you out to the Amphibious Assault Group."

Shen Xun-jun's PAC forces had driven all night stopping only to refuel. As the sun broke the horizon, Shen Xun-jun cursed the lousy Congolese roads. It would have been a far journey on a *good* highway, but bouncing along roads that went from asphalt to gravel to dirt and back to asphalt was making the driving torturous and slow.

Shen Xun-jun radioed to Wong Fu-jia. "We're moving slower than I expected. These roads are worthless. We'll continue without stopping, but we may not make it by tomorrow morning."

"Has anyone stopped you or asked questions?" asked Wong Fu-jia.

"No. Police in a couple of villages tried to ask questions, but I shooed them away. Their security is worse than their roads. How long will it take you to get from your position to your targets?"

"We'll be moving in the dark on foot, so it will be slow here as well. I estimate ninety minutes."

"Unless you hear otherwise, the timetable remains the same. I still can't reach Sergeant Major Han's patrol, though. It's troubling."

"Radios and phones in this country may have trouble with signals."

Shen Xun-jun frowned. "I'm speaking to *you* without a problem. And Sergeant Major Han's radio was fine prior to reaching the camp."

"No matter what, we must continue our mission. We don't need Sergeant Major Han for that."

Shen grunted. "I'll contact you by nightfall with our location. We should still make Kinshasa for our oh-four-hundred strike."

CHAPTER 49

USS Makin Island

Captain Simms sat with his XO and senior chief in a command room watching a live feed from a UAV they had launched an hour earlier. A pilot sat in front of them, flying the UAV. It was cruising at 30,000 feet, and was so small that it would be unnoticed on the ground. Its cameras, however, were powerful enough to zoom in and pan around to view the convoy of vehicles that snaked along a dirt highway called the N-1. The convoy was halfway to Kinshasa in a lowland area of gently rolling hills, small forests, and villages of brown mud huts every twenty miles or so. It was a desolate part of the country, and an excellent place to drop a few thousand pounds of high explosives that would utterly destroy two miles of convoy.

"What have we got on the Harriers?" asked the captain.

"Squadron commander has them armed with MK-20 Rockeyes," replied the XO.

The MK-20 Rockeye was a cluster bomb that opened up to deliver 247 armor piercing bomblets. It had been used extensively in Desert Storm, and had proven extremely effective in destroying tanks, APCs and anything else that dared move across the desert. Each aircraft carried six Rockeyes, which mean 5,928 armor piercing, high explosive bomblets would be hitting the column.

"Location looks clean. Have the UAV sweep a few miles in all directions, and if it's clear of civilians, release the hounds," ordered the captain.

"Aye, aye, captain," replied the pilot, who continued to fly the small aircraft on his mission while the XO radioed the flight deck and had the Harriers readied for takeoff.

CHAPTER 50

General Shen was looking at his laptop, confirming his position on his map. They were on the N-1, a godforsaken, never-ending road in the middle of nowhere, almost twenty miles from Luputa, the nearest village. The sun was up, and it was a hot day out in the lowlands. The trucks lacked air-conditioning, and the men were hot and tired as they rumbled and bounced.

Shen Xun-jun was antsy, and called Wong Fu-jia again to make sure his troops were still undetected. Wong Fu-jia was annoyed at being "checked-up on" by another general of equal rank, and made no attempt to hide it.

"You just get here on schedule, and we'll be ready. Can't you move any faster?"

"I told you, the roads here are terrible!" Shen Xun-jun stopped and looked up. Four objects in the sky formed a tight diamond shape, leaving white contrails behind them in the clear blue sky. They were getting larger. Shen Xun-jun's face showed his confusion. Where would jet aircraft come from?

"The Americans!" he screamed. His driver looked up at the aircraft that Shen Xun-jun was staring at.

"What should I do?" Asked the driver.

"Just keep moving. They're looking for us. All they'll see is a column of relief supplies. By the time they figure out what's happening, we'll be in Kinshasa."

Shen Xun-jun's eyes opened wider as the aircraft formation changed shape and they began bearing down on them with incredible speed. He watched in amazement as objects began floating out from the jets, which opened up in a cloud of smaller objects. His brain understood what was happening, but wouldn't allow him to process the information to his mouth. He just sat in the cab of the truck, watching the surreal scene above of him.

Wong Fu-jia continued to ask questions, but received no reply.

"Alpha Mike Foxtrot," said Wolf, the pilot of the lead jet as he released his payload. AMF was acronym for "Adios, Mother Fucker." The jet pilots watched as the column below transformed from a long line of trucks to an endless, rolling cloud of fire and smoke. Secondary explosions from the ammunition went on for several minutes as the vehicles flew through the air for hundreds of yards. Black smoke billowed in huge clouds that could be seen for miles. The smell of burnt flesh would bring the animals in for an abundant meal.

The Harriers finished their bombing run, circled back slowly, and dropped lower with video cameras on with live feed to the ship. Whatever was once there had simply ceased to exist. Not since "The Highway of Death," when American forces annihilated the Iraqi army as it left Kuwait, had there been more carnage along a roadway.

"Wolf to base, bomb damage assessment confirmed. Returning to base." The squadron commander hit his afterburners, and the others followed suit. Within a few seconds, the jets were roaring west towards the USS Makin Island.

Captain Simms studied the video. "Get the admiral on the horn. Tell him the convoy is destroyed. If there *are* any survivors, they're not invading anything."

CHAPTER 51

18:00, Near Kinshasa

Cascaes and his team watched the "New Congolese Air Force" land in the grassy field. It was a great relief to have the team fully reassembled. The plane rolled to a stop, and Mackey was the first out. He had just paid the pilot more cash in one lump sum than the man had ever seen at one time.

"Keep reading the newspaper. In a couple of days you'll see how you helped save your entire country," Mackey had told the nervous pilot. "We were never here." He faked a quick smile.

The pilot was all too happy to take off and turn towards Kinshasa airport. He would be having a very good dinner in the city that night.

Chris led the team back into the woods, where they had set up a quick camp.

"You're just in time for dinner," said Chris to Mackey and his team. "We pulled out all of the stops." He tossed him a few MREs.

The team spent a few minutes putting gear away and getting a few tents up for the night. Mackey pulled the satellite phone and called in to Langley. He and Cascaes sat in one of the newly erected tents.

"Good news," said Dex. "Navy air destroyed the PAC column en route to Kinshasa. It's over. President Kuwali and Prime Minister Gugunga will be addressing their nation in the morning, and the remaining Chinese diplomats will be expelled shortly afterwards. With Mboto Kangani dead and the PAC forces destroyed, this little chapter in DRC history should be over. I was going to pull your team tonight, but the boss asked me to wait until after tomorrow's speech to make sure everything went smoothly. We've also requested that Kuwali's people have Cory Stewart's body returned to us at the American consulate. We're trying to arrange it so you can escort him back to the Makin Island. We'll have helos sent to N'djili Airport to pick all of you up. I'll get back to you with the exact time."

"Roger that."

"Great job. Extend the president's thanks to your team. And we're all sorry about Cory, Mac. At least you got Kangani."

Mackey hung up. Kangani being dead wouldn't bring back Cory. Neither would a few thousand dead second-rate soldiers. It was just more death—more killing. It just never stopped.

Cascaes looked at Mac. "What is it? Cory?"

"Yeah, Cory. And getting old. I'm just too old for this shit, brother. Time to get out while I can walk and become a civilian."

"I'm pretty sure you told me the exact same thing a hundred times after the last mission," said Cascaes.

"Yeah, I probably did. But I mean it this time. And you too, man. You've got a nice thing with Julia. It won't work in the field. You two get out together and go do something fun. Travel the world without having to shoot anyone for a change."

"Man, you do sound old," said Chris with a smile. "But, yeah. You're right. I don't want to blow this."

The team finished setting up camp, ate a lousy meal of MREs, and set up patrols. The rest of them relaxed and talked quietly about the mission, the countryside, the wild animals, and the mission.

$\oplus$

It was almost three in the morning when Ripper barged into Mackey's tent and shook him awake.

"Skipper, we got company. Large enemy force coming down the hill heading straight for us. We're talking a whole fucking *army*, boss."

"How long before they get here?" Asked Mackey, already up and pulling on his boots.

"Minutes, not hours. Moose was using his thermal scope and spotted something weird when we were on patrol, so we moved out to investigate. We got about a mile out and stopped. They're moving fairly quickly. *Way* too many to count—we're talking *thousands*."

"Jesus! Where the fuck did they come from? If that's the PAC army, then who the fuck did the navy blow up today?"

"I hope it wasn't the *real* Red Cross," said Ripper.

Within five minutes, the entire team was fully assembled with all of their weapons and gear, including night vision. Mackey was back on the phone to Dex Murphy, who was in his bed at home.

"Thousands? We have zero intel on any other PAC forces out there. Zero!" screamed Dex. "Are you sure it's PAC army? Could it be refugees moving through the area?"

"Boss, we went back and took another look after Ripper spotted them. Estimate a force of several thousand guerrillas. These looked like real commandos with proper gear and weapons, moving with quiet discipline through the forest. They were up in the hills, and they're headed right for us. We're between them and Kinshasa. I can give you coordinates for a fire mission, but we need to move, pronto!"

"Jesus, Mack! I'll need presidential approval, and he'll need approval from President Kuwali. There's not enough time. Get your asses out of there. Fall back to Kinshasa and find a defensible position. You may end up being a delaying action until the DRC regular army can get out there, or until we get approval for fire or air support. God damn it! Why didn't we know about this?"

"I'll call back when I can. Out." Mack hung up and quickly spoke to his team. "Listen up. We got a whole army heading this way towards Kinshasa. We'll need to boogie to the outskirts of Kinshasa and keep track of these guys. There's twelve of us and a few thousand of them. Not a good time to pick a fight. Smitty—you got any more claymores?"

"Negative, Skipper. We used everything we had at the fish farm. We can set a few little booby-traps with grenades, but nothing big enough to slow down *this* many guys for too long."

"Alright, skip it. Let's beat feet. I hope you all feel like going for a nice long run. You may have noticed the Africans do pretty well at the Olympic marathons."

Earl Jones smiled. "Y'all follow me. This African American can run faster than them skinny-ass bitches. Especially when I got 5,000 mutherfuckers *chasing* me…"

The team ditched the tents and extra supplies, taking only battle packs and supplies. They started their run through the woods, snaking down through the dark forest wearing night vision goggles to assist them through the tangle of woods and myriad of streams.

CHAPTER 52

Wong Fu-jia began his move towards Kinshasa as planned, moving his troops as quickly as possible in the dark towards the outskirts of the city. At oh-four-hundred, Shen Xun-jun's coordinated attack would begin, and Shen Xun-jun would be supplied with heavy weapons at the designated rally point. General Fu had tried many times to reach General Shen, but was having the same radio problems that Shen Xun-jun was having reaching Sergeant Major Han's patrol. It was maddening.

Unlike Shen Xun-jun's ragtag army, Wong Fu-jia's men were mostly mercenaries and moved quickly and quietly through the darkness. The only noise was the *shush* of bodies against leaves as the columns moved through the brush. Several small farms were in the path of the army, and these were broken into, the inhabitants murdered quickly, and then abandoned without a second thought. By the time the army had reached the suburbs of Kinshasa, they had already murdered a few hundred civilians.

Hodges and Jones had acted as the rear guard, using Hodges' sniper scope to keep the army's position. The team was smaller and faster than the PAC and had increased the distance between them to almost a mile and a half. Hodges and Jones were dangerously close, but confident that they could evade the PAC as long as it stayed dark, which would be another forty minutes or so. They had called several times to report the attacks on the small farms, but there was nothing they could do about it. As the team fell back towards the city, they called Murphy's line twice and got no response.

Wong Fu-jia was getting furious with Shen Xun-jun. He had tried over ten times to reach him by satellite phone and got nothing. Shen Xun-jun was supposed to take the N-1 into Kinshasa from the east. Wong Fu-jia was supposed to move through the city from the west after the initial attack on the presidential compound, and then move to the N-1 from the west until they could link up with Shen Xun-jun for resupply. After they were more heavily armed, they were simply to be "unleashed" on the capital for as much death and destruction as possible until the city fell. Without word back from Shen Xun-jun, Wong Fu-jia was stuck. To assault the capital too early could give away the whole plan. To arrive too late would mean moving through a crowded city in broad daylight. In a city of that size, with millions of civilians fleeing in panic, their arrival to the rally point would be delayed for hours.

Wong Fu-jia stopped the column and studied his map. They were close enough to the city to see the lights. The suburb of Kimbwala was between them and their target, and was too heavily populated to move through unnoticed. They had a problem. Without Shen Xun-jun's status update, they would have to move farther north and move along the Congo River, which was much less populated. This would waste hours, but they simply couldn't stop and wait without being detected— not with 2,500 armed guerrillas.

Wong Fu-jia ordered the column to move north along the river, not realizing that a recent heavy rain had turned the entire area into one big swamp. Black boulders, worn smooth from a few million years of erosion, made up the banks of the Congo River, and between slipping and sliding over the boulders and moving through thigh deep marshland, the column's discipline began to strain. Their pace slowed, and as the mosquitos woke up in the first rays of sunlight for breakfast, the army became angry.

Hodges and Jones stayed close enough to follow their movement, and the rest of the team fell back to Kimbwala where they finally reached Dex.

"Jesus, Dex! I've been trying you for two hours!" blurted Mackey.

"I've been a little busy! I woke up the president, who had to call President Kuwali. It's one thing taking out a column in the middle of nowhere. Kuwali doesn't like the idea of starting a war in a heavily populated area."

"We're trying to *prevent* the war, Dex! I've got a few thousand guerrillas on my ass. They aren't racing towards the city to sing happy birthday to Kuwali. If he doesn't stop them now, they'll be in his living room in another two hours. They've been butchering civilians along the way just to practice. They make it into the city, it's going to be a bloodbath!"

"Listen, I get it, okay? I totally understand your position. But we can't force another nation to take our help. If Kuwali doesn't approve an airstrike, then we can't touch them. He did say he was mobilizing his own forces, but they won't stand up to the PAC. If you're not careful, you're going to get stuck in the middle. I suggest you break contact, and move south until we get more intel and communication from Kuwali."

"That's *it*? We're just supposed to run from this bunch of thugs and watch them rape and murder their way to the capital?"

"Mac, I don't get to make the call, and neither do you. Stand down and get to a safer location."

"You do realize there's nine million people down there, right? Nine *million*!"

"Mac, you have your orders. Move south to a safer location and await further instructions. Out." Dex hung up.

The other members of the team had been watching and listening. Mac shook his head, his anger palpable. "Okay. Our orders are to move south and go quiet until we get more instructions."

Theresa was the first to speak up. "And what about the PAC army that's about the slaughter a few thousand civilians?"

"Kuwali is mobilizing his army. It will be up to him to defend his city."

"And when the PAC scatters Kuwali's army, then what? We watch the city fall apart right in front of us while we do nothing?"

"I don't like it any more than you do," said Mackey.

Ripper added his two cents. "So this was all for nothing? Cory got wasted in this shithole so we could watch the DRC turned over to the PAC and the Chinese?"

"It's bullshit," added Moose.

"They're north on the river," said Jon. "Not too many civilians out there. An airstrike out there wouldn't have much collateral damage. Once the Pac gets into the city, it's all over."

"Kuwali wouldn't allow an airstrike."

"Well, we can't allow them to make it to the city!" snapped Theresa.

"Boss, we fight a delaying action along the river, we can hold them up until Kuwali's army shows up. Then we split and head south. But we could buy the army a couple of hours. At least trap the PAC with the Congo River at their back. A hell of a lot better battle space than house-to-house fighting," said Cascaes quietly.

"You, too?" snapped Mackey, unhappy that his number two man was also ready to disobey direct orders.

"They gave us a mission. Cory *died* for this mission. And I feel pretty shitty about turning tail last minute. So yeah, *me, too.*" He glanced at Julia, who nodded.

"Fuck," grunted Mackey under his breath. "This ain't a democracy." He looked around at his team. His radio came to life. "Yeah?"

It was Hodges. "Skipper, they're moving along the river real slow. Terrain out here is shit. Swamp up to your ass and thorny shit that attacks your legs. It's a perfect spot to hit 'em."

Mackey's face turned red. "Were you listening to our conversation?"

"Say again, Skipper?" asked Hodges, confused.

"Wait one." He turned to the team. "You all understand that we're going to be going against a few thousand trained guerrillas, not a bunch of rent-a-cops? No air or artillery support—against orders. This is what you want to do?"

"I think it's what we *have* to do, boss," said Moose quietly. "We know what the deal is. We can't go toe-to-toe with them. But we can hit them all over and keep moving fast. Keep them against the river until the army gets there, and then we melt into the forest and disappear. You know what these guys do to civilians in this part of the world. We'd never be able to sleep at night. Let's do it."

Mackey exhaled slowly. "It has to be unanimous. This could be a suicide mission, you dumb fuckers."

"I'm in," said Moose, raising his beefy hand. Everyone else's hand went up instantly.

Mackey spoke into the phone. "Alright, Hodges. Start putting some ideas together fast. We'll be coming up from your southwest. Probably fifteen minutes out."

"Gonna be more like thirty, Skipper," replied Hodges. "I'm serious about the terrain. Great place for an ambush—not so great for moving."

CHAPTER 53

Wong Fu-jia was so angry he broke the stock of his assault rifle off against a tree trunk. He had tried, now too many times to count, to reach Shen Xun-jun and gotten nothing. They were now miles out of their way, stuck in swampy marshland with vicious mosquitoes, venomous snakes, thorny plants that were cutting everyone like bayonets, and a myriad of wild animals that remained unseen but were so loud they were terrifying even to men with weapons.

Wong Fu-jia was already anticipating what would happen. The attack would fail and Shen Xun-jun would blame him for not being in the proper position at the right time. He had considered trying to reach the Ministry of State Security to ask for further instructions, but to do so would show a lack of leadership, if not outright incompetence. No. Wong Fu-jia would not allow himself to be the scapegoat. They would push east along the river, no matter how brutal the trip was, and then sweep through the city annihilating everyone in their path as they moved towards the rally point.

Fu snapped at his officers to push the men harder—they were wasting too much time. The long columns of men stretched out almost a half mile along the Congo River. A dozen mercenaries from neighboring Angola served as scouts a few hundred yards ahead of the main column. Wong Fu-jia barked at them on his radio to find an easier route.

With his night scope, Hodges watched the dozen scouts move through the jungle. These guys were pros, no doubt. They were quiet and concealed, and moved effortlessly through the heavy underbrush. Occasionally, an animal would run out from cover, and the group would stop moving, get low in the brush, and watch carefully before moving again. If not for the fact they were still moving in the dark, it would have been difficult to spot them—a wonderful thing, night vision.

He spoke in the quietest of whispers, but the team heard every word in their ear pieces. "Twelve scouts. Seventy yards in front of my position, moving real quiet. Main body is still out of visual. We should take these out real quiet and set up an ambush route."

"Affirmative," whispered Mackey, ten yards to Hodges right rear. "Team one, flank left and get behind them. Team two, advance slowly."

Team one, composed of Hodges, Jones, Woods, Koches, Jensen, and O'Conner slipped quietly forward through the thick vegetation, silencers on their weapons and knives at the ready. The rest of the team moved quickly to the right and took positions of concealment.

With their night vision, team one moved quickly towards the enemy scouts, who didn't have the luxury of seeing well in the dark. Their only night vision was from the moon. One-by-one, they moved up behind the last scouts in the group, and began taking them out silently with their knives. By the time the remaining scouts reached team two, there were only four left, and those four still didn't know their comrades were already dead. Ripper and Moose killed three with their K-Bar knives, and Chris shot the last one with one silenced pop in the dark. The entire ambush had lasted less than ninety seconds and had been almost completely silent.

The team left the dead scouts out in the open on purpose, propped up on thorny branches, to spook the column behind them. The enemy would be alerted to the team's presence, but it would also make them stop and look around instead of just marching ahead at full speed.

Smitty rigged the few grenades he had left with trip wires along the path to the dead bodies, and the team melted back into the woods, heading back towards Kinshasa. They had gone less than a half-mile when they heard the first grenade go off. The PAC was close.

Cascaes put his hand over his throat mic and whispered to Mackey. "Skipper, we need to find out what's going on. Kuwali needs to have his men on the way here *now*, before the PAC reaches the city."

"Roger that. Let's try Dex. He's going to be pissed. We're in a safe area further south, remember?" replied Mackey.

The Team kept moving as Mackey called in on his secure satellite phone, Cascaes holding the folding satellite dish as they walked. "Dex, we need a sit-rep on Kuwali's forces. The PAC is maybe a mile from the city and moving fast."

There was a pause as Dex realized the team was obviously following the PAC's movements. "Mack, I hope you're not thinking about trading bullets with a few thousand mercenaries."

"Negative. We're just observing from a safe distance, but Dex, you have to get Kuwali to mobilize his troop now before the PAC gets into the city. They've already massacred a few farms along the way. In another twenty minutes they'll be in the suburbs. For Christ sake, get a fire mission in here. I can give you exact coordinates!"

"Mackey! I told you! Kuwali won't authorize a bombing run outside his capital."

"Oh, no? Well, you tell that idiot that tomorrow it won't *be* his capital!"

"Mackey, your job is to keep your people safe. I ordered you out of that area. I have no way of extracting your team if anyone gets hurt out there! Now quit fucking around and get out of there."

"And Kuwali's army?"

"We told him everything you told us. They're mobilizing."

"And when exactly do they plan on getting here?"

"I don't have that information," said Dex, trying to hide his own frustration.

"Twenty minutes, Dex. That's how long before the next genocide starts. And you could have stopped it with a couple of Tomahawks or a couple of jets! Out!"

Cascaes didn't have to ask. He just folded up the satellite dish and shoved it into his pack. "Now what?"

"We'd be a speed bump—nothing more," said Mackey quietly.

"So we just split and let them start butchering their way to the capital?"

Mackey looked Cascaes in the eyes, and without saying a word, flipped his night vision goggles back down.

CHAPTER 54

The PAC forces caught a break. They cleared the marshy mess and found themselves in an open area along the river. Wong Fu-jia instructed his officers to pick up the pace over his radio. A moment later, a frantic voice reported finding the dead scouts. A few seconds later, an explosion ripped through the forest. The troops held their fire and moved around quietly. It was a booby-trap, nothing more. The second explosion killed another two soldiers, and a few soldiers fired blindly into the woods before being ordered to stop. The army stopped moving and remained in firing positions.

Wong Fu-jia was outraged. Who was responsible? Kuwali's forces or outside meddlers? He radioed Shen Xun-jun yet again and got nothing. Fu moved through the jungle at a run until he was at the front of the column that was now scattered and ready for an assault. One of his Chinese officers saw him and reported back what had happened.

"The sun will be up in another two hours. Perhaps we should wait until we can see," said the worried lieutenant.

Wong Fu-jia pulled a map from his pocket. He opened it and showed the rally point to the lieutenant. "We have less than an hour to be *here*! They need to move now! We stop for nothing. Kill everything you see, do you understand?"

The lieutenant snapped a salute and ran off to the point of the column, shouting orders in Chinese and terrible French. The PAC soldiers began lighting torches. This is what they had been waiting for—the moment when the marching turned to fighting or—in this case—slaughtering.

The Team was watching from a small hill and saw the flames light up in their night vision. One at a time, hundreds of bright orange balls popped on below as soldiers lit their torches.

Mackey barked at his team. "We've got maybe an hour of darkness, people. This is our only chance to delay them. When the sun comes up, they're going to come out of the woods fast and furious. Hodges, you and Jon stay here and we'll move north towards the river to try and buy some time. When they get close, you boogie, you understand? We'll rally here," he said, pointing to a location south of their current location on his map.

Jon pulled his spotter scope as Hodges began preparing his sniper rifle. They had good cover behind some large boulders and trees, and plenty of targets below, less than a mile out. Mackey and the rest of the team ran off towards the river. As they ran down the hill, they saw the first farmhouse go up in flames maybe a mile away.

CHAPTER 55

The PAC forces had fanned out in a line that extended half a mile across, moving quickly east towards Kinshasa like a plague. Outside the city, tens of thousands of small homes had been built in what equated to American "suburbs," but they were extremely primitive. Most of the homes were corrugated metal or wood in various stages of decay. The streets were dirt roads, and most homes lacked running water and electricity this far from the city.

The PAC soldiers were animals that were now unleashed on a sleeping population of civilians who were unarmed and unsuspecting. There had been peace in the country for years now, and the Congolese had no chance to defend themselves. The soldiers began bursting into homes and slaughtering whole families in their simple shacks, moving from house to house, killing and burning. A few soldiers took the extra time to rape victims along the way, but for the most part, the PAC moved quickly.

Hodges looked through his scope and tried to find Chinese faces. They wanted the officers. Take out the leadership first, and hope that Kuwali's forces would arrive like the cavalry in an old western. Jon spoke quietly as he scanned with his spotter scope.

"Got one. Come right. 1,200 yards. Near the little yellow shop."

Hodges scanned right and found the yellow building. There were several bodies in the dirt road out in front. A Chinese

221

soldier stood with his hands on his hips, watching the chaos around him in the light of the burning homes.

"Got him," said Hodges quietly.

"1,200 yards, wind quiet at less than two knots," said Jon.

Hodges squeezed gently and hit the Chinese officer right in the face, dropping him like a stone. Jon continued to find officers and radio operators, and Hodges did his best to keep up, nailing everything that was marked by Jon. Most of the PAC soldiers were too busy murdering civilians to notice an occasional soldier's body in the road.

Mackey and the team worked their way down towards Kimbwala, where they could see the glow from numerous fires. The sounds of machine gun fire had people up and out of their homes, running towards Kinshasa barefoot with only the clothes on their backs. Anytime the refugees spotted the team, they panicked, but the team just pointed towards Kinshasa and told them to run.

"Stay together! These streets can meander anywhere— use the main road to keep your bearing, but stay together!" Automatic gunfire interrupted him. The team hustled around the shacks and crouched, looking for targets. Occasional screaming told the story of what was happening nearby. Mackey could see his team getting angry at the massacre and yelled out to them. "We can't save them all, and we can't save *any* if you're dead! Be smart! Stay together and remember that this is a delaying action! We'll fall back house to house when they get here!"

Moose was shoulder to shoulder with Ripper behind some cinderblocks that were maybe going to be a house one day. Moose deployed the bi-pod under the M240 SAW and readied for an assault. "Happiness is a belt-fed weapon," whispered Moose.

"Except when you're humping it in a hundred degrees," replied Ripper.

"*So* worth it," whispered Moose.

The team was hunkered down, ready, when a wave of humanity crashed through them. Thousands of villagers began streaming towards them, many carrying small children. Their faces showed an understanding of what was behind them— Rwanda and their own civil wars were well remembered. Cascaes spotted Theresa's face, showing her horror at the panic stricken civilians.

"Hey!" he snapped, "Stay frosty! It's the shit *behind* them you better worry about!"

"Aye, aye," she shouted back over the noise that was getting louder. "I'm good."

Koches came running up the street with the fleeing villagers. He ran towards the house where Mackey and Julia were set up and screamed over the noise. "Right behind me! Prepare for assault!"

"There's fucking civilians everywhere," said Jones. "How are we supposed to shoot the enemy?"

The words weren't out of his mouth when the civilians in the road began falling down all over each other. Machine gun fire behind them was nonstop as the PAC soldiers simply annihilated everyone in front of them. Rounds began impacting the shacks and bricks that the team was using as cover.

"Fuck this," mumbled Moose. He aimed over the downed civilians and began firing short controlled bursts at the PAC soldiers running down the road towards them. At first, the PAC soldiers didn't realize they were being hit, as they hadn't anticipated any kind of resistance. When a dozen or so of them were dead in the dirt road, the others began screaming and taking cover. Ripper fired his grenade launcher at a few groups of soldiers, the deafening explosions sending bodies flying.

"Okay! That's it! Fall back!" ordered Mackey.

The team fired their weapons as they moved backwards, house to house. The PAC was getting close, and the stream of enemy soldiers seemed to come from everywhere. Up on the hill, Hodges kept firing until he ran out of ammunition—a first for him. 130 rounds, and 122 killed enemy soldiers.

"That's it, Jon-O! I'm out!" Hodges snapped the lens covers on the M40A5 sniper rifle and shouldered it. Jon tossed him an M-4 carbine, and the two of them began making their way down the hill towards the fighting. They'd find a spot and wait for the others to fall back to their position in the designated rally point. As they moved down the hill, they could see thousands of fleeing Congolese racing through the streets towards the capital.

CHAPTER 56

Wong Fu-jia was listening to one of his officers talking a hundred miles an hour about enemy fire. It was infuriating. He slapped the man's face so hard the lieutenant almost dropped his weapon.

"We have three kilometers to go before the sun comes up! You need to move faster!" screamed Fu. The soldier bowed and ran off, more afraid of Wong Fu-jia than of enemy fire, which is exactly how the military is supposed to work.

The city was ablaze, and there was now plenty of light. Wong Fu-jia wasn't interested in excuses. He followed the sounds of machine gun fire and screaming, bringing up the rear of the attacking army. Up ahead, his soldiers continued the carnage, the death toll now into the thousands among the civilians. Certainly, the capital should be under attack from Shen Xun-jun's troops, but what of the president and prime minister? They needed to be taken out quickly for the plan to work.

Fu tried to reach Shen Xun-jun once again and got nothing. There was nothing to do but attack. Fu radioed his second in command, who didn't respond. He wanted to smash the radio into a million pieces but needed it. He cursed and called the captain on the far right flank, who reported heavy casualties. Someone had been firing at them, and several Chinese officers were dead. Fu was screaming. *Who was firing?* This was a bunch of villagers! It had gotten to the point that he had no choice. He was without any information whatsoever. He would have to call the Ministry of State Security.

Fu found an abandoned shack and stepped over the bodies inside to a table. He pulled his satellite phone and prepped his call until whimpering interrupted him. He stood, alarmed at first, until he saw it was a small child, still in the arms of her dead mother. She had also been shot, but not mortally, and was crying. Fu pulled his sidearm and shot her in the forehead, then sat back down and dialed the number with a knot in his stomach. He was transferred and put on hold and transferred yet again, until he had the commander responsible for monitoring the attack. Wong Fu-jia explained that he had been unable to reach Shen Xun-jun all night and morning, and they were facing resistance, although they didn't know from whom. Where was Shen Xun-jun?

The commander was very quiet when Fu finished his report. It was very unusual for an operative in the field to call into headquarters directly. He made Wong Fu-jia wait while they tried to reach Shen Xun-jun from headquarters. They tried several times and got nothing. Fu was told to wait. Deep inside the Ministry of State Security, special officers adjusted their live satellite feeds to the last know GPS coordinates of Shen Xun-jun's army and began scanning the route he was supposed to take. It was hundreds of kilometers, but with the last known GPS location, it narrowed the search to a much smaller area. As Fu paced around the small hut trying not to step in blood, the officers in China stared in disbelief at the shattered column that had been Shen Xun-jun's army.

The Chinese officials in the Ministry conferred for several minutes before coming back on the phone.

"It appears that Shen Xun-jun's army has been attacked and destroyed."

That hung in the air for a moment. Shen Xun-jun had thousands of troops. How could they be destroyed?

"By who? When? How is that possible?" Fu was shouting in anger more than really asking questions.

"The Americans most likely. We've been monitoring activity on their amphibious group near the coast. Will you be able to finish your mission without Shen Xun-jun's troops?"

Fu kicked over the table. He walked outside into the burning village. A soldier was raping a woman on the floor of her shack while two others watched and waited for their turns. This wasn't an army. How could he take the capital with this bunch of undisciplined animals? He thought about the repercussions of returning to China having failed to achieve total victory.

"I will continue to fight towards the capital. Will we have support from anywhere else?"

There was silence, followed by a quick, "No."

Fu hung up and pulled out a pack of cigarettes. He sat on a stool and smoked, staring at the dead mother and child on the floor near his feet. The background noises of screaming and gunfire all melted together as he pictured his own family. Failing his objective would not go well for them. He drew deeply on the cigarette, flicked it into the pool of blood, and exhaled. Drawing his sidearm, he stepped outside into the chaos.

CHAPTER 57

The team was falling back towards the city on the heels of the escaping population. The noise was deafening, as tens of thousands of human beings panicked and fled, with loose livestock and dogs mixed in among the masses. Explosions and gunfire went on non-stop, as homes and stores caught fire, blowing up gas and propane tanks randomly in the pandemonium.

"They're close, man!" screamed Ripper as bullets ricocheted off the cinderblock walls of a house next to them.

"How you doing on ammo?" yelled Moose.

"I'm good for a while, but I gave you all the SAW rounds. No grenades. You?"

"Not much. Four mags, no frags. We're gonna' be fucked pretty soon. We better borrow some guns and ammo from the skinnies."

"No way—it's way too crazy. We need to boogie out of here, bro."

Moose looked around them at the running street battle, civilians being slaughtered in every direction. "Fuck. Okay, you're right. Find the others and let's fall back into the city. Maybe the Skipper can get us some help before it's too late."

Behind them, Theresa fired off her M-16 until she clicked empty. "My last mag," she said as she popped it in. She flipped to single shot firing. An explosion and long bursts of automatic weapons fire behind them made them drop for cover.

Ernie P. began screaming at them from across the street. "Move! Move! We're gonna be flanked!"

The approaching army was a disorganized mess, but there were hundreds of them pouring through the narrow dirty streets. Bodies were dropping all around, mostly civilians. Moose yelled at Theresa and Ripper. "Go! I've got you covered! Move!"

He stood up and aimed his SAW at the approaching invaders, firing short accurate bursts. Theresa and Ripper ran across the street to where the rest of the team was reorganizing. When they reached the other side, they opened fire so Moose could run and join them. A three round burst hit him square in the back when he was half way across the street, dropping him flat on his face. The Kevlar vest saved his life, but he was winded and fully prone out in the open. Ripper and Theresa raced forward with the team opening up in every direction to cover their friends. Ripper rolled Moose onto his back, bent over grabbing his arm and leg, and then did a dive roll over Moose which used his body momentum to pick up the giant man onto his back. Theresa watched in amazement as Ripper ended up with Moose on his back, running across the street. She fired until her rifle was empty, then sprinted across the street to cover.

By the time they got behind cover in a small store, Moose had coughed himself back to consciousness. Ripper checked Moose's back, saw he wasn't wounded, and poured some water from his canteen on Moose's face. "Welcome back. We need to haul ass."

Cascaes and Mackey raced into the small store they were hiding in and took cover. "We have everyone?" asked Cascaes.

"Everyone except Smitty and Ernie," reported Ripper.

"Where the hell are they?" snapped Cascaes, in between returning gunfire.

"We're out of explosives and getting low on ammo. Smitty had an idea for some IEDs to slow down the PAC. He and Ernie said they were going shopping."

"How long ago?"

"Maybe fifteen minutes. They'll be back in a couple of minutes."

"We need to fall back now. Let's get out the back of this building and drop back a couple of blocks." Cascaes thumbed his mic and called out to Smitty.

"Smitty! Sitrep?"

It took a few seconds, then Smitty's mic opened with heavy gunfire in the background. "Hey Skipper, we're two streets behind you. If you can hold that intersection for another three minutes, we'll have a surprise ready for the PAC. Almost done."

"Three minutes! That's the best we can do, it's getting hot over here! Out!"

An incoming RPG rocket exploded against the wall of their building, dropping part of the wall and roof inside the small space.

Moose was back up and took a knee to go through his pockets and small field pack. He pulled his two remaining magazines and threw them to Theresa, who snapped one into her M-16. His SAW was empty and lying out in the street. Ripper handed Moose his .45 and popped a new mag into his M-4.

"Two mags, that's it," he said to whoever was paying attention.

Cascaes ripped open his pack and pulled out his last two grenades, which he tossed to Moose. "You're the pitcher. Make them count!"

Jon, Hodges, Jones, and McCoy checked weapons and slipped out the back door, taking firing positions on each side of the small shack. The PAC rebels were opposite them on the other corner, firing assault rifles and RPGs in their general direction. Their rifle fire made up with volume what it lacked in accuracy. The hut was slowly coming apart.

"Another minute and half and we're out," said Mackey.

Two exploding RPG rounds knocked the wall open next to Julia, and she went down hard next to Cascaes. Smoke and debris filled the room, and the team members helped each other up, returned fire, and began exiting through the rear door.

Cascaes screamed into his mic over the incoming fire. "Smitty! We're coming! So is the PAC army!"

The fourteen of them regrouped quickly behind the building and began running, stopping only briefly to take a few shots to slow down their attackers. Most of the civilian population was either dead or had already fled the area. The team ran down the dirt road, taking cover along the poorly constructed buildings.

Smitty's head popped up from behind a small brick wall, which was about waist high. "Hey! Almost done! Hold them off for another few seconds!"

The team fanned out in defensive positions and braced for the assault as the PAC forces moved closer.

Ernie yelled from across an alley that he was "done," whatever that meant.

"Okay! That's it! You need to take off!" yelled Smitty.

Cascaes and Mackey started grabbing their people and yelling at them to move. Smitty hunkered down behind the small wall and started shooting at the incoming army.

"You, too! Let's get moving!" yelled Cascaes to Smitty.

"No can do, Skipper. I don't have detonators. This needs to be a manual job. When they get close, I'll set it off and catch up."

"Then I'll stay with you," said Cascaes. He ducked as impacting rounds started whizzing around their heads.

"I got this, boss," shouted Ernie. "You go. Me and Smitty got a special present for these fuckers. We'll catch up."

The PAC was getting more daring, sensing their enemy was a small force that seemed to be retreating. They advanced faster as their rear guard caught up and bolstered their numbers.

"Shit. Don't stick around too long!" Cascaes moved out quickly with the others, racing from building to building to avoid incoming machine gun fire. The team ran and stumbled along the dirt road, occasionally glancing back at their two teammates and urging them silently to hurry up.

CHAPTER 58

Dex hung up the phone and exhaled a soft, "Thank God."

President Kuwali had ordered his presidential guard units and army to defend the city. Alarms began sounding around Kinshasa, rousing the population from their sleep. Although they were a small, poorly-equipped army, there were a couple of thousand of them, and that was better than the small platoon now trying to hold off an entire rebel army.

Dex called Mackey, but Mackey didn't answer. There was no way to know that Mackey was fighting for his life at that moment.

Mackey and his team had retreated to a cluster of small open buildings that served as "open air restaurants" of a sort. There were a few small knee walls of cinder blocks that provided cover, and the team fanned out to try and hold the street, waiting for Smitty and Ernie to join them.

Two blocks ahead, Smitty was opening the valves on all of the propane and fuel tanks they had found and piled up next to the road. Ernie had filled a few buckets with whatever metal objects he could find in an attempt to make a makeshift shaped-charge, pointed down the street at the attacking PAC forces.

Bullets were ricocheting all over their position, and it was getting untenable.

"You figure out how to set this shit off yet?" asked Ernie.

"Gas. We'll leave a trail of gas as we exit and hit it with a lighter. It should set off the pile and blow the shit out of this place."

232

"We need to go now, man!" screamed Ernie as an RPG round exploded nearby. "This shit's gonna' blow up with us sitting in it!"

"Go! I'm almost done!" screamed Smitty, as he opened the last couple of tanks. He grabbed a gas can and opened the top as Ernie backed away. Smitty started pouring fuel as Ernie fired a few rounds at a group of guerrillas that had moved up on the flank. He killed two of them before a bullet hit him in the head, sending up a mist of blood and bone right in front of Smitty.

"Ernie!" he screamed, as he dove on top of him. One look and it was clear he was dead. The enemy was overrunning their position. Smitty rolled off of Ernie and began firing his assault rifle at the soldiers, who now seemed to stream in from everywhere. A bullet struck his shoulder, breaking his clavicle and spinning him around before he fell. A PAC soldier jumped over the small pile of rubble and cinderblocks and aimed at Smitty who raised his weapon with one arm. They fired simultaneously, knocked each other flat. Smitty cried out in pain, reached into his pant pocket and pulled his lighter.

"Fuck you!" he screamed, as he threw it into the pool of gasoline.

The fireball leveled the entire intersection, taking out three small buildings and several dozen soldiers. Smitty disappeared into the fireball alongside his friend Ernie P.

The team saw the explosions and giant fireball, and Ripper looked over the wall towards their friends. Black smoke billowed, and fire shot to the sky, but there was no sign of Smitty or Ernie.

"Skipper, I better move forward and take a peek," said Ripper. Moose groaned, his back aching, and moved alongside his partner. Ripper looked at Moose just for a second, and then the two of them raced forward along the buildings towards the inferno. They hadn't gone ten yards when PAC soldiers started emerging through the smoke.

"Shit!" yelled Ripper as he saw the men pouring through the smoke. He fired his weapon, joined by Moose, who yelled at him to fall back. The two of them radioed that they were about to be overrun, and kept moving back towards the rest of their team. By the time they got back, the PAC was less than a hundred yards away.

"Where's Smitty and Ernie?" yelled Mack.

"No idea, boss. There's a million skinnies heading this way. We need to go *now!*"

Moose fired a few rounds and yelled to Cascaes. "Skipper, they're either dead or had to run for it. We'll be next if we don't go now!"

An RPG round added emphasis by exploding behind them. Two yards lower and they'd have eaten it.

"Move! Move!" Yelled Cascaes.

The team ran down the street, no longer returning fire. They were simply trying to put some distance between themselves and the attacking army. They zig-zagged through smaller side streets, still heading for the city, but trying to avoid being seen. Their training kept them running, despite the pain.

"I need to get a sit-rep from Langley," said Mackey to Cascaes as they ran down a quieter side street. The background noises had gotten slightly quieter. The team crashed through a door and moved through several buildings and courtyards until they were in a crammed group of tiny houses.

They broke out the satellite phone and called in to Dex, who answered right away.

"I've been trying to reach you!" exclaimed Dex when he picked up.

"We're on the run. I only have a second. We're still trying to get back to Kinshasa. Team is taking casualties and we're low on ammo. What's the situation?"

"Were are you?"

"Near the city. Fighting is house-to-house. We had a change of plans. Are we getting help?"

"Mack! Damnit! I told you to get out of there!"

"Are we getting help?"

"The president ordered his army assembled. They're moving out to defend the city. We have a dozen birds inbound, but they're still an hour out, minimum. Can you get to the presidential palace?"

"Not sure. We'll try. Exfil?"

"At the palace if you can get there. Marines will help secure the area. Stop trying to fight and just get the hell out of there, Mack!"

"Roger. Out."

Mackey turned to Cascaes. "Army is on the way. Marines heading to the Palace for our ride home. We need to hustle before we end up in the middle of these two armies."

"Smitty and Ernie?"

"If they're alive, we'll figure something out."

Cascaes knew in his heart they were dead, but leaving Santos in the jungle on their last mission still haunted him. "Okay, let's get the fuck out of here." Cascaes relayed the info to his battered team. They were no longer a fighting force, they were simply trying to escape and evade back to the palace.

CHAPTER 59

Wong Fu-jia stood over the two mangled bodies staring at their uniforms. One was Caucasian, the other perhaps Hispanic, but both were Americans, no doubt. He knelt down and looked closer at their uniforms. No markings of any kind. Both bodies were badly torn up, but these two had been professionals judging by their uniforms. American Special Forces. He made a sour face.

General Wong looked around at the carnage. Improvised bombs had leveled the area killing many of his soldiers. He wondered how many more Americans they were facing. One of his Chinese officers ran to him, out of breath and snapped a salute.

"General! I can't find any of our officers. Only you and I are left, with the PAC soldiers."

Wong Fu-jia stared at the man, a captain, and contemplated that. With General Shen's army out of contact and perhaps destroyed, and his officers dead or wounded, there was very little chance left for success. Without even thinking, Wong Fu-jia pulled his sidearm and emptied it into what was left of Smitty's dead body. He kicked it and cursed at the top of his lungs. When he got control over himself, he snapped at his last remaining officer.

"Can we get this army reorganized?"

The captain looked terrified to answer, but quietly responded. "They are spread throughout the city, moving towards the palace. Without our officers, there's no way to communicate with them. I'm sorry, general."

General Wong pulled out his cigarettes and lit one. He stared at the captain and offered a cigarette to him. The man looked terrified. "Go on," he said. He watched the man accept it with a shaking hand, and light it. Wong Fu-jia thought, "These may be our last."

The two of them walked quietly after the sounds of weapons, following the fire and smoke as the out-of-control army burned its way towards the presidential palace.

⊕

President Kuwali had made a speech over the radio and television, advising his country that they were under attack from rebels, but that his army would defend the city to the last man. He hoped his fire and brimstone speech would help motivate an army that might drop their weapons and start running if things looked bad.

He now stood in front of the presidential palace on the wide avenue where his troops had assembled and begun to move out towards the approaching army. President Kuwali waved and smiled at his troops, although deep down, he was extremely worried. The Americans were sending marines by helicopter and promised to defend his capital, but what if the PAC arrived before they did?

As the army headed out down the highway heading towards the fight, tens of thousands of refugees walked back in the other direction. Kuwali's wife and children were inside the palace with his own bodyguards. He scanned the skies, praying for the marines.

The team shared ammo and reloaded, drank some water, and began the perilous run to the palace. Jones and Hodges took point, Lance and Cascaes covered the rear. They moved at a slow run, listening and stopping to look around every fifty yards or so. The PAC wasn't doing anything to hide their movements, and the team knew where they were just from the gunfire and burning buildings. Still, they could have scouts out, so they were cautious.

They fourteen of them moved silently through countless small streets and courtyards. The houses and business were crammed together, and there were still some civilians trying to save personal belongings before fleeing east towards the presidential palace. A couple of hundred yards east of the palace was "Martyr's Stadium," an appropriate name for an assembly point for stricken masses. It was there that the president had instructed his people to seek shelter. A decent plan, unless the city fell to the PAC, in which case it would become a very large mass grave.

Mackey checked his watch every few minutes. Like President Kuwali, he silently urged the marines to fly faster.

Jones jogged back from his forward position and found Cascaes. "Hey, Skipper. Highway One is at the end of the block. The good news is, it'll take us right to the presidential palace. The bad news is, it's a real road. It's wide open highway. If the PAC's around, they'll spot us in two seconds. We need to get across the highway, and follow a parallel route."

"Okay, so let's do it…"

"Yeah, well, the other side of the highway is a mess. All residential, and real tight. No line of sight. No straight parallel route that we could find yet. Your call. Run up the highway and hope we don't get spotted, or take the long way."

"Easy call. We're not equipped to fight. We take the long way and keep trying to evade. Let's haul ass across the highway."

CHAPTER 60

The long convoy of vehicles left the palace area and moved down Highway One like a giant military parade. Dozens of trucks, ranging from old military trucks to pickup trucks with machine guns mounted in the back drove southwest towards the approaching army. The plan was simple: drive towards the burning part of the city, find the enemy, and kill them.

The army had one functioning tank in the capital, which was bringing up the rear. The commander of the tank, President Kuwali's nephew, stood up out of the top of the cold war era M-60. He saluted the president as they drove by and tried to look regal in his invincible armor.

They headed straight for the billowing black smoke, less than a mile and a half away. On both sides of the convoy, tens of thousands of men, women, and children headed in the opposite direction on foot, many carrying whatever they owned on their heads or shoulders.

In direct contrast to the orderly column of government troops headed down the highway, the PAC invaders had fanned out across the outskirts of the city in a wide mass. Even having taken casualties at the hands of the team, there were still over twenty-three hundred troops murdering, raping, and burning their way through the city. Without their Chinese officers to keep them focused on their mission of taking the presidential palace, the mercenaries had gotten distracted and turned into a barbaric horde. While most of the civilians had fled, there were still plenty of targets left behind—the elderly who were too slow to escape, the shopkeepers who tried to protect their livelihood, not understanding what they would be facing, and families with smaller children who made the mistake of trying to save too many possessions. The savagery shown to these people was medieval.

By the time government forces were within fighting distance of the PAC, the city was burning in a half mile wide swath of billowing black smoke. The government troops were the first to take casualties, their lead vehicles being hit with RPGs on Highway One. The first explosion happened only a few hundred yards away from the exhausted American team that was still pushing towards the presidential palace.

As soon as the lead vehicle exploded, the long column scattered to both sides of the road and fanned out. The shooting started sporadically, but like a symphony, quickly began to crescendo as PAC rebels engaged and reinforced their lines. The team watched from cover on the other side of the highway, carefully moving northeast. They stopped and assembled the sat-phone, and called Dex Murphy.

"It's on, Dex," said Mack. "PAC troops are engaged with government forces about a mile southwest of the residence. Where are the Marines?"

"Marines are inbound. Should hit the LZ in maybe fifteen minutes or so."

"They need to hit the PAC on their way in. It's a large force, Dex. We're low on ammo and have three KIA. The Marines could save this fight."

"They aren't supposed to engage unless fired upon..."

"Bullshit, Dex! We can call in fire support right now! If the PAC moves through this government force, Kinshasa is gone! Let us direct fire and take out these rebels."

"I'll need to get approval. You're confident that you can direct fire without hitting friendlies?"

"Dex, if I was any closer to the targets I could put them on the phone with you! Hurry up! Out!"

Mack turned to Cascaes. "You heard the conversation. As soon as he gets the green light, I'll direct fire. I want you to take the team back to the palace."

"Mack, I appreciate the gesture, but this is my job. I'm also faster than you when it's time to run like hell. You go. I got this."

Mackey started to protest but Cascaes put his hand on his shoulder. "Hey man, this isn't macho bullshit. I'm good at this, and I'm faster on my feet. You go."

"Okay, but keep a couple of shooters with you." He yelled over to Hodges and Jones. "You two stay with the Skipper and provide security. He's going to call in air support. The rest of you, on me. We're moving to the palace."

A series of explosions made them all duck and cover. "Jesus, they're getting close," said Moose.

"I'm low on ammo and out of Lapua rounds. Can someone spare a few mags?" asked Hodges.

Jon, Ray, Julia, and Pete began pulling out magazines and handing them to Hodges and Jones. "Give me your rifle and I'll hump it back for you," said Jon. "You'll be faster without it."

Hodges reluctantly gave up his rifle, kissing it first before he handed it to Jon. "Thanks, Jon. Take good care of my girlfriend."

"You know it, brother." Jon pulled his .45 and handed it to Jones. "Just in case," he said.

Jones gave him a quick fist bump and shoved the extra pistol into his web gear.

The sound of an artillery round being fired, followed by an explosion, got everyone's attention. Ripper pulled binoculars and peered around a house towards highway One.

"Hey! Someone's got a tank! That should help even things up," he said.

Moose moved alongside and took a turn with the binoculars. "Holy crud, Rip. That thing's older than the boss."

"Fuck you, my *hearing's* just fine," said Mackey.

Mortar rounds and RPGs impacted within fifty yards of the team as PAC forces began focusing on the single tank. The tank fired blindly in the general direction of the enemy, and opened fire with its machine gun, but without modern gun sights and a highly skilled crew, the tank was more bark than bite.

Cascaes smacked Mackey's leg. "Okay, that's it, bro! You go! See you at the palace." He looked at Julia, whose face showed her worry. "It's okay, it's what we do, right?" He forced a smile.

As the team began moving, Julia leaned over, not caring who saw. She kissed Chris on the mouth quickly and whispered, "Be careful," then turned and ran after the team, which was already moving down the alley way.

Cascaes scanned the battle space with binoculars, praying for air support. Hodges and Jones had the flanks and were watching for any incoming soldiers so Cascaes could focus on enemy troop movements. He was thankful that Julia and the rest of them were running back towards the palace.

The tank fired another shell, rocking after the shock, and then moved forward with infantry moving along behind it. Several RPG rounds impacted the front left tread almost simultaneously. The government troops watched in horror as the tread rolled off the tank, leaving it immobile in the middle of the road. Like a giant sign that read: *Shoot Me*, the tank became the focus of every weapon the PAC guerrillas carried. And while the small arms fire did nothing but bounce off, the repeated hits from the RPG rounds began to have an effect. The armor was failing. The top hatch opened, and President Kuwali's nephew emerged quickly, trying to climb on the back of the tank and avoid incoming fire. He was shredded by machine gun fire and hung off the top of the tank. As the crew tried to follow him out, several more RPG rounds hit the tank, and it exploded, with secondary explosions as the shells inside went off. The infantry following the tank took heavy casualties and retreated into the surrounded structures, some of the troops as close as fifty yards away from Cascaes.

"Hey Skipper, think we should pull back a little?" asked Hodges. "We're getting rounds singing over our heads, man."

"Not yet, it's too hard to see," replied Cascaes. It was true, the burning tank and tremendous amount of gunfire had put up a dark cloud that obscured most of the troops movements ahead. He pulled his satellite phone and called in to Dex. "How we doing, Dex? They're almost in my lap!"

"Marines are maybe five minutes out. They only have one gunship with them as an escort. Once they drop the marines at the palace, their orders are to evacuate the president and his family to the ship while the marines hold the palace if they can. Real air support won't be there for another twenty minutes at least. You've got F-18 Super Hornets inbound from the *Iwo Jima*. Listen, Chris, you don't want to be anywhere near there when they start hitting their targets. I suggest you pull back."

"Dex, the army and the PAC are almost on top of each other. If I don't direct fire, they'll be hitting the wrong targets. Let me get online with the squadron commander and make this work!"

"Okay, okay. Let me make this happen. Sit tight and let me get back to you. If I can, I'll have the Super Hornets on the horn directly to you. Out."

Jones was looking through his sights. "Hey Skipper, I don't want to fire and give up our position, but these guys are moving closer."

"How many?" asked Cascaes grabbing his binoculars.

"Looks like their main force is flanking the tank to this side. We gotta move!"

Hodges scrambled over the rubble he was hiding behind and moved next to Jones. He could see at least a couple of hundred guerrillas moving and shooting as they worked past the destroyed tank to their side of Highway One.

"Shit. Skipper, we need to pull back *now*!" said Hodges.

Cascaes broke down the phone and shoved it into his back pack.

"Go! Move back a hundred yards and find a place with a decent line of sight, and we'll be there right behind you," said Jones.

Cascaes sprinted out the back of the alley and kept running in a low crouch, zipping in and out of old primitive houses. The mortar rounds and firing was continuous and getting closer.

Mackey called in on his radio. "We're almost to the palace. Marines will be here any second. Where are you guys?"

Cascaes was running and trying to talk as he moved. "Pulling the FOP back. We'll set up again and guide the Super Hornets. Out."

Cascaes found a low wall that he could use for cover and still see back towards the highway. He radioed Jones and Hodges, and they moved back towards his location.

CHAPTER 61

President Kuwali huddled with his family in the rear courtyard of the presidential palace. His guards surrounded the compound, and eyed the sky above them when they heard the rotors of incoming helicopters. First came the AH-1 Super Cobra gunship, which roared overhead and then slowed and began large circular sweeps of the area. Behind it, four large CH-46 Sea Knight helicopters began descending on the open compound. As soon as they touched down, the rear doors descended, and out charged thirteen United States Marines from three of the four helos. The extra Sea Knight was for the president and his family.

Three thirteen-man squads made a full rifle platoon, and they moved out at the barking of their sergeants and corporals. The lieutenant in charge of the rifle platoon jogged over to the president. There was no mistaking who President Kuwali was, wearing a dark business suit and sunglasses, surrounded by his wife and five young children, as well as six heavily armed guards.

The lieutenant snapped a salute at the president. "Mr. President, Lieutenant Conor Hamill, United States Marine Corps. On behalf of the President of the United States, I'm here to offer you and your family safe conduct to our carrier until the situation here is under control."

The president shook the marine's hand and smiled. "I thank you so much for rescuing my family. I will stay, but ask that you please allow them to leave with you."

"Mr. President, my orders were to escort you as well. Enemy forces are moving in very quickly. They're within two kilometers of this location."

"This is my country, lieutenant. If you would please take my family to safety, I will be forever in your debt—but my place is here. Please. Take them now."

Lt. Hamill snapped a salute and jogged back a few yards, screaming at his platoon sergeant. "Gallo! Get these people loaded and out of here!" The president hugged and kissed his crying family, who begged him to join them, but ultimately ran for the helicopter with their marine escort.

Hamill grabbed his radio operator and called into command aboard the amphibious assault ship *USS Iwo Jima,* part of the 24th Marine Expeditionary Unit. The colonel aboard ship was not happy about the president's refusal to leave. His orders were to rescue the president and his family. Of course, he couldn't force the president to leave his own country, but if anything happened to President Kuwali, it was his ass on the line.

"Lieutenant, you are to secure the presidential compound. Have the president take cover inside somewhere that's well protected and you make sure he's safe. I have a squadron of Super Hornets from the *Bush* inbound and I'm told I've got Special Forces on the ground to direct fire. No one gets inside that compound, you understand?"

"Ooh-rrra, colonel. Out."

The lieutenant screamed for his sergeant, explained their revised orders, and had two marines escort the president inside to a basement office where the two marines would stand post outside the doors with the president's personal body guards as a very last line of defense.

The rest of the rifle platoon took up posts along the perimeter and hunkered down, prepared to fend off a larger force. Lt. Hamill watched his sergeant direct their positioning and shook his head. They were United States Marines and would defend this post as ordered, but they were thirty-six men against a couple of thousand. It was not ideal.

CHAPTER 62

Wong Fu-jia had managed to find a few of his PAC officers and remind them that the presidential palace was the target, not whatever women they could find to rape and murder. The destruction of the enemy's lone tank had been a huge morale booster, and had re-energized the PAC soldiers. They now had the National Army on its heels, and were keeping up the pressure.

Wong Fu-jia checked his hand-held GPS and looked at the map. The palace was a little over a kilometer away, due east. The fact that he had no reinforcements was infuriating. With only the littlest help of heavier weapons, they could be in the palace within minutes. He cursed his luck and tried to rally whatever men he could find.

The PAC soldiers were slowly reorganizing near the burning tank and began advancing up the highway. Wong Fu-jia shouted orders in Chinese that weren't understood by the African troops, but he was pointing and screaming, and that was close enough. *That way.* He raced up the street, hoping the troops would follow him.

Over 500 PAC guerrillas were now moving forward. The president's army was retreating, some of them in an all-out broken run. Cascaes hung up the sat-phone with Dex Murphy and switched his radio to Aqua fifty-four as Dex had instructed.

Cascaes keyed his radio. "Northstar, this is Voodoo Three actual, stand by for danger close polar."

"Roger, standing by," replied the pilot, his engine hum loud in the background.

"Grid as follows, R2P 2348 1474."

"Roger, grid R2P 2348 1474."

"Good copy, stand by for target location."

"Standing by. R2P 7783 1499."

"I copy R2P 7783 1499."

"Good copy. Request immediate support, whatever you can send my way, troops are currently in contact. Several hundred guerrillas advancing on the palace along Highway One. If you can take a low slow run you'll see a burning tank on the highway. That's ground zero. Friendlies half a kilometer south and east, advise when fast movers are on station."

"On station in a few seconds. Suggest you take cover, over."

Cascaes hugged the small wall and scanned the sky to the north with his binoculars. He couldn't help the smile as he made out the four fighters leaving white contrails in their direction.

"Northstar, you are making a direct line to my position. Hit that tank and anything west of it. I'm south of that tank less than half a click, so don't overshoot! Out!"

Cascaes, Hodges, and Jones kneeled behind the wall and peered out to watch the show. The fighters roared in low and slow and began firing rockets and machine guns. The lead jet dropped a CBU-87 cluster bomb over the tank, and as soon as Cascaes saw it open up in the air releasing the bomblets, he screamed, "*Down!*" to his men. They covered their ears and opened their mouths, crossed their ankles and squeezed their eyes shut as the earth began to come apart. 202 small bomblets exploded over the area almost simultaneously, and hundreds of PAC soldiers simply disappeared into the explosions.

When the shock waves finished rolling over Cascaes, he knelt and peered over the wall. The destruction was beyond comprehension and Highway One looked like a lunar landscape. The jets banked and rolled and began tearing up everything they could find west of the tank. The rear guard of the PAC forces took massive casualties, as the jets pounded an area almost half a square kilometer.

"That's it! Palace, double-time!" screamed Cascaes.

The three of them began running along the narrow alleyways, heading northeast towards the palace. The smoke was thick and blowing towards them, making it difficult to see beyond twenty yards. There was still random gunfire, evidence that PAC forces were still engaged with regular army troops, and the jets were still making runs overhead.

By the time the three of them reach Boulevard Triomphal, which made a right turn to the palace, the remnants of the PAC forces were literally across the street. The three of them found a small bungalow of a house and Cascaes called in to Mackey.

"Mack! We're a half mile out but we've got a large force here. The Marines here yet?"

"Affirmative, but there's only one rifle platoon, and they're here to secure the palace. How many PAC at your location?" he asked.

"Not sure. Visibility is lousy. We're going to keep pushing east and—"

Automatic gunfire opened up and rounds began ricocheting all over their location. The three of them hit the deck and crawled for cover.

"On our six!" yelled Jones. He spun around and began firing his weapon at a few stragglers that had accidentally come up behind them, dropping three PAC soldiers at ten meters in the smoke. More rounds began singing off the bricks.

"Shit! They're all over us!" yelled Jones.

Hodges scurried over a small pile of rubble and moved around a corner in the tight neighborhood. It was hard to see anything, and the lines of sight weren't more than a few yards with too much smoke and too many buildings. Hodges stood up and peered around the corner of a beat up house. A PAC soldier slammed into him without ever having seen him. The two of them crashed to the street and began fighting hand-to-hand. Jones ran to them and jumped on the pile, grabbing the PAC soldier by the throat and jamming his K-Bar knife into the man's chest. He pulled him off of Hodges and threw him to the side.

"You good, bro?" he asked.

Hodges rolled away and screamed "Look out!" but it was too late. Two more PAC soldiers came up the same alleyway and went wide-eyed when they realized they had stumbled into American forces. One of them opened up on full automatic and emptied half a magazine into Jones at point blank range.

"*No!*" screamed Hodges. He grabbed his weapon and began firing at the two men, dropping them with short controlled bursts. Cascaes was a second behind, charging up the alley, firing at them as well. He reached the pile of bodies and grabbed Jones by the front of his blood soaked fatigues.

"Jonesy!" he screamed. One look was all it took. Earl had multiple gunshot wounds all over his body and was dead. "*Earl!*" An RPG round blew up less than twenty feet away, sending up more smoke and dust, and shrapnel and bits of rock peppered Cascaes and Hodges. The two of them dove for cover, Cascaes over Jones's body. They returned fire and quickly realized the enemy was being reinforced.

"We gotta move!" yelled Chris.

Hodges moved up to Jones and hoisted his body over his back.

"He's gone, man. We gotta leave him!"

"No way, Skipper! Let's go!"

Hodges began running down the alleyway with Jones over his back, and Chris ran backwards, shooting at the enemy in the smoke behind them. Incoming rounds were singing past their ears, dangerously close.

"Chris! Sitrep?" yelled Mackey into Chris's earpiece.

"Jones down. We're trying to make it back. We need help, Mack!" yelled Chris as they stumbled along the narrow smoke-filed alley. An RPG round exploded above their heads, but sent the wall down all over them. They fell in the torrent of bricks. Hodges was under Jones's dead body and a hundred pounds of rubble and couldn't move. Cascaes had been hammered by bricks all over his body and was trying to summon all of his strength just to uncover himself. The PAC soldiers moved closer.

CHAPTER 63

"Shit!" yelled Mackey as the radio went dead.

"Where are they?" asked Moose.

"Close—half a click, max. That explosion must have been them," he said, pointing at a billowing white smoke not too far off.

Moose and Ripper exchanged a quick glance and began running towards the smoke.

"Wait!" yelled Mackey. "Let's stay together!" None of them had more than a few rounds left, but no one hesitated. They were within sight of the compound and safety, but there was no way they would leave their friends behind. Moose was out in front, racing down the street with Ripper and the rest of them close behind. By the time they got to where the smoke was coming from, the PAC forces had descended on the area and had Cascaes in a wicked crossfire. Hodges was pinned under the bricks and Jones's body, and couldn't free himself.

Ripper and Moose were still on point and began shooting down the alley at the PAC troops that were assaulting their friends. Bullets ricocheted off of the walls keeping Chris on the ground in the pile of bricks. Hodges was still pushing bricks off of himself, one at a time.

Julia, Theresa, and Jon ran down a parallel alley on the left and tried to move around behind the PAC force. Instead, they found themselves facing another dozen troops and engaged in a heavy exchange of fire within a hundred yards. Woods and Koches heard the gunfire and reinforced the three of them, being extremely careful to conserve ammunition.

The rest of the team crawled up the alley and tried to free Cascaes and Hodges from the bricks and debris. The incoming fire was steady and heavy, and they didn't have enough ammunition to return heavy fire themselves. It was slow and perilous as they moved down the alleyway.

Mackey, seeing the alley was too dangerous to move ahead, slipped out the back and moved around to the right slipping through shanty-type houses in a flanking maneuver. He kept creeping along forward on a parallel alleyway until he could hear troops speaking in Kikongo. He slowed to a crawl and pulled his knife and .45, slinging his empty assault rifle over his back.

Mackey leaned against the wall and waited, listening to the two voices argue, most likely over who was going to have to move down the alley towards the Americans. When Mackey heard them moving, he slipped behind them and fired two rounds into the head of the man in front of him, then two more into the other soldier. He grabbed the man's rifle and started rummaging for ammunition when several more soldiers popped up from behind another short wall in the crammed alleyway. They started spraying automatic weapon fire at Mack, who dove for cover and fired a few rounds from his .45 before scrambling away. He had dropped the rifle and ammo, cursed himself, and kept moving.

There was more screaming in Kikongo, and then something else—Chinese? Mack rolled over several times to get out of the incoming stream of bullets and ended up kicking his way through the wall of a shanty. He pushed through the wall and found himself in a one-room house, with several dead civilians on the dirt floor.

Mack tried to listen for sounds to help reorient himself. He was separated from his team and most likely surrounded by PAC guerrillas. He crawled on his belly out the front of the small house, through pools of blood, and watched and listened as he moved inch by inch.

Wong Fu-jia was screaming at his soldiers. He had finally seen Americans. He wanted them dead. His troops outnumbered what were most likely Special Forces forward observers or attack controllers. General Wong grabbed the PAC soldiers around him and pushed them towards the alley where had seen the American run away. He pointed his own rifle down the alleyway and moved up behind his mercenaries. A few more PAC guerrillas arrived behind them, and Wong Fu-jia used hand gestures to get them to spread out and move through the decrepit houses. A serious firefight was raging one alley over, but he had an American cut off from the rest, and smelled blood. He whispered harshly in Chinese, but the PAC forces had no idea what he was saying without the interpreters there to help. *Forward. Kill.* That seemed to be the general idea.

Mackey crawled faster, moving away from the sounds of the firefight. He knew he needed to start circling back around to reach his team, but the alleyway didn't go that way, and there were PAC forces everywhere. He needed help, but there was no way he was going to jeopardize any of his people to try and get to him.

Back in the other alley, Moose and Ripper were inching their way up towards Cascaes and Hodges, firing only single shots when they could see a target. In contrast, the PAC forces were pouring a heavy rain of lead down the alley, keeping Cascaes and Hodges pinned to the floor, still tangled in bricks and debris.

Julia, Theresa, and Jon had flanked around the side alley and came to a connecting path. They got low and peered around to see the guerrillas firing down the street from behind knee walls and piles of bricks. Jon raised his rifle and pointed to the men on the right. Theresa and Julia aimed at the targets on the left.

"Now!" whispered Jon, and he opened up on them.

Julia and Theresa fired until they both clicked empty. They dropped the empty magazines with the sick realization that they were completely out of ammunition. Jon had one grenade, which he pulled and tossed down the alleyway. The three of them covered up and allowed the blast to roll over them. Jon moved forward with Theresa and Julia behind him, each brandishing knives.

Jon used his throat mic to call to his team. "Moose! Where are you?"

"End of an alley. Was that your grenade?"

"Roger."

"Good kill. We're clear right now. Move up."

The three of them raced up the alley and hung a right, then ran down the tight alley to where Moose and Ripper were pulling bricks off of Cascaes, Jones, and Hodges.

"Where's Woods and Koches?" asked Ripper as they reassembled their people.

"No idea," said Jon, looking puzzled.

"They were behind you! Shit!" Ripper keyed his mic. "Woods? Koches? Sitrep?"

No reply. He tried again. Nothing.

"Mack? You copy?"

Nothing, and then a very quiet keying of the mic in double short bursts. He was alive and could receive but couldn't talk. "This is a clusterfuck," said Ripper as he continued to pull bricks with Moose. "I don't know where Mack, Jake, or Lance are. Skipper? You okay?"

He pulled Cascaes out of the pile of bricks. Cascaes's face was white from dust, except where blood was leaking through from multiple small cuts.

"Get Hodges," was all he managed to say. Julia moved to him quickly and pulled her canteen, pouring it on his face. "Hey. You okay?" she asked quietly.

"Yeah, I'm good. Help Moose."

Theresa had managed to pull Jones out of the rubble and saw his condition. She checked for a pulse for several seconds but knew he was gone. She looked up at Moose. "He's dead, Al."

Hodges was conscious, but badly beaten up and bleeding from dozens of welts. "Jonesy?" he croaked when he saw Theresa place his limp hand down on his chest. She shook her head at Hodges, whose tears cut through the dry dust on his face.

An explosion nearby ended the conversation. Moose stood up, pulling Cascaes and Hodges to their feet one at a time. "We need to boogey, Skipper. We gotta find Mack, Lance, and Jake and they're not together."

Cascaes looked around for a weapon, and ultimately jogged over to a dead PAC guerilla to strip him of his assault rifle and ammunition. Hodges followed him and did the same, followed by Theresa and Julia. The team was foraging for weapons and ammunition when all hell broke loose again. They grabbed what they could and hustled down the alleyway where Julia, Theresa and Jon had come from.

"Lance! You copy? Koches?" asked Cascaes into his mic. A mic opened and at first it was just automatic weapons fire. Finally, Lance responded. "It's too hot, Skipper. You need to get back to the palace."

"Give me a sitrep and location!"

"Skipper, they're all over us. Pull back. It's no good, boss. Sorry. Out."

Moose pointed towards the sounds of gunfire. "Got to be them, Skipper."

The team began moving towards the gunfire. Hodges was last, having hung back to give Jones a kiss on the forehead before leaving. Theresa stayed back waiting for him, concerned about his condition. Concussion for sure, multiple bruises and abrasions, maybe a few broken ribs. Hodges coughed and spit, but kept moving.

Cascaes motioned for his men to follow the sound of the firefight, but took a knee and broke out the sat-phone.

"Northstar, this is Voodoo Three actual. Are you still on station?"

"Negative Voodoo Three. You have a Super Cobra, call sign Jersey fifty-six in your AO. Returning to base. Out."

Cascaes considered that a second. The marines must have brought a bird in with them for overwatch. "Jersey fifty-six, this is Voodoo Three actual. Danger Close Polar."

"Voodoo Three actual, this is Jersey fifty-six. We are not authorized for support at this time, over."

"Jersey fifty-six is Lawrence Taylor and you better be a Giants fan. Broken Arrow. I say Again. *Broken Arrow.* Over."

The pilot of the Super Cobra was, in fact, a Giants fan. Jersey fifty-six was Lawrence Taylor—perhaps the greatest defensive football player in NFL history. Chief Warrant Officer Jeff Cantor had taken his call sign for his favorite player. He shook his head. His orders had been to circle the compound and provide security over-watch to the Marine Rifle Platoon. He wasn't supposed to leave the palace airspace, but an emergency brevity code from an overrun unit trumped his orders.

"Voodoo Three actual, this is Jersey fifty-six. Broken Arrow. Good copy."

"I'm popping smoke." Cascaes pulled two yellow smoke canisters and pulled the pins. He threw them up on the roof of the small shanty next to him.

Less than half a kilometer away, CWO Cantor could see the yellow smoke.

"I have yellow smoke," said the pilot.

"Roger, Jersey fifty-six, that's me."

"Affirmative. Inbound." The Super Cobra raced across the city straight for the yellow smoke.

Cascaes barked into his mic. "Team! We have an inbound bird. Get to the yellow smoke before he hoses this whole area."

The team had been trying to work towards rescuing Lance and Jake and stopped short where they were. Ripper looked at Moose. "Shit! Now what?"

"Lance! You and Jake find a hole! Incoming!" yelled Moose. He grabbed Ripper by the arm and shoved him back in the direction they had just come from. "Let's go! To the smoke!"

It had been a confusing mess, but the team understood their best option. Get back to the yellow smoke where the pilot wouldn't be dropping ordnance and let him do his job. Lance and Jake would have to find cover and tough it out. The roar of the Super Cobra overhead made everyone sprint harder towards the smoke. They could see Cascaes on his knee, still on his radio.

"Mack! Can you see yellow smoke?" asked Cascaes.

There was no response.

"Mack, come in!"

Nothing.

"Voodoo Three actual, this is Jersey fifty-six, inbound on your position."

Overhead, the Cobra slowed and CWO Cantor found multiple targets running through the maze of alleyways and narrow streets below. Cantor watched a small group of soldiers moving through an alleyway towards the yellow smoke. He could see muzzle flashes. The 20mm three-barrel nose-gun opened up and began chewing up everything in its path.

The team huddled close together, taking cover as best they could as they watched the alley way in both directions. They could hear the sound of the gun overhead. It didn't sound like a machine gun, more like a very loud chain saw. Shell casings rained down on the shantytown.

The bird moved very slowly, pouring fire in every direction around the yellow smoke. A few times, Cantor spotted larger forces moving around further out and used his Hellfire missiles to destroy them. For the first time in what seemed like hours, Cascaes and his immediate team weren't under attack. The same couldn't be said for Lance and Jake, and on the other side of the team, Mackey.

CHAPTER 64

Jake and Lance had tried to find cover, but there was no place to hide from the mini-gun. The incoming rounds were destroying everything around them and the shells were impacting way too close.

"Popping smoke!" yelled Jake. He pulled a yellow smoke grenade and tossed it a few feet away. "Skipper! Tell the pilot we're popping smoke before he hoses us!" It would, of course, give away their position, but better to be shot at by automatic weapons fire than vaporized by the Super Cobra.

Cascaes relayed the information to the pilot, who saw the smoke and redirected his fire a few seconds before he would have killed them both. He continued to fly in slow sweeps over the area, inflicting tremendous casualties on the PAC guerrillas. Further out on the other side of Cascaes, Mackey was crawling through the alleyways, taking fire from unseen soldiers.

The noise was deafening as the Super Cobra fired missiles and rained total destruction with its nose gun.

Cascaes radio came to life. "Voodoo Actual, this is Jackal Three Bravo, we are currently en route to your position. We have two rifle squads, reinforced with a machine gun section. Approaching from the north. What do you need us to do?"

Cascaes almost cried with relief at the sound of the marine platoon sergeant from the presidential palace. The Marines. The Marines were coming.

"Jackal Three Bravo, this is Voodoo Actual. The bird saved us, but we're still in contact, with team members isolated.

We're on a narrow road parallel to the main avenue. You see our smoke?"

"I have yellow smoke, roger."

"Just keep heading for the smoke before it disappears. PAC forces everywhere. Close quarters. Out."

Cascaes called over to his team. "We have marines inbound!"

A wave of relief washed over the faces of his team. Moose screamed over the roar of missiles from the Cobra. "Skipper! We need to get to Lance and Jake *now!* They popped smoke. If *we* can see it, so can the PAC."

"Okay. Let's work our way over slowly while the marines get to us. Mack is still out there somewhere, maybe in the other direction."

The team spread out and began moving methodically down the alley towards the sound of gunfire and drifting yellow smoke.

Mackey's corner of the world had gone quieter. Although he could still hear plenty of gunfire, and the gunship overhead unleashing hell somewhere nearby, his immediate area had gone quiet. The quiet scuffling of boots or doors opening and closing was the only clue that troops nearby were hunting for him.

Mack popped the magazine on his .45 and looked quickly. Three rounds left, plus one more magazine. He needed to find a way out quickly. He could hear Kikongo being whispered on the other side of the corrugated steel wall. Mack froze. While he could easily shoot through the wall, he had no idea how many troops were on the other side. He controlled his breathing and watched the shadows around the base of the walls and doorway. They were everywhere.

Moose and Ripper had taken point and were running down the narrow street towards the last of the yellow smoke. Cascaes had informed the Cobra pilot that they were moving towards the other marker and asked for cover fire. Cantor had swept the area repeatedly, keeping Lance and Jake from being overrun. Small arms fire was hitting the helicopter, but Cantor ignored it and continued to wreak havoc on the enemy below. By the time Ripper called over to Jake and Lance to tell them they were coming up behind them, the enemy had broken off and retreated.

Ripper came to the corner and yelled. "Woods! Koches!"

"Here! Come up!" came the reply.

Ripper, Moose, and Theresa charged up the alley and found the two of them lying against the side of a building. They were both bleeding from gunshot wounds.

"Shit!" yelled Theresa. "Why didn't you tell us you were hit?"

"'Cause you'd come running. We didn't want you getting yourselves killed to get here. Thank God for that bird."

Theresa looked at Jake's wounds first. He had been shot through the quadriceps, through and through, and had tied a pressure bandage on himself. The second round had snuck in under his body armor and hit him in the ribs under the armpit, where it broke two bones and lodged itself there. He was bleeding heavily.

Theresa, acting corpsman, pulled another pressure bandage and took off his blood soaked Kevlar. She cut his shirt open and applied the pressure bandage. He was pale and looked like he was fighting the shock and losing.

Ripper helped Lance wrap his left hand, where a round had gone through and broken a few bones. It wasn't life threatening, but it hurt like hell. "I have morphine if you need it," asked Ripper.

"Fuck that, man. This ain't no time to take a nap. We need to get out of here."

Ripper stood up and extended his hand to help him up.

"Blew out my knee, man. Not sure what I did. I can't walk. I told numbnuts over there to leave without me, but he has a man-crush on me or something. He took a couple covering me." Lance was watching Theresa working on controlling Jake's bleeding.

Cascaes got back on the phone. "Jersey fifty-six, this is Voodoo Three actual, request medivac for two wounded, do you copy?"

"Voodoo Three, we don't have medivacs. I'm going to try and get a Sea Knight moved up behind us to that grassy field, but you're going to need to move your wounded, copy?"

"I copy. Keep these guys off our back and we'll try and fall back to that rendezvous point." The loud steady noise of automatic gunfire behind them made them seek cover.

"Voodoo Three actual, this is Jackal Three Bravo. We are coming up on your location. Enemy has broken off. What's your sit rep? I have yellow smoke fading in front of me."

"That's us. Smoke is almost gone, but that's us. We're falling back with two wounded. Wait one. Mack? Mack, you copy, over."

Nothing.

"Jackal Three Bravo, come to the smoke and help us move our wounded."

Within three minutes, a squad of marines appeared down the alleyway. They looked crisp and neat, and very, very young. The oldest of the group, a staff sergeant, jogged to Cascaes when he saw his phone and extended his hand.

"Voodoo Three?"

Chris shook his hand and smiled. "Chris Cascaes. I owe you more than one cold beer."

"Everett Palmer. Lima three-three. Let's get your people out of here and see about that beer. It was hairy as hell getting here. PAC troops are all over, although that Cobra wasted plenty. How bad are they?"

"Neither can walk. One's worse than the other. Chest wound, lost a lot of blood I think."

Palmer whistled and a young marine corporal ran to him. The staff sergeant relayed what he wanted done, and the corporal started barking at the others to help carry the wounded.

"Spare any ammo? We're out," asked Chris. Everett had his men share what they had, and the team took a second to reload and check weapons. Now, almost resembling a fighting force, they were ready to fall back to the field and evacuate their wounded, then find Mack.

CHAPTER 65

The shadows were moving around outside and the whispering continued for several minutes. Mack was screwed, plain and simple. He dared not move for fear of the slightest sound giving away his position. He sat against half of a fifty-gallon drum that had been the family stove with his .45 in his right hand and a K-Bar knife in the other.

He had been eyeing the feet moving past the wall when the old wooden door kicked open. It seemed like slow-motion. The PAC soldier stepped inside the small hovel and saw Mackey sitting there as Mackey raised his pistol at him. The gun barrel of the Type-81 Assault Rifle came up a split second slower than Mack's .45.

The good news was, Mack fired two shots dead center and killed the soldier immediately. The bad news was, as he fell out of the doorway back into the street, another three guerrillas now knew where the American was. They stormed the doorway as Mackey literally ran through the rear wall. The back of the building collapsed as he came through it, right into two PAC soldiers who had been sneaking around behind him. Mack emptied his magazine into them and sprinted down the alley as fast as his legs would take him. Bullets whizzed around him, but Mackey cut through houses, jumped fences, crashed through wooden walls and continued to race for his life, dropping the magazine as he ran and slamming his last one into the .45.

Wong Fu-jia had only been a few feet away when Mack crashed through the rear of the house, and joined in the pursuit, screaming in Chinese to kill the American. While Mackey was putting distance between himself and the pursuers, he was headed in the wrong direction.

The marine rifle squads were running through the narrow streets helping the team carry their wounded. Staff Sergeant Palmer was on his radio directing the Sea Knight to the grassy field, and the Super Cobra continued to provide support. The sounds of fighting all over the city were starting to die down. The PAC had taken such massive casualties that they had started to melt into the countryside to the north, many of them attempting to reach the Congo River and find a way across from the Democratic Republic of Congo into neighboring Congo-Brazzaville.

Reports of the PAC's retreat reached the presidential palace, and President Kuwali left the basement to make a television appearance and assure his people that the DRC was winning the battle against foreign fighters. He stopped short of saying the Chinese were responsible, but Dex Murphy and the others back in Langley watched the president and smiled, knowing that somewhere in China, someone was about to have a very bad day.

The presidential army reorganized and began pressing southwest again. Army units all over the country were moving towards Kinshasa to help, and the only two Congolese helicopters fit for flying had been dispatched from Kinshasa airport to reconnoiter the area. The PAC forces continued to retreat, but there were still over 800 of them killing anyone they saw on their way out.

The team reached the dual rotor Sea Knight and helped Lance and Jake aboard where corpsmen were waiting for them. Hodges walked himself aboard at Cascaes's orders. He was out of the fight for the day. The staff sergeant yelled to Chris over the sounds of the rotors. "We need to get back to the presidential palace. My orders were to secure that compound and provide security to the president. We came when you called out the *Broken Arrow*, but we need to get back. We can't fit your people aboard, but it's only half a click."

"We're not headed back just yet. I've got a man out there somewhere that I need to locate," shouted Cascaes.

"Shit. We *have* to get back, sir."

"I understand. Look, you saved our ass. The PAC is definitely falling back. As long as that Cobra can stay on station, we'll be fine. I can't leave my guy out there."

"Understood, sir. I'm sorry I can't help. We need to dust off."

Chris snapped a salute, shook the man's hand, and thanked him. The staff sergeant handed Chris another magazine and two frags, and wished him luck. He stepped back into the bird and waved, and the crew chief ordered the ramp lifted.

Chris looked around at his team. It was mostly his original SEAL team: Ray Jensen, Pete McCoy, Jon Cohen, Ryan O'Connor, Moose, and Ripper, along with Julia and Theresa. There were a lot of faces missing in his huddle. Jones, Ernie P., Cory and Smitty were dead, and Koches, Woods, and Hodges were all wounded and out of the fight. It had been the mostly costly mission he'd ever been a part of.

"Look, there's only nine of us left. But Mack is out there somewhere and we need to find him before the PAC does," said Cascaes.

"Nine fields a whole team, Skipper," said Moose.

Chris nodded. They weren't playing baseball today, but he understood. They were all on board. "Ammo?"

They all nodded and said they were "good to go." The marines had shared what they had before they left. They were exhausted, but ready to find Mack.

Cascaes tried Mackey on his radio and got no response. It was stressful. Mackey could be dead, in which case he was putting his people in harm's way for no reason. He might be wounded and unable to speak, which would make finding him nearly impossible. Or, most likely, Mack being Mack, he was just not answering so no one would go looking for him.

"We head back on the north side of the highway and track northwest. Mack would have had to travel north-northwest when he was separated. We keep trying him on the radio and work our way over there slowly. I don't think the PAC is looking to fight anymore, but there are presidential troops around now as well. We don't need to get shot by friendly fire, either. We'll be moving into Bandalungwa and then Kintambo. These are packed residential areas like the one we just came out of. Stay together, stay frosty."

Cascaes's radio crackled. "Voodoo Three actual, this is Jersey fifty-six. I am low on fuel and ammunition and breaking contact. Stay safe. Out."

The team looked at each other. No one said a word, but they all knew their edge had just been lost.

CHAPTER 66

Mackey ran until his lungs and legs refused to go another step. He ducked behind what might have been a small bar or restaurant. It had a counter and chairs set up outside, and a small one room cooking area inside. Mack found a case of warm Coke and drank three of them in under two minutes.

The PAC soldiers were close behind, but were carrying heavier weapons and field packs. Mack was down to the clothes on his back, his .45, and knife. The training and running had definitely saved his life as he sprinted for almost a mile and half before stopping to catch his breath and inhale a few sodas. His ear piece buzzed.

"Mack? What's your sitrep? Come in over?"

It was Cascaes. Mack shook his head. "Stay where you are, Chris! I'm E&E!" he barked, referring to escaping and evading the enemy.

"We're not leaving you out there alone. Where are you?"

"Chris, you're gonna get our team killed. There's PAC goons everywhere. I'm fine. I can't stay and chat. Get your ass back to the palace and I'll contact you when I can. Do *not* follow me! I'm very popular right now. I gotta go. Out."

"Mack! Stop it! We're coming for you. We're north of Highway One. Work your way north east and we'll link up."

Mack was already back up and running. Wong Fu-jia and a few dozen mercenaries were only a moment behind...

The team ran across the open highway and started moving northwest as fast as they could run. They could see presidential troops way out in front of them, pursuing the retreating PAC forces. Way down the highway, the remnants of the lone tank still smoldered.

Cascaes looked out at the city in front of him. A few million displaced people moving in panicked masses. Two armies running through the city. Two square miles of residential and commercial neighborhoods connected by hundreds of tiny alleys and narrow roads. He turned to his team.

"No. Mack's right. I'd say the same thing. Risking the entire team in this clusterfuck of a mission for one man doesn't make any sense…"

"Skipper! We don't leave our people behind!" barked Moose, visibly angry.

"Moose, Mack's a pro. He'll figure out a way back if it's possible. But nine of us out there isn't going to save the day. We barely got out of the last fight. We've got dead and wounded enough already. That's it. I'm callin' it. We're done."

Julia looked at Chris in shock. "Chris? That's it? We're just going to leave Mackey out there in the middle of a thousand enemy soldiers and do *nothing*?"

Chris looked at the weary faces of his team. "It's my call. We're done."

CHAPTER 67

Cascaes sat on the grass in front of the presidential palace with his team around him. They were too exhausted, mentally, physically, and emotionally to speak. They each occasionally glanced down the road, as if Mackey would just come walking up any moment, but that didn't seem very realistic. United States Marines had set up a defensive perimeter, and stood their ground around the presidential palace.

Cascaes called into Langley where Dex Murphy picked up. Cascaes reported their killed and wounded, leaving Dex speechless for a few seconds.

"Look, Chris. Your mission was to help prevent the coupe. You did just that. President Kuwali's ambassador to the UN made a plea for UN Peacekeepers to come in, but let's face it—the DRC is surrounded by Angola, South Sudan, Uganda, Rwanda—none of which are in any better shape than the DRC. POTUS authorized more marines to reinforce the palace until this blows over, but in a few weeks, it'll be like this never happened."

"I'll be sure to tell that to the families of the men I lost," said Cascaes.

"Chris, I pushed your team too hard. You had three tough assignments in a row. Your people performed better than anyone could ask for, but it's time to get them home to decompress for a while. I'll work out the details and get you back on the first thing that flies."

"Dex, I can't leave until I hear from Mack. Bad enough I had to leave my dead in the field, I'm not leaving a missing team member."

"Seventy-two hours, Chris. After that, you and your team are on a bird to the Sixth Fleet until we can arrange for international transport."

Cascaes signed off and sat staring at nothing. Julia moved over next to him.

"Hey. How ya' doing?" she asked softly.

Chris rubbed his face and shrugged. "We need to find Mack. I want to retrieve our dead. This whole situation is a mess. We're a small team of special operators, not a combat unit equipped to take on a whole army. I keep thinking about where we started, at the lake, and how we ended up here. What a disaster."

"We stopped the PAC from overthrowing the government. We probably helped stop another African genocide. We didn't *fail*, Chris. It was just costly."

Chris felt a lump in his throat. Jones's big smile flashed in front of his face. "Yeah. Way too costly. And what am I supposed to do? Just get on a plane and leave Mack out there with a few hundred guerrillas running after him? If they take him alive it won't end easy for him."

"What would you do if you were Mack?"

Chris looked at her. Even exhausted and filthy, she was beautiful.

"Seriously, Chris. What would you do?"

He tightened his face and thought for a second. "I'd keep moving. Keep trying to work my way back around to us. The PAC is most likely trying to head north to the river. They'll get across into Congo-Brazzaville and just dump their uniforms. So with them pushing north, Mack will have to keep heading towards us before he gets squeezed between the PAC and the river."

"You called in a broken arrow before. Why not call in for air support again? Or a rescue? Maybe the PJs can get him?"

"It's not I haven't thought about air support, but only Mack can call it in. We have no idea where he is."

"What if the bird can get back on station and try to reach Mack directly?"

Chris nodded. "It's worth a shot. He grabbed his radio."

"Jersey fifty-six, this is Voodoo Six Actual, come in over."

There was no reply for the first few times, and then finally, "Copy Voodoo Six. Was refueling and rearming. What's your sitrep, over?"

"Jersey fifty-six, we have one lost dog approximately one klick west-northwest of the presidential palace. I've been unable to reach him, and believe he may be on the run towards this location with enemy forces on his tail. Can you provide air cover and arrange evac? Over."

"Wait one, Voodoo Six." There was a long pause as CWO Cantor spoke to his CO. "Voodoo Six Actual, this is Jersey fifty-six. Can you give me a grid and narrow the search area?"

Chris broke out his map and he and Julia did their best to guess where Mack would most likely have been. He called back the grid location and listened as CWO Cantor began coordinating other air assets that were arriving on station. The other members of the team gathered around closer and listened to the radio, feeling hopeful for the first time in a while.

CHAPTER 68

Mack squatted behind what was considered an elegant house in the Bandalungwa district. There was still sporadic gunfire, but it was less organized. No less than a dozen men had been chasing him for over two hours, shooting whenever they spotted him. The proximity of the houses on such narrow windy streets had been helpful in evading the troops behind him, but Mack was running out of gas. He looked at his electronic GPS. He had been heading north for his entire run and was approaching the Congo River. He needed to start moving east. The GPS unit was shaking in his hand.

Mack took a few deep breaths and climbed over the wrought iron fence to begin the second phase of his marathon. Feeling a little more secure, he decided to check in with his team.

"Mack to base, come in over."

Nothing.

He tried repeatedly, but it was no good. There were simply too many houses and obstructions in the way. Mack looked around at the neighborhood. They were all basically one-story houses. In the distance, he could see a factory smoke stack, maybe three hundred yards away. If he could get to that, he'd more likely be able to reach Cascaes, who could then call in for an evac.

Mack began the cautious jog through the neighborhood. Occasional civilians would spot him, but would immediately run the other way. It took fifteen minutes to make it to the factory. Once there at the fence, Mack stopped and studied his surroundings. Occasionally, someone would sprint madly down a side street, trying desperately to get to safety. The biggest question was *where* exactly safety was.

A chain link fence surrounded the factory, and Mack hated the idea of climbing it out in the open, but he had no choice. He needed the elevation to make radio contact, and the smoke stack was the tallest thing around. After scanning a few more times, Mack made the dash across the street to the fence, climbed it as fast as he could, and half climbed-half fell down the other side. He hit the bottom, hopped back up, took a quick look around, and then sprinted to the factory.

He was halfway across the open lot when the first two shots cracked behind him. A white man in combat fatigues didn't exactly "blend into the surroundings." Mack jumped on to a fifty-gallon drum and then climbed up the side of a small building to the roof. He raced across the flat roof and started climbing the rungs that lined the side of the smoke stack. There was a small landing about half-way up, where Mack stopped and laid down on his stomach. He turned the radio back on.

"Mack to base! Mack to base! Come in. over!"

Across town, Cascaes's earpiece came to life and he jumped to his feet without

even realizing he'd done it. "Mack? Where are you? Sitrep!"

"Chris, I'm maybe one click west of the palace. There's a small factory over here with a smokestack. It's the tallest thing out here. I climbed it to make radio contact, but I've been spotted. Can you call in any help? I'm out of ammo and jammed up!"

"Do you have any smoke?"

"Negative. I ain't got shit! Maybe half a mag in my .45 and I'm toast, Chris."

"Wait one." Chris grabbed the other radio. "Voodoo Six Actual to Jersey fifty-six, come in over!'

"This is Jersey fifty-six, on station."

"Need fire support and immediate evac. Approximately one click west of the palace. One team member who does not have smoke or 117 Fox for direct transmission. Look for large factory smoke stack. He is in enemy contact. Over."

"Good copy, Voodoo Six. Heading there now. Sea Beast Three, this is Jersey fifty-six en route for fire support. Need immediate evac at same location."

Cascaes listened to the pilots speak to each other, and the rest of the team assembled around the radio to listen. Mackey had been located and had help heading his way. They just had to get there in time.

Wong Fu-jia still had four men with him. One of them had spotted the American and managed to get a couple of shots off, but wasn't sure if he had hit him. The American had fled to a small factory—perhaps they finally had him cornered.

The five of them spread out and moved across the street to the fence that surrounded the property. They studied the grounds but saw no movement. Fu motioned for them to assault. They ran down to the gate and shot off the lock, then raced into the factory property. The five of them ran around the factory knocking over boxes and barrels, searching for the lone American. The sounds of a helicopter rotor made them freeze where they were and scan the clear blue African sky.

Wong Fu-jia's lightbulb turned on. The American had wanted to call for help and needed elevation for his radio. He ran to the side of the building and looked up at the roof, and then at the large smokestack. He had to be up there! Wong Fu-jia was screaming in Chinese to the four men who didn't understand him, but he was pointing and screaming, and they all ran towards the smokestack.

"Jersey fifty-six is inbound on search location. Rescue target does not have smoke or radio. Sea Beast Three, follow my lead and prepare to evac one team member. Over."

"Copy that Jersey fifty-six. We're inbound on your tail. Out."

Mackey let out a long deep sigh of relief when he heard the roar of the Super Cobra. He took a knee to start scanning the sky when the first tracers and ricochets began pinging all over the metal deck he was on.

"Sonofabitch!" he screamed as he hit the deck. All Mackey had was his .45, which was useless at long range. He screamed into his radio. "Chris! I see the bird coming in! Tell him to strafe this position! I'm on the stack platform with incoming!"

Cascaes and his team all heard the incoming message and Chris radioed back to Jersey fifty-six. Chief Warrant Officer Cantor went full throttle and roared in overhead towards the smokestack. "I've got eyes on your guy, Voodoo Six! Coming in hot."

Mackey pressed his body against the bricks of the stack and tried to get small as the small arms fire bounced all around him. Wong Fu-jia and his men had charged against the open ground in front of the factory and zeroed in on the platform where they saw the American. They were standing there taking the platform apart with their fusillade when the narrow grey helicopter came into view. Wong Fu-jia's face showed the sudden realization that it was all over.

CWO Cantor pressed his thumb on the trigger and his triple mini-guns opened up on the ground below. What was a flat courtyard turned into a cloud of dust and body parts as hundreds of 20 mm. rounds took apart everything inside the courtyard. Capable of destroying large, hard targets, the shells were a tremendous "overkill" against the five men below. The bird circled around and looked for more targets, but couldn't find any.

"Sea Beast Three, this is Jersey fifty-six. LZ looks green. Dust off now. I have security, over."

Cantor continued low, slow rounds over the factory grounds as the much larger Sea Knight moved into the courtyard. It landed in the center of the courtyard, touching down on torn up earth and small pieces of what had been enemy soldiers.

Mackey scurried down the side of the smoke stack and ran towards the helicopter with his hands high above his head so no one would mistake him for a hostile. The rear ramp was already opened before the bird had touched down, and two crewmen with machine guns stood at the ramp looking for trouble. All they found was a very happy, very exhausted American soldier who couldn't have been happier to see them.

"Sea Beast Three to Jersey fifty-six and Voodoo Six and, we have your package. Returning to base. Out."

The Super Cobra made another sweep around the factory and escorted the Sea Knight back to the presidential palace before peeling off to find more targets at the Congo River. When the Sea Knight touched down on the large lawn in front of the presidential palace, the entire team was waiting to greet their boss.

CHAPTER 69

After the remaining PAC forces had either been killed, captured or escaped into neighboring Congo-Brazzaville, life returned to normal in the Democratic Republic of Congo. The president had ordered a National Week of Mourning, and the United States and other countries pledged money to help rebuild parts of the destroyed capital. China also offered to help rebuild, and denied any involvement with the PAC forces, but President Kuwali politely refused their aid.

The day after the attack, the team, escorted by Lieutenant Hamill's marines, recovered the bodies of Earl Jones, Joe Smith, and Ernesto Perez. Their flag draped coffins joined Cory Stewart's onboard a C-141B Starlifter back to McGuire Airbase in New Jersey, then a quick transfer back to Langley.

The team mostly slept on the very long flight home. Jake Koches and Lance Woods were flown out to a hospital ship before being sent to Germany. They'd be following the Team home a couple of weeks down the road. Hodges made the flight with the rest of his team, albeit a little black and blue with multiple cuts all over his face and body.

Chris Mackey was fast asleep. The adrenaline that had helped keep him alive had left his body. He had been right all along of course—he was too old for this shit. He snored loudly, but the engine hum drowned it out.

Julia and Chris sat together, speaking quietly over the sleepy drone of the plane. Julia leaned over and smiled. "It was a hell of a romantic getaway, but I think maybe we started thinking about a different line of work."

Chris nodded. She could always make him smile, but he was shot. It had been a terribly costly mission, and he had calls to make when he got home. "I think Dex would give us as much time off as we wanted. He even said something like that on the sat-phone. Where do you want to go?"

"I only have two requirements about location. We're together, and no one is trying to kill us."

Chris looked around to make sure no one was watching, then he kissed her hand. "Deal."

EPILOGUE

One Month Later

Chris and Julia were sitting up in Julia's bed, sharing a bottle of wine and eating cheese and crackers.

"I could get used to this," said Chris, leaning in for a kiss.

"Which part, the crumbs in my bed, or being naked with me on nice clean sheets while drinking wine with no one trying to kill us?" asked Julia with a smirk.

"All of the above. The DRC seems like a movie we watched. I've never gone so long without training or being around my guys. Six weeks off? Who gets that?"

"You complaining?" she asked. "Prefer the smell of a half a dozen unwashed SEALs to my perfume?"

"Nope." He kissed her again, and smelled her hair as he buried his face in her neck. "Not a bit. In fact, just the opposite. I thought it would take a long time to get used to the idea of 'being out' or retiring, but the truth is, I've never felt more relaxed in my entire life than I do right at this moment."

Julia smiled. "Won't get bored if no one is trying to kill you?"

"Based on what happened an hour ago, I think you might be trying to kill me…"

"Oh, you poor thing!" she said with a laugh, and leaned in for a long hug.

The television grabbed their attention, and Julia grabbed the remote and turned up the volume.

"...with China vetoing the Security Council's recommendation to send aid and support to the Democratic Republic of Congo. Chinese Ambassador Li Quingshui said that China opposed the UN resolution because the current corrupt government had accused China of participating in the attempted coup. He went on to say that China's peaceful attempt to aid the suffering people of the Democratic Republic of Congo had proven that the current US backed regime was a puppet government that was corrupt and committing genocide on its own people. Because of this, China would not allow any aid into the impoverished nation until the government faced new elections..."

Chris took the remote from her hand and clicked the television off.

Chris Mackey sat in Dex Murphy's office looking stoic.

"I understand Mack," said Dex. "What about an inside job? Being a desk jockey isn't as boring as it sounds. You'd still get to run missions, do some good in the world..."

Mack shook his head. His eyes filled with tears. "All three agents, Dex. Smitty. Ernie. Cory. I put three stars on that wall downstairs. No, sir. I'm done. I was too old for this gig a few years ago. It's time."

Mack stood up and extended his hand. Dex stood and gripped Mack's hand tightly with both of his. "You're one of the best agents we've ever had, Mack. I'll miss you. Stay in touch."

Mack nodded, knowing full well that once he left that office, there was no staying in touch.

"Take care of yourself, Dex," he said quietly. He forced a smile and headed for the door to parts unknown.

ABOUT THE AUTHOR

David M. Salkin is the author of thirteen thrillers in various genres, including military espionage, crime, horror, science-fiction, action-adventure and mystery. With a writing style reminiscent of the late, great Michael Crichton, Salkin's work keeps his readers turning pages into the late hours. His books have received Gold and Bronze medals in the Stars & Flags book awards, and David has appeared as a guest speaker all over the country.

David is an elected official in Freehold Township, NJ where he has served for twenty years in various roles including Mayor, Deputy Mayor, Township Committeeman and Police Commissioner.

When not working or writing, David prefers to be Scuba diving with his family. He is a Master Diver and "fish geek," as well as a pretty good chef and wine aficionado. Some of his famous recipes were perfected in the parking lot of Giants Stadium.

Visit DavidMSalkin.com for all the latest news on book releases and appearances.